MIDNIGHT MOVIES

DAVID A. KAUFELT

DELACORTE PRESS/NEW YORK

Published by
Delacorte Press
1 Dag Hammarskjold Plaza
New York, N.Y. 10017

Manufactured in the United States of America

First printing

Designed by Leo McRee

LIBRARY OF CONGRESS CATALOGING IN PUBLICATION DATA

Kaufelt, David A
Midnight movies.

I. Title.
PZ4.K199Mi [PS3561.A79]   813'.5'4   79–19664
ISBN 0–440–05244–0

For Dick Duane

PROLOGUE

On April the first, the night Jean Rice Halladay caused a sensation among the dowagers at the Eye Ball, I wrote in my diary: "Life has got to change." It didn't occur to me then—although it might well have—that Jean would be the catalyst. Jean and Dutch.

The Eye Ball is, undisputedly, the one yearly charity function you must attend in order to qualify for entry into Old New York Society. The Texans, the politicians, and the Jews are traditionally given the least desirable tables—those farthest from the dance floor. Still, they continue to buy tickets.

It's officially designated The American Guild for the Blind Cotillion, and those tickets cost a bundle. The farther away from society you are, the higher the tariff to get in. The Texans, the politicians, et cetera, pay fifteen hundred dollars per plate and consider themselves fortunate in being allowed the opportunity.

The patron seats—those located at tables adjacent to the dance floor—cost only one hundred dollars each. But they are reserved for members of the families who helped to found the Guild in eighteen hundred and eighty five.

The Eye Ball has always been held in the Grand Ballroom of the Waldorf-Astoria. Ever since I can remember, Lester Lanin and his Society Orchestra played the music Aunt Alice and her pals like to tap their toes to. But that year, an upstart entertainment committee drafted Peter Duchin and *his* Society Orchestra, and Aunt Alice had to be content with the unspoken solace that "after all, dear, he is very nearly one of us."

During his second break Peter came to our table and asked BaBa to dance. BaBa was being demure in front of Aunt Alice: she looked to me for acquiescence. I nodded encouragement, and she went off with Peter to the dance floor, some twelve inches away.

They began to fox-trot to the music Peter's men seem able to manufacture in their sleep. He and BaBa are old friends, their acquaintance stemming from the hundreds of balls and benefits BaBa has supported or chaired or in some way involved herself with during her Young Concerned Matron era (1972–1977). At that point in our marriage, I wouldn't have cared if she'd committed adultery on the Grand Ballroom floor. Actually, I might have welcomed the diversion. My dinner partners, invited by Aunt Alice to share her (the) table, were pretty heavy going.

Two of them, aging gentleman lawyers in custom-cut dinner jackets, were reassuring each other, over their wives' discreetly blonded and tiaraed heads, as to the rightness of their eating habits.

"I usually get home from the club around seven, have another highball, relax, and we dine about eight thirty."

"That's the way we do it, too, Arch."

I looked around that cavernous space, which had been decorated by Lilli Ruben with the five thousand dollars the Guild gave her and five more from her own purse. There was a theme. There always is. April in either Portugal, Brazil, or Paris. I seem to recall huge gold umbrellas on every table and a great many overripe purple and white lilacs.

The woman sitting on my right was a person I had often heard spoken of but had not actually met until that evening. Madam Lizzardi was afflicted by the lilacs, sneezing into an appropriately floral silk handkerchief every now and then. Each year Aunt Alice reserves one place at her table for someone who is "deserving" but who can't easily come up with the one hundred requisite (and deductible) dollars.

Madam is a retired opera singer who had climbed onto the stage of the old Metropolitan Opera House at a time when nice girls, according to Aunt Alice, "remained in their boxes." As a result, she was ostracized by Aunt Alice's world. (Aunt Alice's social code invariably brings to mind Edith Wharton heroines and their bridge debts.)

To worsen matters, Aunt Alice confided in me during dinner, making yet another of her incredible and assumedly unintentional puns, "she married an Italian composer of little note."

I didn't laugh. Aunt Alice lost her sense of humor the morning Uncle Garfield died, leaving her in charge of eighty-seven million dollars. "Not a responsibility I bear lightly," Aunt Alice likes to say.

Nor is Madam Lizzardi a responsibility to bear lightly. She suffered, she told me, not only from hay fever (or lilac fever, to be strictly accurate) but from a variety of diseases, which necessitated her popping little yellow pills and drinking quantities of ice water throughout the evening. She was covered in venerable black silk and yellowed diamonds and smelled like vanilla extract.

Her chief asset to Aunt Alice is that she knows exactly who everyone is, where they've come from, and where they are going. "I'm amazed," Aunt Alice says, "how dear Amelita manages to glean all that information from her little house out there on Long Island."

"Who is that?" I heard Aunt Alice hiss as I watched BaBa and a new partner two-step around the floor, smiling at everyone in sight.

Madam adjusted the mass of her body so that she could see who Aunt Alice was staring at with her uncompromisingly American cornflower-blue eyes. Also curious about who had caught Aunt Alice's hard-to-get attention, I turned and looked in the direction of a table that bordered on the limit of acceptability.

"*Cara*," Madam said in her awful, knowing voice, "that's Jean Rice Halladay."

"Really," Aunt Alice said, pausing to allow Madam a delicate sneeze. "Who is she?"

"*Cara*, don't you recall . . . ?" Madam proceeded to draw a detailed sketch of The Scandal, while I looked at Jean Rice Halladay for the first time.

She was wearing a white coat-dress, filigreed with silver thread that matched her eyes. As I and a good many others watched, she began to unbutton it down the front. I heard Madam wheeze and Aunt Alice catch her breath. Under the coat-dress, of the same material, was a gown that depended upon two thin silver straps to keep it up. When she moved, the cloth touched her body in a way that made it clear she was wearing nothing under it. At the same time, the gown appeared as if it might be transparent. One had to look very carefully, and then one still wasn't sure.

Lawrence Rockefeller, at the next table, said that it was the first time anyone had ever done a striptease at the Eye Ball. Aunt Alice swiveled around and glared at him.

My attention stayed with Jean. Her silver-blond hair had been twisted into a French knot and her face, so clear and soft and young, devoid of makeup, appeared as if it were being seen through gauze, the kind cameramen use when they want to be kind to aging film stars.

She looked very much like a film star. Not any one special star, but one we all should have known and didn't. She was impossibly glamorous in a way that made Old New York assume its blankest, most disapproving expression.

It was as if the makeup, the bleach, the publicity poses for the airbrushed glossies assumed by her mother and her grandmother—all the paraphernalia of being a star —had been absorbed by them and passed down to her through their genes.

And then, of course, there was her past.

"... and I understand, though it never came out at the trial, that *she* pulled the trigger." Madam was breathless with hay fever and climactic excitement.

I excused myself. Aunt Alice barely noticed, but Madam Lizzardi shifted her bulk once again so that she could follow my movements. I smiled at BaBa and her latest partner and walked to the table at which Jean was sitting.

"Dance?" Buddy Ruben was asking as I approached.

"Are you out of your mind?"

I said hello to Buddy, he introduced me to Jean, and then I asked her to dance.

She didn't answer, and for a moment I thought I was going to get the same answer she gave Buddy. But she stood up and led the way to the dance floor.

"Poor Buddy," I said, taking her in my arms, feeling her skin through the thin, possibly transparent dress.

"He asks for it."

"And you give it to him?"

"We don't fuck, if that's what you're getting at."

It wasn't. It was only much later that that piece of information became of interest to me. At that moment it served to cut off any further conversation. We continued to dance, but our contact, such as it was, had ended.

We completed a circle of the room; I thanked her; she looked at me appraisingly, apparently found me wanting, and turned to a dark man standing with his back to us, talking to Buddy, who was still sitting at the table where we had left him.

"Can we please get out of here?" she asked the dark man, and I thought her voice was going to break. I had been left standing on the dance floor in a fairly foolish position (I had been dismissed, but it took a moment to realize it) and beat a hasty retreat to Aunt Alice's table. I asked if she was enjoying the sherbet.

"Very much," she said, looking at me directly with those disapproving yes. "A little tart."

BaBa muffled a laugh, Madam concentrated on her own dessert, and David Littlefield engaged me in a conversation about Louie Auchincloss's latest novel, which I admired and David "deplored."

After I'd had a conciliatory, redemptive dance with

Aunt Alice (which was rather like pushing a giant Good Humor stick around the room), BaBa and I said good night. Then we said good night fifty or so more times as we made our way to the exit doors.

Jean was still in the ballroom, talking to the dark man, who seemed to be giving her much the same sort of treatment she had been giving Buddy Ruben.

When he turned, I recognized him as Bert Brown. He was one of BaBa's fast friends. He had married well, turning a dubious social standing into a solid one. At that point in time, he was trying to parlay his social success into a political one. I didn't take to him then. Now, of course, I find it difficult to be in the same room with him.

"Where's Catherine?" BaBa asked, insisting on stopping, on saying hello. He kissed her, shook my hand, and moved slightly, blocking my view of Jean. He made no effort to introduce her.

"Le Flu. Catherine's insisting it's the French strain." I could just see Jean's hands. "I left her sitting in front of a fire, eating chocolates, pretending to read *Madame Bovary*." Her right hand reached for a crystal holder filled with cigarettes. She knocked it over.

"I'll call tomorrow," BaBa promised, "and conduct the entire conversation in flawless Parisian French." Jean's hand lay still for a moment, then righted the holder and chose a cigarette. As BaBa and I moved off, I turned and saw Buddy Ruben leaning over Jean solicitously, lighting her cigarette. She put her hands around his as if to steady him, but it seemed clear—again it was only an impression—that it was she who needed the steadying.

"Odd table for Bert Brown to be at," BaBa said as she adjusted her fur wrap and examined herself in the corridor mirror. "What was she like?"

"Who?"

"Buddy Ruben's date."

"We didn't say much."

"I don't suppose she has to."

We had been standing under the Waldorf marquee for some minutes, searching for Aunt Alice's vintage black Cadillac. She had lent us the car for the evening, her own transportation being supplied by David Littlefield's Daimler.

I spotted Thurmond, Aunt Alice's driver, on the far side of Park Avenue and waved at him. He nodded reassuringly and started the car. Behind him was a long maroon Mercedes, sleek and modern, all business, with a TV antenna and a uniformed chauffeur. Getting into it were Buddy Ruben, Jean, and Bert Brown.

It was to be some ten months later, when he was trying to educate me, when he was trying to instill in me "a little zest for living, dolls," that Dutch Cohen was to hear where and how I first met Jean Rice Halladay. "Darling!" he said, rolling his heavily made-up eyes. "Darling! You're not going to sit there in that ridiculous suit and tell me it never occurred to you that Buddy Ruben was the beard?"

CHAPTER 1

She had been living in New York nearly ten years, not
five blocks from where I lived, shopping at the same
drugstore, cashing checks at the liquor store I used, moving in circles that often overlapped mine. Yet I had never
seen her until the night of the Eye Ball.

"You must have seen me a zillion times, James. You
just didn't notice me."

"Not noticing you would be like not noticing World
War II."

"Is that supposed to be a compliment?"

"Not exactly."

During the nine months following the Eye Ball, I saw
her perhaps half a dozen times. The first was early in
May, five weeks or so after the ball. I was lunching at
Charles Chevilliot's La Petite Ferme with BaBa.

BaBa was insisting on a regime of weekly luncheons.
"Important husband-wife luncheons," she called them.
They invariably began with BaBa ordering a double gin
martini and saying, "Now listen, James. We must be
sensible about this." Since BaBa was also popping little
white pills, "ups," two or three times a day, I suggested

she start being sensible by cutting out either the pills or the martini. This advice she ignored.

At any rate, it seemed to me then that I *was* being sensible. I was waiting, in the words of Aunt Alice, for BaBa to "ride it out" (another of that woman's classic, unintentional puns). Now, when I look back at our lives, at the way I was behaving, like a zipper on a fat man's trousers, threatening to burst, I realize I was far from sensible. That afternoon, under the thin layer of controlled cool I wore, I was on the verge of taking one of Charles's steak knives and plunging it into BaBa's tiny preserved artichoke of a heart.

"Isn't that that woman who was with Buddy Ruben at the Eye Ball?" BaBa interrupted herself to ask in machine-gun staccato.

Jean was waiting for her luncheon partner—a blue-haired lady with a fixed, self-involved smile—to gather together all the items unhappily postmenopausal women are always gathering together on the point of leaving restaurants. Gloves, purse, keys, lipstick, the earring she had removed during the soup course and played with during the entrée.

Again it was Jean's hands—long and slim, reaching for a cigarette—that gave her away. They shook as she lit it with the other woman's lighter. I remember wondering if she were an alcoholic and dismissing the thought because no one with skin and eyes as clear as hers could be drinking enough to make her hands shake.

When they finally walked out, the older woman fussing with her name-designer-purse clasp, Jean looked at BaBa and then at me, seemingly amused and patient, giving no sign that she remembered either of us.

"Masturbation fodder?" BaBa asked, the pills and the

gin making her nervous and vulgar. "You do masturbate, don't you, James? You must do. Unless you have some little woman tucked away on West Fifty-eighth Street. Or perhaps it's a boy. You know, James, I always thought you should try the man thing. You'd be a marvelous fag. Lord knows you have the waistline for it."

I stood up, edged my way out of the table and the restaurant, and went back to my office, where I spent too much time wondering who the blue-haired lady was whom Jean had been lunching with, wondering about Jean.

The blue-haired woman was a virulent type named Babs Raymer. I learned, when we put the pieces of the story together, that Jean lunched with her again on Friday, January twelfth, several hours before she was to meet Dutch Cohen for the first time. (I, of course, had been firmly ensconced in Dutchy's firmament for some time.)

She had returned to that apartment on Seventieth Street late in the afternoon and realized that she hadn't really eaten all day. She had skipped breakfast and moved her food around the plate during lunch. Though it makes her feel lightheaded—or maybe because it does— she often goes for an entire day without food.

That Friday afternoon, she shed her fur coat and lay down in the center of the huge, satin-covered bed that took up most of the available and expensive space, and closed her eyes.

She still hadn't become accustomed to the fatigue. Though she didn't particularly like the job, she enjoyed working. Earning her own money was a novelty that, like the fatigue, wouldn't wear off.

She had discovered, working for Lilli, that she was what her father would have approvingly called a conscientious worker. She found herself putting in more hours than anyone else, going in at eight, not leaving until it was time to go to dinner or a party.

"I was afraid all of the time. Afraid that I was going to be fired. Even though I knew I was the best she had, even though Lilli constantly reassured me, I always felt, in the back of my mind, that she was going to let me go, that she was waiting for the appropriate moment. The littlest error would make me crazy for weeks. And the major ones! The day I realized I had mismeasured a room in a town house on Seventy-fourth Street and ordered carpeting a good square foot too short was the day I seriously considered suicide."

That Friday in early January she was too tired to eat. She had been shopping fireplace mantles with Babs Raymer who, in addition to being blue haired, was thin and hostile and in her late fifties.

"They were all thin and hostile and in their late fifties. That's the time when women of a certain class and mentality think about redecorating." Babs Raymer knew all about Jean's mother. She pointed out that Jean was lucky not to be a permanent resident at Dobbs in Connecticut or at Doctor Siegel's place out on the end of Long Island. Babs Raymer is a woman, I gather, who prides herself on not mincing words. "It's a wonder you can keep a job," she said, echoing Jean's thoughts. "With your background."

That afternoon, which was unseasonably warm for January, she made herself a cup of tea in the chorus-girl kitchen, which was separated from what was designated the living area by a series of mirrored panels. She sipped the tea, jasmine, and tried to obliterate the insistent image of Babs Raymer, sitting in the back of her black limousine, her gloved hands clasping each other.

The letter was mixed in among the bills from Bendel's and Bergdorf's. It was from Auntie Mae Bonita. Auntie Mae had been the only female friend she could ever remember her mother having. A hairdresser, reputedly Rita Hayworth's henna expert, she would show up at the Bel-Air house when Jean was a child, ostensibly to do everyone's hair.

"We'd sit in the kitchen—which, like every room in the house, was sixty foot square—on huge mock-Gothic chairs. Enoch, the butler, would schlepp down the back stairs from the dining room, assisted by whoever was the gardener of the moment. We ran through a terrible lot of gardeners.

"Auntie Mae would tailor her gossip to the age of the person she was working on. Lita would always be first. At that point in her life, she was experimenting with lilacs and mauves and would descend to the kitchen from her third-floor suite in the gilt elevator she had had installed, wrapped in a sheer purple dressing gown trimmed with what I like to think were maribou feathers. Auntie Mae would chat, through her mouth stuffed with bobby pins and curlers, about the silents and the scandals of the twenties when both Lita and Auntie Mae were featured players with Lasky.

"When Auntie Mae got to mother, to Lorraine, and started smearing the ugly henna through her hair, she would change decades and go into the forties and fifties when the scandals all had to do with divorce and adultery and homosexuality. 'I don't suppose you know that A. and L. are sharing a house in Palm Springs,' she would say as her strong hands worked the solution into Lorraine's hair. 'And I hear that ain't all those two girls are sharing.'

" 'No!' Lorraine would say, as if she, too, hadn't read *Confidential*, as if she hadn't been to a party the night before where L. and A. showed up holding hands. Dear God, I loved those stories. I'd hang on every word. A morning in the kitchen with Auntie Mae Bonita is the closest to a Norman Rockwell family scene I can dredge up."

The letter was written in red ink on gray paper. Jean, suddenly hungry, started to read it while hunting around in a cabinet over the half fridge, hoping to find a can of something. After the first sentence, she stopped hunting and went back to the bed.

The letter read: "Dear Jean Rice, I am so sorry that your mother, the divine Lorraine, has passed over and so quietly, too. Too quietly for a star of her magnitude. You know, I didn't see all that much of her after the trial and all the hoopla that followed. I was living up the Coast in Selvan which is a community for tourists all tricked up to look like a little piece of old Scandinavia. Lorraine hated to come up there. Said it made her nauseous to see all those tiny reproductions. She always liked my little house out in the Valley.

"They wouldn't tell me exactly what it was that took her. All they would say when I called was that she had passed over. I didn't see any notice in the LA paper or hear anything on the TV. If I were pressed, I would say it was from the big C. Whenever I read the cards for Lorraine, the big C was always mixed up somewhere in the background, looking as if it was ready to pounce.

"I know you two didn't get on all that well and probably had little contact in recent years but I did want to say that I thought it was a shame a star like Lorraine Rice dying like that, with absolutely no publicity and thus I am expressing my heart felt condolences.

"If you ever do get out to the Coast, you make sure you come and visit me here in Gardena. I have a nice little stucco cottage right in the middle of the Japanese community and though it can be a touch lonesome, they sure are better to me than some folks I could name.

"With sincere affection and hoping this letter finds you in the very best of astral health, yours truly, (Auntie) Mae Bonita, Hairdresser to the Stars."

She spent two frantic hours on the telephone, attempting to reach all the people in Southern California who would talk to her. There weren't many, it being lunchtime in Beverly Hills on a Friday. Most of the people she called were unwilling to put down their salad fork or their hand-strung racquet or their masseuse's middle finger to take a call from Jean Rice Halladay. Long-distance conversations with any of the Rice women hadn't proved overly profitable in the past.

Finally, she got through to her mother's last husband's house in Malibu. He sent a woman named Sybil to the phone. "We didn't see any reason to trouble you, Jean, dear. I mean, what would have been the point? That's what I said to Rex. 'What is the point?' Ringing you up in New York and making you fly all the way back here for what you must realize was a very simple, extremely private ceremony out at the Lawn. Of course, she was cremated. No one wanted any publicity. You certainly can understand that, Jean dear. The media would have unearthed everything all over again and all our private lives would be raked over the coals. And, to put it bluntly, there wasn't any money for the sort of extravagant funeral Lorraine would have liked to have had. She didn't have a sou, my dear. The house was only on loan, thanks to Rex and his brother. The car and the few pieces of genuine jewelry barely paid for the funeral as it was."

"How much do I owe Rex?" Jean asked. "I'll send him a check."

"Don't be that way, Jean dear. Please."

"Let me speak to him."

"Actually, he's not here at the moment. He's all involved in Valley real estate these days. Up to his neck in it."

"He always was up to his neck in it."

"Jean dear, leave your number and I'll make absolutely certain Rex calls you the very second he comes in."

She slammed the receiver down on the cradle with so much force the plastic jacket cracked. Then she tried to phone Auntie Mae Bonita, who didn't appear to have a telephone, and that made her feel even more disconnected and alone. She tried to drink some tea, but her hand was shaking. She dropped the cup into the sink, where the fine Rose Medallion porcelain cracked into a great many pieces, and she began to cry.

"I wasn't crying for Lorraine," she said.

"Then who were you crying for?"

"Me, you dope. Who the hell do you think?"

CHAPTER 2

Jean was educated at first in a private school for movie millionaires' children and then by a series of governesses and tutors. She has wild gaps in her knowledge of history, geography, and English literature. She is very good with numbers. "It's in my blood," she says. "Daddy was an accountant at heart. And Lorraine always knew where her last penny was and when not to spend it."

Dutch Cohen liked to claim he had no formal education whatsoever, that he spent the years at Yeshiva smoking cigarettes in the boys' room, that the six months he attended classes at Pratt were a joke. The gaps in his knowledge of almost everything save fashion and film were bottomless holes, never to be filled.

Though I have what passes for an upper-class education in this country, Dutch and Jean both, at various and simultaneous moments, have expressed amazement at the holes in *my* knowledge, at the gaps in *my* experience.

"Darling," Dutch said, his painted eyebrows rising a good two inches over his mascaraed eyes, "how could you not know about Jean's mother's trial? It's been televised, novelized, made into two motion pictures and a rock opera. Darling!"

"I was aware she had had some unsavory trouble. I didn't know the details," I said, defensively.

"Darling," Dutch said, taking two steps back from me as if I were a carrier. "Darling!"

That unseasonably warm January afternoon, after confirming the fact of her mother's death, after she had stopped crying and realized she was going to do nothing about the noncelebration of that event, she put her arms around the cherry-colored satin teddy bear she had carried with her everywhere and examined her life.

Not reviewed it. Examined it. Even now, every so often, when events go very wrong, when she's about to lose control, she will step back and go into one of her psychoanalytic reveries, presenting a laundry list of important events, explaining what part they have played in making her who she is.

That she grew up in Hollywood/Beverly Hills is apparent to anyone who has ever had anything to do with Southern California. By the time she was eight, she had been to Europe twice, Asia once, and New York half a dozen times.

"I used to go with Daddy when Lorraine was drying out or getting it off with someone or lapping up ersatz motherly comfort at Auntie Mae Bonita's out in the Valley."

Daddy—Lewis Fisher Halladay—came from a long line of Californians (well, as long a line as a Californian can have). He was one of the few local men to become a power in the film industry. "The Wall Streeters who were actually running the studio at that point trusted Daddy because he wasn't a Jew," Jean says, as if that made sense. He would go to the studio every day of the week, to check the budgets. He had a navy blue Buick sedan and a chauffeur got up in navy blue livery. "The car and the driver were New York's idea. Hollywood is a great respecter of controlled luxury."

There's a photograph of him in her collection. "He didn't have a title. That's how important he was." Tall, blond, and worried, he wears—in all the snapshots—a dark double-breasted suit. There's something of Truman's mid-American determination about him, his rimless glasses making him look firm, dedicated, and sincere.

It was only after his death (so unlikely for a man who looked like that), when she was going through his papers, after the seal in his office in the Bel-Air house had been broken, that she found the plastic picture-fold section of his surprisingly pedestrian wallet. In it were a dozen photographs of Jean, taken at different ages.

"He'd whip them out at a moment's notice," Lorraine told her. "Baby, your father was crazy about you."

"I wish he had let me in on the secret."

Both her grandfathers had died by the time she was born. The grandmother she knew and liked best was her mother's mother, the silent film star, Lita Rice. Lita was born in a working-class section of Cleveland in 1900. She lasted in Cleveland until she was twenty and ran off to California with a married beer salesman who deserted her fairly promptly in the then village of Hollywood. It was she who had caused the Bel-Air house to be built. She lived in one of the third-floor suites while Jean was growing up, with a collection of costumes from her films and Rudolph Valentino's Ouija board.

"She was a dedicated craftswoman," Jean says of her. "Dead serious about Film As Art, about the crucial importance of glamour in a star's career." She died soon after Jean turned seven and had a quiet funeral, attended by Jean, Lorraine, Lewis, her maid, and two of her ex–leading men who looked, according to Jean, as if they had been released from Madame Tussaud's for the day.

Jean rarely speaks of her other grandmother, and when she does, she doesn't speak well of her. Jean and her paternal grandmother, Mary Halladay, were the only mourners at Lewis Halladay's funeral. Lorraine was in protective sedation in the Bel-Air house, guarded by two policewomen, awaiting arraignment on charges of killing her husband after he shot her lover.

"It was the last of the great Hollywood scandals. Now," Jean says, "they embezzle sixty thousand dollars and think *that*'s a scandal.

"I was clear at the other end of the house, half an acre away, sleeping with my teddy bear and the governess, a terrible dyke named Anya," Jean says, sometimes. "The first thing I knew was that Teddy and I were being wrapped in a fur blanket and being carried down the two hundred black marble steps, through the grand hall and out into the black Packard Grandmother Halladay kept as a symbol of her old California lineage, her apartness from anything to do with film."

Jean spent the next few years of her life with Mary Halladay, then a ripe seventy, learning to be a lady. They lived in a house Frank Lloyd Wright designed at the top of Gower Street where it becomes one of the Hollywood Hills. "That was the agreement. She would get mother off if mother would give me to her. I don't know where her head could have been. Mother would have given me to her for a very dry martini."

Sometimes Jean will give another version of the night her father died. They vary, depending upon her mood, her audience, the day of the week.

In the one she likes best, she remembers hearing gunshots and running down those two hundred steps that made up the central staircase, Teddy in her arms, pushing open the paneled library doors. "Mother was sitting in one of the Cecil B. DeMille biblical chairs, a silver pistol in her hand. Her lover, a Mexican boy who helped with the grounds, was lying on the flagstone floor in front of her. It was a hot, dry, California desert of a night. He was wearing khaki shorts, the kind boys wear in the army. Father was standing just inside the French windows. He walked across the room, a movement which seemed to be endless, took the gun from mother's hand and wiped it carefully with the handkerchief he always carried in his breast pocket.

"He raised the pistol to his head. I remember hearing the click of the trigger and then the shot. An enormous spurt of blood came pouring out of the side of his head. It was as if someone had stuck a tap in his temple and turned it on. The blood was the same color as the Chinese rug he was standing on. He fell. Mother began to scream, theatrically. Seeing me, she stopped and said, 'Now what am I supposed to do?' She said it casually, as if the laundry had forgotten to deliver the sheets, as if she were stuck in the middle of a scene and needed direction."

There are several other renditions, all of them beginning with Jean and Teddy in bed and ending with her mother's screams. On rare occasions, she'll smoke a cigarette and pick up the story. "After Grandmother Halladay bought off the judge, the jury, and the prosecutor, after it was 'conclusively proved in court' that the Mex shot my father and then himself, I would see Lorraine once every month. That was when the three of us would

21

make an appearance at either Chasen's or Jean Leone's or the old La Rue. They would all stop speaking the moment we were shown to our table and start in again the moment we were seated. They loved her. Lorraine played a magnificent widow.

"Naturally she wore all black. Black turban, black sheath, black gloves. Grandmother Halladay and I were in the southern color for mourning: your pure white. Grandmother would order, would set the tone for the conversation, would keep up the entire conversation by herself. Lorraine would smile and nod and look wistful.

"I wouldn't say a word. Once in a while I'd see an old classmate like Valerie DeVine, sitting with her mother and friends laughing or fighting but certainly living, and there was I, stuck in a banquet at the Bistro between my mother the murderess and her unlikely protectress, the victim's mother. Playing our roles out in front of a loving, appreciative audience.

"They did adore Lorraine. They just wouldn't let her forget the scandal. It was un-American. Hollywood was as closed to Lorraine Rice as if she had done a benefit for Joseph Stalin."

A blood clot in her brain struck down Grandmother Halladay one morning while she was shopping for gloves in May and Company. Jean moved back into the Bel-Air house with Lorraine. Jean was seventeen and Lorraine was forty-seven.

"Baby," Lorraine said to her, surprised, "we don't have any money." The Halladay oil wells had long since run dry, and Grandmother Halladay had spent what was left of her fortune (after reprieving Lorraine) on keeping up appearances.

"Maybe," Jean said, having to raise her voice so Lorraine could hear her (the acoustics in the dining room were not what they could have been), "you should marry Rank."

"Baby, I couldn't."

She did. Rex Rank was a Brentwood lawyer–real estate–investment man who was forty-five, twice divorced, and who had been Lorraine's lover for seven years. He was as hopelessly in love with Hollywood as was Jean's father. He wanted to marry a legend.

Rank tore down the Bel-Air house and put up sixty condominiums, in the luxest of which he installed Jean and her mother.

He was a man who would have liked to have lived in the Bel-Air house but claimed practicality as one of his virtues. He was a man who did not regard intimacy with his stepdaughter as incestuous. "He had the biggest cock I've ever seen. It was as long and as thick as a typewriter carriage. And just as relentless. For a long time I thought all men were equipped like Rank."

He was her first. His best friend, Jack Royce (né Greenberg) was the second, seducing her on the reclining front seat of his white Rolls-Royce convertible on a Tuesday afternoon high up in D.W. Griffith Park. He and Rank had a history of "trading dates," but Royce fell in love with Jean.

"I was his Lolita. He used to tell me that as he fucked me from behind: 'You're my little Lolita, honey.' It was the only way he could get it off."

Royce was forty, worked out in Pete's Gym in the Valley five days a week, and owned—along with his unappetizing wife—a series of expensive boutiques in Beverly Hills, Palm Springs, and New York. "Nancy Sinatra used to shop in the Beverly Hills store all the time," Jean told us. Seeing Dutch's expression, she threw him a bone. "As did Dietrich."

When Royce suggested Jean skip junior college (San Fernando Valley State) and come to New York with him, where she could work in the Fifty-seventh Street shop, Lorraine was enthusiastic.

"You're a big girl now, Baby," she had said. "I had hoped you would continue with your education, but Jack's offering you a marvelous opportunity. . . ." She gave Jean a check for five thousand dollars and had her husband, Rank, drive Jean to the airport. They went via the Sunset Marquee Motel on the Strip "for old time's sake."

"The day I arrived in New York, I was wearing a very short, white skirt, a pink blouse, and candy-striped knee socks. Jack Royce nearly came in his pants. He met me at the airport with his East Coast Rolls."

The seats in that automobile did not recline, but that was unnecessary as he had the Seventieth Street apartment. "It was Jack's pad, the place where he scored." Jack's scoring days, for the time, were over. Jean was installed.

She saw Lorraine only once after she left California. Jean had been in New York for five years when the Ranks, on their way to London, stopped in New York. They stayed at the Plaza (not a good sign, real California money checking into the Sherry Netherland) and took Jean into the Edwardian Room for dinner. Lorraine's skin looked as if it would crack if it were touched, "like one of those alligator purses Lita used to carry around in the forties."

It had been seven P.M. The headwaiter had made a

little fuss over them. There were no other diners. The three of them sat in the middle of that vast, improbable room, listening to the sounds of cutlery and china being shuffled by the white-coated staff.

Rank, a little drunk, said, "You've turned into quite a beauty, Jean." He took her hand and put it on the bulge between his legs. "Say hello to an old friend, Jean."

After that, there were only Christmas cards and checks, even after Rank and Lorraine divorced.

"Darling," Dutch asked her at this point in her narrative, "what more did you want? Lorraine Rice was a double legend: a movie star *and* a murderess. Nine tenths of the world would trade you mothers without blinking a false eyelash. You couldn't expect her to be so fabulous and give you motherly love, too."

"I didn't even want the checks."

"You're all too sentimental about mothers, dolls," Dutch went on, lighting a joint, talking about Fay, his own, far from satisfactory mother.

Two years after Royce installed Jean in the Seventieth Street apartment, his wife divorced him, taking the two children, the Holmby Hills House, the Palm Springs and Manhattan shops in the settlement.

Disappointed, Jack announced he was returning to California to take care of business. Jean was not to accompany him. "Honey, you are not cut out to be a shop girl," he said, giving her a check for ten thousand dollars, half of which she spent on a black fox coat she saw at Bergdorf's.

She wasn't exactly alone in New York. "I knew a thousand men," she says. "Not one woman. I didn't trust them then and I'm not sure I do now." After Royce came

Peter Antonucci. After Peter Antonucci came Richard Wright Langston. After Richard Wright Langston came Sonny Velasquez. Etcetera. They were all there in her photograph collection. Handsome, thick, for the most part young and privileged.

She lived on her mother's Christmas checks, on the largess of the men she was having sex with.

She took sketching at the New School. She read the *Daily News*, the *Post*, and the movie reviews in the *Times*. She met men for lunch. She went to a daily dance class. She shopped for clothes. "There was always plenty to do," she says when I ask her what she did with the time she wasn't in bed.

It came to an end, that lazy period of indiscriminate, endless sexual activity, when she met—more or less simultaneously—Bert Brown and Victoria DeVine.

CHAPTER 3

It's a weekend Jean analyzes almost as often as she does the scandal.

"It was late June and it was hot and this man I was seeing, Dickie Hull—he had these long, muscular legs—asked me if I wanted to go to Southampton for the weekend. He didn't sound particularly enthusiastic, but he never did. Friends were giving a house party for someone who was running for a minor city office and there was going to be a big benefit party—Bella had promised to appear—all very swank and timely.

"I asked Dickie if I needed to bring a long dress and he said he rather thought that I did.

"We flew out in Dickie's little plane. A car picked us up at the East Hampton Airport and drove us into Southampton to one of those Gin Lane houses on the ocean that look as if they ache to be in Southern California —all Moorish arches and twirled balustrades.

"The guest of honor and his wife were delayed, we were told by the host, an ex-senator with jowls. Edward Arnold would have played him in the film. 'Bert's campaigning his ass off.'

"Dickie and I were shown to our rooms by a starched

maid. We had sex and showered and changed and went down to the balcony which was a hundred feet long and twenty feet wide. It had terra cotta tile flooring and faced the ocean. It reminded me of our house in Bel-Air (we didn't have an ocean but we certainly had a pool).

"The women all had rich girls' names and expensive haircuts and talked about Dale Collins's party at the River Club. As it happened, I had been there so that was all right. I knew two of the men, but we were being repressed and polite and I pretended not to. Someone lit a joint which wasn't unusual in that time and place and everyone was getting a little drunk.

"I recognized Victoria the moment I stepped out onto the balcony and took a glass of champagne from the butler's tray. Difficult not to, Victoria being six feet tall and having undisguisable hips. She said later that of course she had known me, too. 'Instantly.'

"Her father, Max, had been a hotshot director in the fifties, working at Daddy's studio. She and I attended Tuller School together along with a couple of dozen other Hollywood brats, three of whom became failed actors, two of whom committed suicide, and one of whom became a writer specializing in books detailing 'intimate' secrets of her neurotic upbringing.

"I had always adored Victoria. At the same time I was jealous. She had a mother and a father, always swooping down on the school and taking her off for forbidden treats. After the trial, after Grandmother Halladay had withdrawn me from the Tuller School (and life), the only time I ever saw her was across rooms in restaurants.

"Victoria smiled and I smiled but we made no move to come together across that balcony laden with guests, servants, food, and Italian summer furniture, the sort decorated with tons of cast-iron grapes. There was a moment when I wondered if Victoria would regale the assemblage with the Tragedy of Lorraine Rice, and decided, after looking at her, that she wouldn't, that she hadn't changed. As a child she had oozed maternal solicitude, always the first with the colored Band-Aids and the candy pills.

"Bert and Catherine still hadn't turned up by the time dinner was over. No one knew where they were, whether they were actually coming. The senator, who had sat me on his right, kept going to the phone, trying to find out. The handsome young quiet type on my right, whose name I didn't get then, told me the senator was trying to decide whether or not to call off Bella and Sunday's fete. He looked at me with mournful eyes.

"We all trooped back out onto the balcony to sip cordials and watch the black sky and the white moon. A young, plain, and tough woman came up to the wicker love seat where I was sitting with Dickie, planting her feet firmly in front of me. During dinner, after the lobster salad, she had said that she liked to think of herself as a 'neon Hedda Hopper.' She was in her early twenties and had already achieved a certain notoriety, publishing articles in the lesser magazines, taking cheap shots at easy targets like Streisand and Jerry Brown.

"She was just another California girl, a couple of years after my time, compensating for what she looked like.

" 'You're Lorraine Rice's daughter, aren't you?' she asked, though it was more of an accusation than a question. There followed one of those drop-dead silences.

"I said that I was.

" 'Tell me,' she said, in her upholstered shotgun voice, 'is it true she was getting sandwich fucked by two wetbacks when your father strolled into the room?'

"It was then that Victoria DeVine covered the full length of the balcony in four seconds flat and slapped whatever-her-name-was across her wide horse's mouth and said, 'You're not a neon Hedda Hopper, kid. You're a neon cunt.'

Victoria put her long arm in Jean's and escorted her down the steps that led to the beach. They took off their silver sandals (California girls always wear silver sandals back east, Jean believes) and walked half a mile up the beach to the two-story, two-room folly built in the twenties by the then owner as a "little place to get away from it all."

They propped themselves up against a wicker davenport and smoked joints Victoria carried in a Cartier case designed for that purpose. They didn't speak until Victoria looked over at her and said, "Nothing could make the little princess smile." And Jean smiled. "It's been that bad, huh?"

"No," Jean said and burst into tears.

Victoria put down her joint and put her arms around Jean. After a while, Jean looked up and saw that Victoria was crying, too. "What're you crying about?"

"I always cry when other people cry. I'm eccentric. Listen, what're you doing with Dickie Hull?"

"What do you think I'm doing with Dickie Hull?"

"That's what I thought. Do you have a job?"

"Are you out of your mind?"

"Listen—the first thing we're going to do is get you a job. The second thing we're going to do is find you a man. Or vice versa. What'd you think of Buddy Ruben?"

"Who was Buddy Ruben?" Jean asked, borrowing Victoria's handkerchief, blowing her nose into it.

"He sat next to you for two hours during dinner."

"Not my type. Too nice."

"Listen, Jean. I think you're going to have to change your type." They sat up until dawn, talking about Hollywood, smoking joints, and crying.

The remainder of the weekend is a vague memory to Jean. The Mouth had been asked to leave and had done so the following morning. She had gone too far, and the senator's wife didn't want her own name showing up in the wrong columns.

Jean and Victoria played tennis, swam, and hiked down to the public beach with the rest of the house guests to look at poor people. They filled in one another on their biographies. Victoria was editor-in-chief of *Interiors, the* decorators' bible. "I've always adored playing house," Victoria said. She was married to a weak-chinned man named Morgan, who kept out of her way. "I felt as if I had been adopted," Jean says.

Bert and Catherine arrived in time for the fete, and Jean shook their suntanned hands. Catherine had enough poise to float the Titanic, she remembers thinking. "They looked mean and leathery, like all those rich kids with a mission. I was too overwhelmed with Victoria, with the warmth and comfort she was giving me, to notice much else."

Afterward, they saw each other daily. She learned a great deal, she says, from Victoria. "I couldn't believe one person had so many opinions. About so many subjects. I've always felt, more or less, that I had to agree with anything anyone said. That is, when I was being agreeable and wanting to be liked. When I was being disagreeable, I would say 'fuck' a lot or be quiet and withdraw. It never occurred to me that I could be vocal about what I hated and still be accepted.

"Once, in the living room of that triplex Morgan had bought for her in the Dakota, Victoria said, 'I hate, loathe, and despise people.' I thought she was going to be struck dead. I felt the same way. But I couldn't imagine admitting, out loud, that I did. I remember saying 'People are disgusting, aren't they?' and feeling very naughty."

She lit a pipe filled with hash—we're terrible dopers whenever we're together—and said, just as Dutch might, "People are the woist."

Victoria felt that though there were several suitable careers a woman might engage in, there was only one for Jean. At least one in which she might help her. Jean was to become a decorator. Or, as Dutch would say, a decoratress.

According to Victoria, Buddy Ruben had fallen "immediately and hopelessly, head over heels in love with Jean" during the Southampton weekend.

I have known Buddy Ruben since he was a freshman and I was a senior at the same university. He always made the right club, the right team, the right alliance. Still, there was something in Buddy's makeup that made people think he was ashamed of himself in some subtle way, that he was always aware of some hidden, inner flaw in his character. He looks like a prizefighter and comes on like the early Gary Cooper. He was popular, when I knew him well, with vain women and overbearing men. Jean, after Victoria's party for her, still wasn't interested in Buddy Ruben.

"I've never liked 'nice' men," she enjoys saying. "And don't tell me that's because my father wasn't nice. And don't tell me you're nice. You're not. You miss by a mile, James."

Despite Jean's apparent lack of interest, Buddy and Victoria arranged an interview with Buddy's mother. Lilli Ruben, of Lilli Ruben Associates, is a famous Jewish dragon, the sort for whom they weed out the more vocal anti-Semites when she deigns to accept an invitation. She appeared in New York in the mid-1930s—a refugee, it is said, from Hitler's Germany. It is also said that she was married to one of the von Papens and that Buddy was the issue that resulted from that union. Perhaps that's what Buddy is embarrassed by.

Lilli is small and ugly and chic and as fascinating as a diamond-backed snake in a glass cage. When she declares shirred walls, shirrers are busy up and down Fifth Avenue for months.

BaBa used to have weekly consultations with Lilli in Lilli's simple little gold-and-blue consultation room, for a time, immediately after BaBa's sessions with her charlatan analyst in his simple little silver-and-mauve consultation room. BaBa used to wonder, aloud, which of them did her more good. My money, in more ways than one, was on Lilli.

She hired Jean at something like one hundred and fifty dollars a week, declaring she would be, at the least, decorative. Jean asked if Lilli knew who her mother was. Lilli tut-tutted and waved her tiny, beringed, wrinkled hand. "That can only help, darling girl."

"You've changed your life," Victoria said when Jean told her about her job. Over jasmine tea and Thai sticks, they congratulated one another. "Listen, Jean—you've taken charge."

"No," Jean said, puffing slowly on the Thai stick, letting the drug work its potent way into her mind and body, "you and Buddy and Lilli have."

"I never slept with Buddy Ruben," she says.

"Darling!" Dutch said. "You didn't do it with Buddy Ruben and you could have? I'm flabbergasted. I, personally, would pay five grand to do it once with Buddy Ruben. They ran a picture of him in *After Dark* when he was running for something or other—councilman?—and he didn't have a shirt on. The sexiest hairless chest, with a wonderful—I mean wonderful—tapered waist. Oy, what I would do to Buddy Ruben if I could get him into that bed."

"I was saving him," Jean says. "When things were at their worst with Bert, I used to have this fantasy. Once I was really finished with Bert, I would go to Buddy's apartment, ring the bell, and get into his bed where I would be petted and loved and made to feel a wife. I never identified with Judy in the Andy Hardy film. Or, for that matter, with the vamp Mother played. I wanted to be Judge Hardy's wife, bustling around the kitchen, worrying about the kids' hot lunches, being secure.

"That's what I believed life with Buddy Ruben would be. One sunny Sunday in May we would drive down to City Hall, be married by the mayor, and overnight I would become this adorable junior league matron with a Jewish husband who would end up governor and a benevolent despot of a mother-in-law with pots of money and influence. . . ."

"But, darling! How could you restrain yourself? Darling, Buddy Ruben's a knockout."

For Jean he was, then, a technical knockout.

Besides, Bert was just then lurking on the perimeter, about to step mid-circle and take over.

CHAPTER 4

Bert Brown's mother was once married to BaBa's father.

"No shit," Jean commented.

Bert Brown doesn't come from "great stock," as Aunt Alice would have it, but his ancestry is more than acceptable in the circles in which he revolves. He is a man who shares, with what I assume is a greatly diminished few, the American dream of becoming President of these United States. ("The American Dream," Dutch once said, "is easy suicide.") I can't think of a single reason why someday he shouldn't be just that.

Taking into consideration Jean's mistress fantasy, her relationship with Bert would seem to have been an adultery conceived in heaven. It is a fantasy that Dutch Cohen shared—begun when, coincidentally enough, he saw a revival of *Another Woman*, a film in which Jean's mother played a tycoon's backstreet dalliance.

"Even though Lorraine died in the fadeout—she dropped about one thousand Nembutals, one by one—I personally thought she had the best of both worlds," Dutch told us. "She had a little maid, a little house, a little car, and she only had to see the leading man twice a week when he could get away from his frigid wife's endless cocktail parties. And she had the most stunning Adrian clothes."

One never thought of Bert's wife, Catherine, as being frigid. Not then, at any rate. Bert is so undeniably good-looking. Smooth and handsome in the contemporary nostalgic style. He wears his hair slicked back. He has sleepy eyes. He seems to be in control, always. Though he comes from a longish line of Americans, he has developed a sort of indefinable ethnicity, one that reminded me of George Raft and Dutch of Robert De Niro.

"He reminds me of no one on earth," Jean says. "He's a very special kind of monster."

If Bert remembered that he had met Jean during the weekend of his Southampton launch, he never said so, and she never reminded him. They met again when she was redecorating the mayor's bedroom, the job of adding luster to the mayor's new home falling quite naturally on Lilli's slightly hunched shoulder. Not only was Buddy Ruben part of the new administration, but Lilli Ruben was a power in her own right.

"The mayor," Jean says, "had ordered humor and austerity, and I was going nuts trying to decide what was humorous and what was austere. Ronnie LeBonne, that little red-haired screamer who's been with Lilli for years, was doing the public rooms downstairs, which were a hell of a lot easier. I was stuck with the bedroom.

"The color wasn't a problem as the mayor's taste ran the gamut from white to off-white and the furniture was strictly Abraham and Straus. It was the accents, as they say in the trade, that were making me so crazy. Every time I saw a little painting that I thought might be perfect, I had to ask myself if it were humorous *and* austere and of course it never was. If it were the Lindsays I would have hung a Warhol or borrowed something old and great from the Met and have done with it. Even the Beames would have been easier. A small, homey Chagall and I would have been on my way. But this one wanted humorous *and* austere.

"Finally I schlepped a huge papier-mâché bunny I found in a Madison Avenue *haute* junk shop up to his bedroom and propped it in a corner.

"Betty Pollette, that glorified thirty-two-thousand-five-hundred-dollar-a-year housekeeper, had taken one look at the bunny—it was pale pink and six feet long—and sniffed.

"Though I told myself Betty Pollette with her DVF dress belonged in New Jersey where she came from, that sniff made me insane. Was the bunny too austere? (It had seen better days.) Was it too humorous, too off-the-wall? I would have given my fur coat for a joint, but that obviously wasn't possible so I sat down and studied the fucking bunny.

"The door opened just as I decided I had better take it back to the junk shop and Bert waltzed in with that choreographed Jimmy Cagney strut of his. He and Buddy Ruben, as elected minor officials with their own reservoirs of power, were both habitués of Gracie Mansion. He had come up to see what Betty Pollette had been sniffing about.

"I don't know if I can explain the effect he had on me. It's never stopped. Even now, if I saw him, I know I'd feel a bit of it. You know that phrase, 'weak in the knees'? I actually felt weak in the knees when he walked into that room. I don't know why he didn't do that to me in Southampton. But that day in the mayor's bedroom in Gracie Mansion, I was totaled.

"Knowing you, James, I don't suppose you've ever been hit like that, that overwhelming sexual punch, getting you square in the solar plexus, not to mention other areas. It supersedes everything. All civilization, all restraints get stripped away. I would have done anything in the sexual line Bert Brown wanted me to do five seconds after he came in.

"He has those big, wide hands that have nothing to do with the rest of his body, and when he took mine in his, by way of introduction, I thought I was actually going to pass out. We couldn't have said more than half a dozen words to each other before I was in his arms. I lifted my face to be kissed but he only smiled, released me, went to the door and locked it. Then he came back to me, put those outsized hands on my shoulders, and pushed me to the floor.

"I remember noticing, as he undid his pants, that he had fly buttons, which meant that he went to an old-fashioned custom tailor. He dropped them and then he undid his undershorts. They were the Brooks Brothers kind with snaps at the top. He undid them slowly. Everything he did was slow and measured and beautifully performed.

"He has a gorgeous cock. Not circumcised, perfectly shaped. It's like a cannon, astride two round, almost hairless balls. 'Kiss it,' he said, and I did. Then he forced it into my mouth. It smelled of sweat and that incredibly cheap talcum—Lilac something-or-other—they give out in club barbershops.

"He did all the work, pushing himself in and out of my

mouth for what seemed like hours, slowing up when he was about to come, exercising that control of his. When he did come he told me to swallow it and I did.

"He disengaged himself, to coin a phrase, pulled up his trousers, went to the phone and made a call, telling someone that he was delayed, that he'd show up in an hour. Then he came back to me. I was sitting on the edge of the bed, absolutely out of it. I felt as if I had been hypnotized.

"He pushed me back and, just as in a naughty Victorian illustrated book, he lifted my skirt and pulled my panties down. He put two of his oversized fingers in me and, with his other hand, undid his trousers and opened his shirt.

"It was all so slick, so pornographic. He removed his fingers and then his shirt. He has one of those torsos with one million beautifully defined muscles, as if he earned his living posing for anatomy text drawings. He pulled me to the edge of the mattress, propped my legs up against his chest and went directly into me.

"I couldn't see what was happening. My skirt, one of those long crepe-de-chine numbers we were wearing then, was in the way. All I could see were my legs against his shoulders and his face. He was looking down, watching himself going in and out of me with those quick, brutal thrusts he specializes in.

"I must have come half a dozen times. When he came, I could feel his sperm shooting inside me, but his face showed nothing but a kind of polite disinterest. He pulled out of me and went to the bathroom. I lay there on the bachelor mayor's superfirm king-sized bed, my skirt up around my tits, my legs dangling over the end of the mattress, wondering what the hell had gone through me.

"He emerged from the bathroom, all buttoned and slicked, nodded at me as if I were some casual but not particularly attractive acquaintance, picked up his briefcase, unlocked the door, and was gone.

"I got myself to the bathroom, cleaned up, found a stain on the mayor's coverlet that was not going to come out, reversed the coverlet as Betty Pollette walked in. 'What's Bert think of the bunny?' she asked. 'He thought it was hot shit,' I said, moving past her and out the door, leaving her in a high state of sniff.

"All the way back to Lilli's in the taxi, I kept my mind occupied with the little things. The towels in the bathroom; the stain on the coverlet; the goddamned bunny. But in the back of my mind, that tiny, dark space I rarely let even myself into, I knew I had just had sex with a man who hadn't kissed me, who hadn't even pretended to enjoy touching me. It was the most exciting sex I had ever had. It was, at the same time, the most unsatisfactory. I wanted more.

"He called me at the office the next day and arrived at the apartment in the early evening and that was the beginning of that."

She loved it. She loved the way he rarely spoke directly to her. "She needs a new wardrobe," he had told her, surveying her closet during the early part of their— for want of a better word—romance, touching the white satiny dresses. He went with her and bought her softer, richer dresses. He became, almost instantly, her entire social and sexual life.

"Suddenly I was a one-man woman." She'd see him four or five times a week. "It wasn't an all-out undercover relationship. Catherine knew about it. Buddy would come along when we went anyplace where we might see people (like your Eye Ball), but we never avoided restaurants or parties or clubs. Bert has a certain honesty, I'll give him that."

"Were you in love with him?"

"James, you can be naive. I needed Bert Brown. I needed him to make me feel terrible about myself. He was all the hit-and-run sex—all the impersonal, angry sex I had ever had—all rolled into one perfectly shaped cock. I didn't need strangers with Bert around.

"There I was, feeling pretty good about the fact that I, Lorraine Rice's little girl, was actually working for a living, doing pretty well, supporting myself. And then I'd come home and wait for Bert to show up and do his fucking-without-touching trip. Intellectually I knew what I was doing to myself. No shrink had to tell me. I could not allow myself to feel good about myself. It's a hard habit to break after a lifetime."

Then the letter came from Lorraine Rice's ex–henna expert, and Jean cried for the first time since her father died, and she didn't seem to be able to stop.

CHAPTER 5

She was still crying an hour later when the phone began to ring. She let it go on for a while and then, when she realized it wasn't going to stop, put down the teddy bear and the crumpled letter and answered it.

It was Buddy Ruben calling for Bert, who wanted to know where she was.

"Something's happened, Buddy. I don't think I can . . ."

"He told me to tell you he wasn't accepting excuses tonight."

She was silent for a moment. Then she said, "I'll be there in a half hour, depending on the taxi situation."

"There" was the Tavern-on-the-Green, where one of the more powerful Democrats' clubs was having a political smoker in the room studded with crystal chandeliers. Bert was very careful about the events to which he draped his wife around his arm and the events to which he draped Jean. Political smokers, for the most part, were definitely a mistress affair.

Jean went to her closet and pulled out a pre-Bert dress. It was a white satin wrapper with feathers on the sleeves and around the hem. "Its neckline," she says, "stopped just short of my vagina. It was the kind of dress that leaves nothing to the imagination except how much it cost. It was actually more Lorraine's sort of thing than mine." She wrapped ice cubes in a face cloth and lay down for five minutes with it over her eyes. Then she soaked cotton balls in witch hazel and used up another five minutes in the same way. "My eyes were so red, they looked like radishes." The swelling went down, and she attached three-carat aquamarine earrings in the shape of hearts to her ears and applied eye makeup, gingerly, to match. She searched for and found her highest, whoriest heels, dropped half an up, and walked over to Madison, where she hailed a Checker cab and asked the driver if he minded if she smoked a joint. He said he didn't, as long as he got a toke, so they split the joint as they drove down Fifth and across the Park to Central Park West and Tavern-on-the-Green.

The Crystal Room has a quantity of priceless chandeliers hanging from its vaulted ceiling and a glass wall fronting Central Park. That early evening it was filled with men in dark suits and vests, balding, fat, and jovial. They smoked cigars at each other, told each other old dirty jokes, and pretended to drink more than they did.

There was a perceptible reduction of noise as a waiter held the door open and Jean came through, hesitated, got a fix on the crowd, and pretended to look for Buddy who was signaling to her from a far corner. Only after she was absolutely certain that she had everyone's attention did she walk across the room, around the tables, with as much hauteur as her mother ever emanated in any of her films.

"It was a memorial performance for Lorraine." That

wasn't the end of it. She allowed Buddy to take the fur coat from her shoulders and then help her into a seat facing the room. Bert sat opposite her, talking to a short, tobacco-colored man who came from Brooklyn and was a key cog in the party machinery. His name was Delabowski and he began every sentence with "Now listen, pal." Neither he nor Bert affected to notice Jean, not missing a beat in their conversation when she sat down.

She ordered a double scotch from a waiter who was hovering over her, trying to see down her dress, and ignored Buddy's attempts at small talk.

She surveyed the room as the room surveyed her. It was certainly not the first time that she had managed to stop traffic at a social event she considered either beneath her or so far from her brand of reality that it didn't count, but she was enjoying it more than usual. Causing a stir among New York's mid-level power brokers gave her, that evening, some idea of her own power.

"Ask her why she's dressed in Frederick's of Hollywood's catalogue special," Bert said, when she had ordered another double. Virtually every eye in the room had shifted from Jean to the waiter bringing her the drink and then back to Jean again as she knocked it down in her best Rancho Notorious gesture. "Ask her why she's looking like a hooker on her last date."

Buddy looked at Bert, with big, pleading, plaintive brown eyes, but Bert only said, "Go ahead and ask her, Buddy."

Jean reached over and picked up Buddy's drink. It was some sort of rum concoction. She stood up, waited for the crowd to come to attention, and then threw it at Bert. First the liquid and then the glass.

"Since you weren't accepting excuses," Jean said. She

hooked that coat over her shoulder and started across the room, making her way through the tables, passing the uplifted, absorbed, red, fat faces.

Bert caught up to her at mid-room, below the green chandelier. His slicked-back hair was wet from the drink she had thrown at him. There was a red welt on his cheek where the glass had hit him. The expression on his face was of polite concern. He raised his big, soft right hand and slammed her across the face. She tried to kick him in the groin but he was prepared. He caught her foot by the heel and upended her. She landed on the carpet, the clasp on the white satin dress coming undone, revealing even more of her.

"Get Miss Rice out of here," Bert said, turning to Buddy. "Take Miss Rice home."

Jean pushed Buddy's helping hands out of the way, stood up, refixed the clasp, and proceeded to shout across the Crystal Room, across those short, fat, dumpy politicians with their cigars and their stomachs. "I shouted so loud, my throat hurt for days. I shouted so loud, I thought the goddamn chandeliers were going to fall on our heads. I shouted the first thing that came into my head: 'You'll never get elected to dogcatcher in this town when I get through. I'm going to drag you through every court in this state. I'm going to tell Barbara Walters that there's a practicing sadist on the staff of the mayor of New York. I'm going to . . .'"

Three quiet men had come into the room and, by this time, had escorted her to the emergency side door, which gave out onto a driveway where the limousines stood. Buddy was sitting in the one in which they placed her.

"They must have a lot of practice at this sort of thing,"

Jean said. "They barely touched me. Wonderful how gentle contemporary bouncers can be."

"You shouldn't have done that, Jean," Buddy Ruben said.

"I shouldn't have done what, Buddy? Throw the glass at his face, try to kick him in the nuts, or threaten him with coast-to-coast exposure?"

"You shouldn't have done it, Jean."

Buddy Ruben kept shaking his head, and suddenly she was thoroughly scared. Visions of acid being thrown in her face went through her mind.

Buddy had used the limousine telephone to call Victoria, to tell her that he thought Jean needed to be with someone. When Victoria and Morgan arrived, they insisted, with their sure sense of occasion, that she go with them to a dinner party.

"A dinner party! My God, it's two in the morning," Jean said.

"It is exactly nine seventeen," Morgan said, consulting his Rolex.

"Give me one good reason why I should," Jean asked, trying to hold her hand steady enough to light a cigarette.

"It will be amusing," Morgan said, studying his complexion in a blue glass mirror, not liking what he saw.

"It will be as amusing as a *berith*," his wife contradicted him. "There'll be forty fags and three undercooked lamb chops."

"So why on earth should she go?" Morgan asked, turning away from the mirror.

"She has just found out that her mother has been dead for months. She has had, to employ understatement, a sensational fight with Bert. She gets suicidal after fights with Bert, though only she and I and now you know that. Furthermore, she is likely to look on this day as a sign from above, thanks to her early a-religious training and her *mishuganah* grandmother. There is every reason for her to come."

"Victoria," Jean began to protest, weakly.

"Listen. This is not a night for you to stay home, put your hair in curlers and your feet up. So slap on your makeup—that is a nasty bruise—and move your exquisite ass."

Though Victoria DeVine is not one of the people I admire most in this world (*"au contraire,"* as her husband would say), she has had a certain positive influence on Jean's life. I will allow her that. After all, Victoria introduced her to Dutch.

CHAPTER 6

Victoria first met Dutch Cohen when her father, Sam, was making his farewell film (there have been seven more, to date) in Hong Kong. Victoria, eighteen and just out of school, was beginning and ending her motion picture career as a production assistant (read *go-for*).

Sam, being a firm believer in democracy and cutting costs, insisted that Victoria stay at the Hotel Woodrow Wilson along with the other lower-echelon members of the cast and crew. He and his redheaded mistress were at the Hong Kong Ritz, taking bubble baths, drinking Russian champagne, and otherwise comporting themselves like people making a movie.

"It was one hundred and eighty degrees in the shade," Victoria recalls, "and my hair took to coiling itself into millions of tiny spitcurls, and them were the days when straight hair was *à la mode*. I would just about make it in from location to the hot, damp cavern that was billed as a fully air-conditioned lobby and wait for the energy it took to face the elevator, which looked like one of those prisoner-of-war cages in which you can neither stand nor sit.

"After a week, I wasn't talking to any of the members of the crew or cast. I was on the verge of tears every minute of every hour of those hellish, interminable days. I was dying to get on a plane and head for somewhere civilized like Vegas.

"The one bright spot, the one moment of hilarity, came every evening at seven, while I was sitting in the lobby's cracked green-imitation-leather chair, panting for a drink—there was no bar. All the little bellhops—there were dozens of them—in their little blue pajama uniforms—would gather in the far corner around this fat, Jewish, balding pouf, absolutely mesmerized.

"Of course it was Dutchy, wearing Bermuda shorts, a thrift shop shirt from Second Avenue, and his high-heeled clogs. If you ask, he'll tell you what he was doing in Hong Kong, but it would take several hours so I'll make it short and snappy and tell you myself.

"An insane New York clothing manufacturer, at the end of his rope, hired Dutch to supervise the Hong Kong production of his shirt line. He sent Dutch to Hong Kong, put him up at the Woodrow Wilson, and gave him a tiny salary. All Dutchy had to do was go to the factory every morning to make sure they were putting the shirts right to front. It was his first job on being expelled from Pratt. One of his mother's Seventh Avenue boyfriends got it for him. Naturally he blew it.

"After a week or so of standing around the factory being bored, he took to dropping in every other day. Then once a week. And so on. Of course he was spending all of his time doing what he liked to do best: shop. He was buying *chatchkas*. The worst of all possible *chatchkas*. Tiny dragons painted in psychedelic colors. Little waiters' jackets with shoes to match. Plastic candelabras in the shape of snake heads. Pink teacups and yellow and black metal trays and rainbow-colored kimonos and anything else that cost less than a dollar and smelled remotely exotic.

"He was getting ready, he said, for the time when he would have a loft in New York, one of his recurring fantasies.

"Be that as it may, each night he'd bring his treasures back to the Woodrow and the bellhops, very shy and very sweet, would corner him in the lobby. 'What you buy today, Meester Dutch?' the one who spoke English would ask. Then, like a Polish-Jewish peddler, circa 1898, he would unwrap his wares. At first sight of the cellophane parasols and the ceramic ducks and the nylon happy coats, the little bellhops would go as wild as their natures and stations in life would allow, running off in all directions, recongregating in the opposite corner, tee-heeing themselves to death.

"One night, after witnessing this performance I don't know how many times, I went over and introduced myself to Dutch as he was wrapping his finds. 'Would you like a little opium, dolls?' he asked me after the preliminaries and naturally I said I would and we trotted on up to his room which fronted a clogged air shaft and made the Black Hole of Calcutta seem like the City of Light.

"We lit pipes, as they say. I had never done opium. I was out in two minutes. But you know Dutch and drugs. So there was I, sprawled on his lice-infested mattress in downtown Hong Kong, OD-ing on opium, captive to Dutchy Cohen who, the more he smoked, the more he talked. He gave me the full story of his life, the eight-hour version. I can't tell you how I felt. I thought I had gone mad."

Dutch was subsequently fired from his job by the irate manufacturer when the first shipment of shirts reached New York with three sleeves and other aberrations. Victoria had had enough of the movie business. She and Dutch teamed up and decided to travel through the East on their way back to New York. They had many exciting adventures, all of which Dutch related to me at one time or another.

Getting Victoria's version is difficult. She will only shake her head when I ask about the months they spent traveling through Korea, Japan, and India, saying, "You don't have the stomach, James, and I don't have the time."

Looking through my diary, I find that it was exactly two nights before Victoria was to introduce him to Jean that Dutch went to Le Dirt.

Le Dirt is a serious cruising bar in the neighborhood (Twenty-first and Sixth) where Dutch picked up a twenty-year-old hustler who had coal-black hair and size twelve shoes.

The hustler easily persuaded Dutch to go with him to Jersey City. Easily, because Dutch made it his cardinal rule never to bring a hustler home to his loft ("You're only inviting trouble in the door when you schlepp home one of those hustler kids, James"); because Dutch was stoned on hash, and when he was stoned on anything, he could be persuaded to do most anything; and because Jersey City was a place that smelled attractively of lower-class sex in Dutch's imagination. "Darling, what do you think of when you think of Jersey City? Boys. Cheap, white Irish boys with skinny chests and heart tattoos on their tough little biceps. What could be sexier?"

In a deserted building on Grove Street right off Bay Avenue, the hustler beat Dutch fairly badly, punching him around the brick walls of a long vacant store, knocking him down, kicking him in the left eye with the scuffed and rounded toe of his oversized work boot.

Later Dutch was picked up by the police in front of the Jersey City Polish Community Center. Blood was streaming out of his injured eye. There were random bruises on his face and body where the hustler had punched and kicked him. He was taken to something called the Auxiliary Emergency Shelter Unit on Bergen Avenue, where his eye was cleaned and bandaged and he was allowed to call me.

I found a cab driver willing to cross the Hudson River at one in the morning on a winter night, and I went and picked Dutch up.

He seemed not totally unhappy about the experience. "If I ever see that cocksucker again, dolls, I'm going to murder him." He paused and touched the gauze covering his left eye as if it were a medal won in heroic combat. "But I must admit he was cute, that I have to give him. Six feet tall with shoulders out to here and the funniest, sweetest space between his two front teeth. . . ."

The temperature had begun to climb in the afternoon and was in the upper fifties on that January night when Victoria brought Jean to the loft. "Such a freaky night," Dutch said. "Watch. All the kids will come running in with little short-sleeve shirts. They love to rush the season."

Dutch was giving a dinner party in honor of his then boyfriend Angel (born Andrew Reilly), who had been celebrating his purported twenty-first birthday for an entire week with drugs of all descriptions and sex of all genders.

It was Angel's behavior, Dutch said, that had sent him into the arms of the Jersey City hustler. "If I lose the sight of my left eye, we have only Angel to blame. And don't tell me I didn't tell you so when he comes roaring through that door, begging for me to get into bed with him. 'Come on, Mister Dutch, let's have a little sex.'"

For the record, Angel never got into bed with Dutch unless he was very stoned, drunk, or being bribed with clothes or money.

A more valid reason for the party was that Dutch had sold a dress he had designed to Bloomingdale's, a high-water mark in his career, not to mention his life, justifying the continued expenditure of the money his father had left him.

He claimed he wasn't worried about his eye, though he spent a lot of time that day looking at the disconcerting blood spot in its white area when he wasn't teaching me how to roll joints.

"James, darling—pay attention. Nothing worse than a sloppy joint."

"A perfect occupation for a sedentary recluse," I said.

"Dolls," Dutch said, putting his arms around me, kissing me on the cheek, "when I get through with you, you're going to be as reclusive as Perle Mesta."

No man, not even my dim, departed father, had ever put his arms around me and kissed me before. Yet I found it immeasurably comforting, even natural.

I suppose this is the appropriate moment for me to explain what I was doing living in a loft building on Twentieth Street between Fifth and Sixth Avenues, a loft building occupied by The Living Guerrilla Theater, an artist in her late fifties who called herself Tallulah, assorted Manhattan cottage industries (e.g., the making of beaded evening hats), and Dutch Cohen.

BaBa had chosen to spend the summer following that memorable Eye Ball in the Southampton beach house. I showed up on two or three occasions, always at her request, always to appear at her "stuffy" parties. Poor BaBa. She must have led an exceedingly schizoid life that summer.

She went to Europe in September, returned (a surprise) in October, and we spent a couple of months attending dinners, galas, theater parties, museum and gallery openings, and all the other nonevents that made up the fabric of our social life. I'm not certain what thread held the fabric together during that fall. Perhaps it was simply that BaBa was having trouble cutting it. I was just having trouble.

And occasionally I would see Jean. Usually at the party after the party. Going out some door. She is the sort of theatrical person who makes exits rather than entrances. She was always dressed in some muted Hollywood outfit. White satin. She looked like one of the current crop of child stars: impossibly young, impossibly knowing. She moved through the crowds beautifully, causing a quiet sensation, convincingly unaware.

Once, when we were entering an elevator that would carry us to a skytop discotheque party for Louise Nevelson, she was, characteristically, coming out. "You're the girl in my husband's wet dreams," BaBa, drunk and high on little white pills, said.

Jean kept walking, wrapping a long and white fur around her. BaBa began to follow, but one of the girls she went to Miss Spence's with (they are legion) put an arm through hers and led her off to the ladies' room. The elite take care of their own.

BaBa left me during the first week of December. I had already taken the loft and was spending most of my non-office time there, though I don't think BaBa was aware of that.

"I won't leave if you don't want me to, James."

"I want you to, BaBa."

"It doesn't mean I'm going forever, James."

I didn't reply.

"I think you want me to go, James."

"I do."

She stood in the center of the sitting room that faced the park, dressed in her abandoning wife costume, holding a vintage Vuitton traveling bag, looking ill at ease, perplexed.

"I'm not sure I want to leave, James. I'm not at all sure," she said in her little girl's voice.

"If you don't, BaBa, I'm afraid I'll have to go first. I have a breakfast date with old Hopkins."

"Fuck you, James," BaBa said, going out the door into the foyer, struggling into a dark sable coat. "I had hoped this was going to be civilized." She jabbed at the elevator button. "I might have known . . ."

I never knew what she might have known, because the elevator arrived at that moment and, whatever her sins, BaBa has been brought up not to argue in front of elevator men. She gave me one last querying look and finally, irrevocably (as far as I was concerned) went.

I breakfasted with Hopkins, who told me all about a novel his nephew was writing, a sort of male Gothic. "But it's got a twist, Jimmy, my boy. A genuine twist." I gave him appropriate encouragement, and then I had

Miss Lustig make arrangements for the apartment to be sublet (with the cooperative board's approval, of course) and for some of my furniture to be moved to Twentieth Street. I gave the couple who "did" for us—the Albas— two months' wages and was relieved to be told that they had already lined up a new situation. Couples like the Albas are a vanishing breed, but the people who hire them seem to be flourishing.

I wrote a check for a large sum of money and sent it to BaBa in care of her lawyer.

It was December the fifth according to the diary I try to unashamedly keep (who has diaries in this era of dime-thin tape decks?), and I felt, if not wonderful, at the very least unburdened. I couldn't wait to see Dutchy.

I had begun thinking about lofts that fall, when BaBa had come back from Europe and took me to a party in SoHo in an artist's loft. It was clean and wide and spacious, a place for everything. It was like walking around the inside of a huge, old-fashioned roller-top desk. "*Un peu* anal, don't you think?" BaBa had asked when we left. I told her I thought it was very neat.

Not too long after, I called Ed Oppenheimer who is in real estate (BaBa used to say he *is* Real Estate) and asked him about lofts. He laughed, and we had lunch. He tossed around a lot of unfamiliar terms. "You want a full conversion, raw space, or one of those uptown-downtown jobs in TriBeCa?"

I told him what I did want (a lot of glass and space), that it was confidential (Ed gave me one of those winks as if we were both in on some smutty secret), and that I was really just investigating the possibility.

That was the truth. I was toying with the idea rather

than intending to do it. I couldn't actually imagine myself leaving the twenty-block radius I had grown up in and moving downtown, in with the addicts and the orgiasts.

Still, I dutifully spent several afternoons allowing Ed Oppenheimer to lead me up and down stairs, in and out of elevators as we looked at lofts that were either too large or too small, too dim or too converted.

After a time, Ed stopped going with me and began sending keys and directions via messenger. I had just about decided that taking a loft was not going to be the panacea for my broken marriage when Ed's secretary called and told me about a "really exquisite" conversion "not too far downtown." She was so enthusiastic, I agreed to look at it.

I took a taxi to Twentieth Street and, armed with the key, viewed the fifth-floor loft. I thought that if I were serious about taking a loft, I would be serious about this one. Like all the lofts in the building, it was in the shape of an *E*. There were glass windows on all sides, and the previous tenant had put in all the amenities without making it look like a ranch house. It was white and spacious, and the buildings towering around it made it a very New York sort of living place.

But I had decided that when BaBa left—and I thought she would leave at any moment—I would remove myself to London for a while and perhaps work in our office there. I would take a large, damp apartment and furl myself as tightly as an umbrella and read a great deal.

Thinking of London and its protective insularity, less alien than this loft building and its foreign open spaces, I stepped into the large industrial elevator, expecting it to descend when I pressed the appropriate button. Instead, it went up and stopped at the sixth floor.

The door slid open, and Dutch Cohen stepped in, saying, "Howdy." I looked at his mascaraed eyes, said hello, and congratulated myself on my decision to visit London for an extended and perhaps even permanent stay.

The elevator began its descent, Dutch staring at me while my eyes remained riveted to the panel board. Suddenly the elevator gave a great wheeze, then a small cough, then a shudder, and then it stopped. Numerals two and three were lit up on the panel. We had stopped between them. Ravel's *Bolero* could be heard being played over and over again on a piano in the second-floor loft.

"That Tallulah is such a nut," Dutch said, banging on the elevator door with his big, meaty hand. "Divine. But a nut." It took him some time to attract her attention, but eventually the music stopped and they had a kind of shouting dialogue. She agreed, after some persuasion, to call "that scumbag of a managing agent." Perhaps an hour later a man arrived who experimented with the wires above us, which could be seen through a small, square hole in the ceiling of the elevator cage.

"The emergency bell didn't work, huh?" he asked, and I agreed. He went back to doing something to the wires, occasionally shouting reassurances down to us.

"We're not worried, dolls," Dutch called back. He was in the middle of the condensed version of the story of his life, smoking a joint the size of a Corona Corona. I was no longer worried, either. Like the Chinese bellhops in the Hotel Woodrow Wilson, I was fascinated, vastly amused, and tee-heeing all over the place as Dutch unwrapped and put on view the facts, embroidered, of his life.

He was recounting how, when he was in his teens, in the early 1960s, he was in great demand to do wedding makeup. "When my cousin Sonia walked down the aisle of the Beth Israel Congregational Synagogue in Hewlett, Long Island, and slowly removed her veil and then turned to the congregation, you could have heard a pin drop until her mother began screaming. I had given Sonia the Japanese look, all matte white powder and black painted eyelids. Intense Kabuki. Sonia was a sensation, dolls, but nothing like her sister, Marlene, whom I did in blackface in honor of the Civil Rights Movement."

He stopped for a moment and examined me. "You're not gay, are you, James?"

"No, I'm not," I said, feeling as if I were confessing my disbelief in God.

"Isn't that a riot? All this time I was sure you were gay, and suddenly I realized you're only wearing that suit because you're a *shagitz* from uptown. What do you do for a living, darling?"

I told him. I also told him, under examination: the state of my finances; the extent of my family's social connections; the fact that I was about to be separated from my wife; that I was considering moving into the loft below him because I knew when BaBa left I would be forced to make some changes and I wanted to be prepared. I did not mention London or my furled umbrella fantasy.

All of this fascinated Dutch. Like Jean, he was interested in amassing details. And then there was his exotic obsession. I was as exotic to him as he was to me.

The single confession I made that afternoon in the

stuck elevator that excited him most, however, was that I had never been in bed with a man.

"Do you mean to sit there and tell me, James, that you never sucked a cock?" he asked, lighting one more joint. "It's not natural, darling."

"As God is my witness."

"You must have jerked someone off." He inhaled deeply. "You at least jerked one of your friends off when you were fourteen."

"I didn't."

"But, darling, boarding schools are hotbeds of homosexuality."

"Not the one I went to."

"What about circle jerks?"

I admitted I didn't know what a circle jerk was.

"Darling!" He took another deep puff and stared at me to find out if I was "putting one over on him." He decided I wasn't. "That's when you go to camp and everyone in the bunk stands around in a circle and jerks off. The object is to see who can come first. My one and only summer at camp, we used to get up in the middle of the night and do it over Ricky Seltzer who was always homesick. I don't know how that kid slept through it but I bet you a dollar he has beautiful skin today. Did you know that come is extremely beneficial for the complexion? Pure protein. Makes a wonderful face mask, but never get it in your eyes. You can go blind from it."

Soon after I told him where I had gone to college and he expressed further amazement that I had never engaged in the Princeton Rub with my roommate, the elevator began to move. He was going to see a buyer at Bloomingdale's (the buyer, as it turned out, who eventually bought the first dress), and we shared a taxi uptown. By the time I let him off, I had decided to take the loft.

"People like us don't live in lofts," my sister, Bernice, called to say, literally moments after Ed Oppenheimer told her husband that I had taken one. She made the word *loft* sound like an unsavory dish.

"I know this thing with BaBa is very unsettling, but there's no need for you to go off the deep end, J.J. Think of what Aunt Alice would say. Now listen. Winston and I have a perfectly splendid idea. Sublet your old barn of an apartment if you must, and go take the Rhinebeck house for the rest of the winter. We'd only come up on the odd weekend and I promise we'll tiptoe around like perfect little deaf, dumb, and blind mice. Heather and Allison can play in father's trophy room. You know how they adore it."

"What about my work, Bernice?"

"J.J., you say the funniest things."

That afternoon, I arranged with McCrae to move some of the furniture I had stored with them into the loft. It did not seem particularly at home there. The uphol-stered sofas, the Chippendale desk, some odd but good English tables and chairs my mother had left me, were particularly out of place.

"Paint every stick of it pink, dolls," Dutch said, sitting heavily on a light eighteenth-century love seat, crossing his legs. "Then get some queen in here who's clever with decals . . ."

His own loft was, to use his word ("and such a yenta word, dolls"), eclectic. The work area, set up on the bottom bar of the *E*, was filled with sewing machines and cutting tables. The long bar was home to an eight-foot-square Bronx Renaissance dining table, which Dutch held very dear. "I inherited it from *my* stepmother. It's an imitation of an imitation that never was." The rest of the space was filled with extravagantly decorated "recycled" furniture painted a variety of tropical colors, souvenirs from his Hong Kong journey, and gifts from friends who knew his taste.

The walls were a deep and unpleasant red, the floor an unwholesome pink. The windows were left uncovered at all times so that our neighbors, when sufficiently bored, could look in and see a nude boy or two bathing in the molded plastic shower stall, which he steadfastly refused to curtain.

The boys would stay at the loft because, as Dutch explained: one, it was somewhere to crash; and two, "I take care of them, dolls. Every single one of them is looking for a mother." They were young, in their late teens, early twenties, prepared to accept—or so it seemed—whatever came along. None of them hustled. "No hustlers in the home, darling," Dutch said, on more than one occasion. "That's only asking for it. When I find out one of them hustles, out they go. No exceptions."

I wonder where he found those boys. Dutch maintained that he had the same quality Jean does, that he attracted boys because of his physical chemistry. "Darling, that little Victor could not keep his hands off me. All night long he kept rubbing and touching and kissing and hugging and taking little bites out of my neck. I tell you, James, he was driving me nuts."

But Dutch wasn't, as far as I could tell, really attractive to the boys. They seemed to find their real pleasure with each other or with the girls whom they would take dancing. Both sexes were thin and pale and looked as if they were prone to some wasting disease, tuberculosis victims in another century.

Dutch towered over them. He was five foot ten, usually some fifteen to twenty pounds overweight, balding, and wore Vaseline on his eyelids, which gave his ruddy Jewish cherub's face an early cinema hero's glow. Dressed in baggy trousers or shorts, silk shirts, high-heeled sandals or boots, a turquoise kerchief knotted around his neck, he reminded me of an illustration in my boyhood copy of *The Arabian Nights*: "The Keeper of the Harem."

Jean, on the other hand, has always looked, to me, entirely contemporary. Even when she got herself up to look like Harlow or Monroe or her mother, she still had that entirely instantaneous, contemporary look, as if she had just stepped out of *Vogue* or *Women's Wear Daily*.

When she arrived at Angel's birthday party that spring-like night in January, I was talking with a group in Dutch's "first" seating area. I was slightly drunk, and they were very stoned. I was passing joints about, feeling comfortable, even happy, like an earthling pressed into valuable service on Mars.

When Jean came in, wearing an expensive, slinky, funky silver dress, looking distracted, tortoise-shell combs in her silver-blond hair, her fine hand resting in the crook of Victoria DeVine's milk-white and nude arm, she looked like a fragile patient accompanied by her no-nonsense nurse.

Dutch fell for her in very much the same way I had fallen for him: immediately and without reservation.

CHAPTER 7

"Darling," Dutch said. "Darling." He kissed Victoria and Morgan on their pale lips and, taking Jean's hand, stood back. "Exquisite," he said, and one expected him to insert a jeweler's loop into his good eye. "Simply exquisite."

Victoria ignored this and looked in the direction of the dance floor. Fifteen or twenty young people of indeterminate sex were dancing to music from the soundtrack of a popular rock film. Victoria harumphed. "Your usual four hundred for dinner, Mr. Dutch?"

"The kids don't get dinner, darling. You know that. They only get dancing and a joint."

"Just as long as they don't start having sex during the main course."

"As they did the last time," Morgan added.

"Darling, try to think of them as decoration." Dutch sent the DeVines into the first seating area where I was sitting, with an admonition to Victoria "not to let any of those *schnorrer* kids near the scotch."

I sat across from a dress designer, a tall and willowy blond fellow with an improbable name which was not his own. He wore a perpetual pout on his petulant lips and a yellow rose in the lapel of his collarless blazer. He reminded me of a Beardsley drawing. I found him exceedingly unattractive. "But, darling," Dutch protested, "he's the rage of New York." His rich lover was backing him with a multimedia campaign, and one saw his face and sometimes his designs everywhere. There was even a short squib about his newly formed company in *The Wall Street Journal*. "Next year, darling, he'll be designing eyeglass cases."

He was arguing with a tiny interior decorator who specialized, he said, in wallpaper colorations. Dutch referred to him as Miss Self-Destruct. At first sight, Miss Self-Destruct looked like a peculiar but attractive boy, the sort that is always up to something. But behind the blue granny glasses lay eyes the color and texture of old Coca-Cola bottles. After a moment, it was apparent he was in his mid-thirties and had seen, as Aunt Alice would say, a bit of life. He was sniffing cocaine from a device tricked up to resemble a popular antihistamine inhaler. He seemed irrevocably lost.

"She killed herself, Harvey, not because of you and not because she was dropped from that tediola play by that nell director but simply because she was a desperately unhappy, sad, sad, lunatic."

"If you're talking about Stephen," Victoria said, taking a place next to Harvey (Miss Self-Destruct) on a pink, overstuffed nightmare of a sofa Dutch described as a real find, "I couldn't agree more."

They were not talking about Stephen, it turned out, but about his lover, Richie.

I had been frequenting Dutch's parties and soirées and casual get-togethers for several months, but I still found it difficult to believe in the existence of those people. And it wasn't just that the men called each other "she" or that they dressed in the kind of clothes found on the men's fashion pages or that they either stared at my crotch or ignored me altogether. My disbelief was based on the fact that I couldn't communicate with anyone. We came not only from different planets but from different galaxies. I knew a great many people who were deliberately odd and peculiar, but none who were this odd and peculiar, none who were so unaware of what was going on outside, in the world. They talked by the hour about the latest clothes, furniture, lovers, hairdressers, makeup, and movie stars. But if one mentioned Castro and Africa, for instance, then rather a front-page item, they would be perfectly capable of asking if hide-a-beds were coming in some divine new native fabric.

At the same time, they were always amazed at the names I didn't know, the frames of reference I didn't have. "Darling, you mean to sit there and tell me you never heard of the Fire Island Pines Meat Rack?"

It was, I think, a problem of mutual insularity. New York has as segmented a social system as any Indian raj. My entire life had been spent among people very much like myself. I had heard there was an underground society, one that danced all night and slept all day. But part of me thought that that world was a media creation, hype for discotheques and boutiques. I didn't really believe it.

Until I met Dutch Cohen, that is, and began my education.

That evening, while I was continuing my education, receiving a detailed account of how Stephen's lover, Richie, had checked into the Fairmont Hotel in San Francisco, filled his tub with Piper-Heidsieck brut, and cut his wrists with a Rolls-Royce razor after downing a bottle of tranquilizers ("the only way to go, my dear"), Jean was in the kitchen with Dutch.

The kitchen consisted of a General Electric Frost Free Refrigerator with an ice cube maker and a huge chrome restaurant stove. Dutch was preparing his Mixed Grill for Thirteen, pushing spicy Italian sausage around an enormous frying pan, talking about Angel. "The cutest, sweetest boy with the most adorable bowed legs. Smart as a whip. For a kid who never got beyond junior high school, he is remarkable. He'll show up any minute."

Dutch had a need to establish his sexual preference from the outset of any relationship. "It saves a lot of trouble, darling, in the long run. When I tell you about the women who wanted me, about the extremes they have gone to to get me into a bed . . ."

After he added the lamb chops and the green peppers, he asked Jean why she supposed the DeVines had taken so long to introduce them.

This began a long conversation about the DeVines and their habit of keeping their friends compartmentalized, followed by Dutch's version of his Hong Kong meeting with Victoria. Finally Victoria herself went into the kitchen and announced it was midnight and three of the guests had departed and where the hell was dinner.

"Darling," Dutch said to her, "this is not a diner and I am not a short-order cook. Have another joint."

Eventually, dinner was served. Jean sat at a small square table covered with a pink cloth, with Victoria, Morgan, Harvey, and the willowy blond. I said hello and Jean smiled but, as usual, gave no sign that we had met before.

"I gave you an enormous hello," she says. "I even think we had a conversation about the Eye Ball."

That is patently not true.

I was sitting in a corner on a baby-blue leatherette banquette next to a painfully thin young man. His arms, hanging from a T-shirt, looked like much-used jump ropes. "You've got to actualize yourself, man," he said to me. "You got to get to your source, man. All this sex and anger, man, it's bullshit."

Dutch walked by with a platter of potatoes, leaned over, and said to my dinner partner, "Frankie, you can save yourself the effort. James will come out of the closet the day David Eisenhower does."

"Man," Frankie said, hunting and forking and digesting a piece of wayward sausage casing, "what Dutch needs is a genuine primal."

After dinner, I went downstairs to pass out and Dutch showed Jean around his work area. He sat down at one of the sewing machines and she sat on a stool and told him about Bert, about her mother's death, about her mother.

"I felt very comfortable," Jean remembers. "Usually it takes me about seven years to be at ease with anyone, but not with Dutch. He asked me what my mother was like and for the first time I could remember, I began talking about her and not about the scandal. 'She was,' I told him, 'always on stage. Even when she was being motherly. My grandmother was the same way. Consequently —and I know this from years of shrinkdom—I try to surround myself with good, strong surrogate mothers. Witness Victoria. Witness Lilli Ruben. I want a mother, Dutchy.'"

"We all do, dolls. But none of us are going to get one. Tell me about the father substitute, Mister Bert."

"He's muscular and dark and wrote two Triangle Club shows at Princeton. He is currently New York's deputy mayor for policy. He's the toughest, meanest man I have ever met. He is the epitome of the kind of man I always wind up with."

"Have a joint, darling."

"It won't help," she said, lighting it.

"No, but it will give you something to do with your hands. That's a gorgeous bracelet. Plastic?"

"Malachite."

"Stunning. Now, me, darling," he said, taking a drag off the joint, "I'm exactly the opposite. I love my men young and cute and sweet. With a touch of the devil, but I want them innocent. Which doesn't rule out the possibility that they might be malicious and maybe even a *bissel* dangerous. Does he like rough sex?"

"Yes."

"Tell you the truth, so do I." He touched his eye and stood up and kissed her. "Anyway, we all get what we want in the end. I firmly believe that. Don't you, Miss Jean?"

CHAPTER 8

Dutchy said later he wanted to bring us together himself that night—but I was passed out. By four A.M. the party was over and Jean left with the DeVines. She lay her head back against the new, stiff plush of the DeVines' car and closed her eyes, her lids feeling as if they weighed several tons. She asked Morgan for a cigarette.

Victoria knew what Jean's occasional cigarettes denoted and said, "I'm not going to let you go back to that apartment alone tonight. You'll come and stay with us. I'll have Piers call and alert Eve to open up the big guest room." Victoria was pleased with the car and the telephone and Piers and Eve and the big guest room. Morgan, it had turned out, came from landed gentry.

"I'd love to, Victoria," Jean said, stopping Victoria from rapping on the glass window to attract Piers's attention, "but I can hardly turn up at Danny Allesandro's at nine to meet Mrs. Raymer in my Tinkerbelle dress."

"What's Danny Allesandro's?" Morgan wanted to know.

"*The* fireplace mantel shop in town," his wife answered.

They left her off, after much kissing, in front of her apartment. "Shall I send Piers up with you?"

"Don't be silly, Victoria. I'll speak to you tomorrow."

She pulled herself up the stairs to that third-floor apartment, opened the door with its three useless locks, and went in without switching on the lights. "I didn't want to see that goddamned circular bed for some reason. Or the mirrors or the tiled floor or the kitchenette. At that moment, I was very tired of the apartment and of everything in it. I remember regretting refusing Victoria's offer. It would have been nice to have her fussing over me, tucking me into the fourposter in the guest room, force feeding me hot chocolate.

"Anyway, I got out of that dress, dropped it on the floor, and did a few necessary things in the bathroom. Then I got into the bed. All this without benefit of light. I was stoned and foggy and it wasn't until I lay down that I realized I wasn't alone.

"I lay very still. I was badly frightened. Someone was in my apartment, wearing a scent I didn't recognize. I lay in that bed not daring to move. I could see the hands of the luminous clock moving very slowly. It was a contest, you see. Who would speak first.

"I lost. 'Who's here?' I asked, my voice in remarkable control. Not a tremor. He laughed and switched on a light. Bert, nude, was lying on the opposite side of that ridiculous, enormous circular bed. Between us, also without clothes, was Catherine. It came to me that she was a dyke. I don't know why it hadn't occurred to me before. Not that there had been anything blatant: no heavy stud act, no motorcycle jackets or pantsuits with ties and collars. But on the two or three occasions I had seen her, there had been no jealousy, nothing other than a piquant interest.

"She reached for my legs at the same time Bert stood

up and came around the bed. Of course he had a hard-on. This was very exciting for him. He straddled me, pressing my arms against the mattress with his knees, forcing himself into my mouth. At the same time Catherine was pushing my legs up and out, pressing her mouth between them.

"I didn't struggle, after the first few minutes.

"Later, he fucked me from behind while she was eating me, licking his cock as he came out and went back in. Her hands clutched my tits so hard, I thought she was doing permanent damage. When he finished, when he had pulled himself out of me and had come in her mouth, she lay next to me. It was her scent I had smelled. Her skin was as poreless as a pane of glass. She raised her legs and Bert went into her as if he were going into a marshmallow. He fucked her for a long time, going in and out with that brutal, mechanistic thrust of his. I watched his face as he worked on her, as he waited for her to have an orgasm. It was totally blank. No expression, like a man on an assembly line.

"Afterward, they stood up and dressed. It was as if I weren't there. She kept the door open in the bathroom. I saw her using my brush; later, I found red hairs caught in the bristles. They were chatting. 'I'm famished,' Catherine said, 'let's run over to the Brasserie and have a steak sandwich. I could eat a cow.' 'You just did, darling,' Bert said, never able to resist a bad pun. 'Good night, Jean,' Catherine said, from the door. She was in one of those five-thousand-dollar Scaasi gowns, a white mink coat on her shoulders, diamond earrings dangling. Bert was in black tie. He had evidently picked her up after the Tavern-on-the-Green business and they had gone on to some party. They looked alike, as if she were a red edition of his black handsomeness. They stood at the door, smiling at me, the parents going out on the town for an evening. I was the child in my crib. 'We'll have to do this again, very soon,' Catherine said, and left. Bert followed, not saying anything.

"The disgusting thing was, James, that I got off on it. Part of me enjoyed being used and debased. Otherwise I would have protested, screamed, forced them to stop. But I didn't. Those two vampires knew. They helped to perpetuate the bad feelings I had about myself, the feeling that I was only good for one thing.

"I grabbed Teddy and held him to me and tried to sleep. It was seven in the morning; I had been going for twenty-four incredibly awful hours. Of course I couldn't sleep and I didn't want a pill. I kept thinking that I had to be at Danny Allesandro's at nine to meet Babs Raymer. By eight, when it was just starting to get light outside, I got up, took a bath, washed my hair, and called United Airlines."

She caught the ten o'clock flight to Los Angeles and tried to sleep, but Flip Wilson and two people she didn't know were shooting craps at the front of the plane and a man who used to work for her father sat next to her in the first-class cabin and got maudlin over orange juice and champagne.

She arrived at one o'clock in the afternoon, refused a lift from the maudlin man, and got Hertz to rent her a huge white Ford. "It was like driving a truck with a loose steering wheel." She took the freeway to Malibu, driving through the smog, past the palm trees and the state troopers and the familiar landmarks. A Filipino at the gate put up an arm to stop her, but she kept on driving right up to the pink house. The Filipino must have called ahead, because Sybil was already in the foyer when she pushed open the door and went in.

Sybil was wearing her afternoon costume, a bikini and sunglasses. She was thin and taut and uptight. She looked like a cornered alligator. "Jean dear," she said, making a move as if to kiss Jean who stepped back. "*Quelle surprise.*"

"Where's Rex?" Jean asked.

"He's off on one of those real estate—"

Jean pushed her out of the way and crossed the landing which led to the terrace which led to the stairs which led to the beach and the pool.

"He's not well," Sybil called after her. "He's not at all well. He shouldn't have any excitement."

Rex Rank was in a beach chair. The blue pool shimmered anxiously behind him. The pink princess phone sat benignly on a wrought-iron table next to him. His hands touched the phone as she approached.

"Jean," he said, and she could see that he wasn't well. "Little Jean."

She stood over him but didn't feel pity. "Pity is not an emotion indigenous to Southern California," Jean says. If Sybil was an alligator, Rex Rank was an old, captured fish. "Pity is an emotion that atrophies in Southern California," Jean says.

"How did she die, Rex?" Jean asked.

"It was a heart attack, dear," Sybil said, coming forward. "Wasn't it, Rex?"

"I don't know, Jean," Rex said. "I don't know. Sybil took care of everything."

"Your grandmother Halladay left a provision for her remains to rest in the family mausoleum," Sybil said, as if she were reading from an old horror film scenario. "She's next to your father and your grandmother Halladay. It's for the best, Jean."

Jean looked at the two of them, preserved in Bain de Soleil and Malibu sun, and turned and went back up the steps, back to the Ford. "Jean darling, you sure you won't have a bite to eat?"

She went to Santa Monica and had a sandwich and a cup of coffee and tried to think. Then she got back into the Ford and drove to Gardena. Auntie Mae Bonita lived in a neat, ugly, low stucco house on a street of such houses. It looked as if a child had set up the block with toy buildings.

A Japanese mother combed her daughter's long black hair on the neighboring porch. She looked at Jean disapprovingly but didn't turn away.

If Rex and Sybil had been preserved in suntan oil, Auntie Mae Bonita appeared to have been dried, like fruit in a health food store. Her hair was still flaming red, however, and her voice was the same American twang Jean remembered.

"So you got the letter, honey," she said, looking slyly up at Jean, smelling of the mint and herbal teas she liked to dose herself with. Jean stood in the middle of the living room on the linoleum oriental carpet feeling out of scale. All of the furniture in the room was of the squat, overstuffed, Minnie Mouse variety, upholstered in heavy green fabric. The walls had been whitewashed and the windows screened in. Undercutting the tea aroma was the scent of a pine air freshener.

Auntie Mae sat on a green sofa, her penciled eyebrows making her seem permanently surprised, her hands in her lap, her print dress up above her knees, revealing rolled stockings. She sat under a bulletin board on which were thumbtacked signed studio stills of her stars. She looked as if she had had nothing to do but wait for Jean.

"My, you still have that hair. Come here and sit down, honey, and let me touch it. What they would've given for your hair in the old days. Pity you never took up acting. You could have been another Harlow. Or Monroe."

Jean laughed her cynical laugh, which can be a very chilling sound, but it didn't affect Auntie Mae Bonita, who offered her a lemonade. "No more booze for me. Not anymore. Not since I took up the Rodale method. Fresh fruits and vegetables, that's the ticket. And no more dyes, either, Miss. Nothing but your organic henna." She looked at Jean with her startled eyebrows and said, "Guess how old I am, dear?"

Jean stood up and examined the eight-by-ten photograph of her mother. "Seventy?" Lorraine wore a black dress, no jewelry, and a flower, a gardenia, in her hair. She was as sultry in the black-and-white glossy as a tropical jungle.

"I'll be eighty-four next December, knock on wood." She rapped her thick, red knuckles on a wooden side table, not taking her eyes from Jean's face. "I thought my letter wouldn't fool you. You always were a smart cookie, Jean. I remember when I used to go out to the house in Bel-Air—"

"How did she die, Auntie Mae?" Jean asked, lighting a cigarette.

Auntie Mae looked around the room as if she were giving a recital and there were guests in all the green chairs, did something to her teeth and said, "I hadn't seen Lorraine for a good, long time. A bunch of them"—she pointed without looking to the glossies above her—"got together and forced Rank to loan her one of the guest houses on the old Gable-Lombard ranch out in Brentwood. She didn't have any money, not to speak of. I don't mean she was starving. She had a little car and Rank wouldn't let her go on the dole. Be too afraid what people would say. But she wasn't going out dancing at the Coconut Grove every night, that I can tell you.

"No one wanted to know her. Not really. She used to call me and she'd stay on the phone for hours, reminiscing. One day she came, just like that, without even calling, swooped me up in that way of hers and we drove down to see Mary Astor at the Home, but Mary wasn't seeing us. On the way back, Lorraine kept saying that she guessed that the Home was the next stop for her. Rank was going to put up some of those matchbox houses on the ranch, and she had already been told she had to leave.

"You know, honey, she didn't have any interests. She didn't knit or care about nutrition or have a spiritual life like her mother. Lorraine had only lived for the men and the music and now there weren't any of either. Not for her.

"The last time I heard from her was on a Saturday right after my ladies and I had begun on the Ouija board. I wasn't going to answer the phone, but something told me I had better and sure enough it was Lorraine. 'I'm feeling blue, Auntie Mae.' I can hear her now. That's what she always said. Whether a zipper was stuck on a dress or she was getting a divorce or the world was coming to an end. 'I'm feeling blue, Auntie Mae.'

"Well, I had an inkling it was more than a stuck zipper so I got one of my ladies to drive me all the way to

Brentwood. Her car was in the driveway—a little red thing—but the shades were all down and the door was open. I did not like the vibrations in that house, I can tell you that, but I steeled myself and forced my way to the bedroom. I knew what I was going to find.

"Lorraine was all curled up on her bed with her hands clasped under her head like a sleeping child. A big bottle of Johnny Walker Black and a little bottle that once held sleeping pills were on the night table next to her. There was a note written on her peach-colored stationery that said, 'I am sorry. I am very, very sorry.' It looked like a kid had written it with a crayon. Someone once told me she had never learned to write properly, not at the studio school, and now I believe it.

"She must've called Rank, too, because he and Sybil arrived about two minutes after I did. Rex wanted to know what I was doing there and I said I knew him before his name was Rex Rank and that maybe he ought to pay a little more attention to the woman on the bed. He collapsed in a chair when he looked at Lorraine. Sybil went right to the bed, took Lorraine's hand, and felt her forehead. She dropped the hand after a moment, looked at me, blinked her eyes, and then went to the phone and called first an ambulance, then a man she knew who was connected with the police, then her lawyer. When she was finished with the phone, she took the peach-colored note out of my hand, read it, shook her head again, and burned it in an ashtray. She took the Johnny Walker out to the kitchen and came back for the pill vial which she put in the big, black, quilted purse she was clutching like it contained her life savings.

"When the ambulance men and the police and the

lawyer arrived, she went into the living room with them, shutting the door on Rex and myself and, of course, Lorraine. I could hear her voice but not what she said. Later, she and Rex drove me home (naturally my ladies had long since left). Sybil didn't even tell me that I had to be quiet. That was understood. The official verdict, I found out later, was pneumonia. At least that's what it said in the L.A. *Times* in the tiniest notice I've seen since Trixi Friganza passed over.

"I knew right well they hadn't told you. Don't ask me how; I knew it. That's why I sent you that letter, because I thought it'd be a terrible shame for you not to know."

Jean refused a second offer of lemonade. They sat quietly for a few moments and then Jean asked Auntie Mae Bonita if she had enough money and Auntie Mae said, "I don't know anyone who does," but she was getting along, what with the social security and her ladies and the gifts They—she pointed to the photographs— sent at Christmas.

There was a discreet knock on the door and two Japanese-American women in pastel visiting dresses came in for their Ouija session and Jean kissed that round, knowing, startled face good-bye and got into the Ford and drove to Forest Lawn.

"Why did you go to California in the first place?" I asked her.

Jean looked away and said, "I didn't want to feel guilty for the rest of my life in case she had really died of cancer or pneumonia or a heart attack. I didn't want to have to feel terrible because she had been so brave and goddamn bullet-biting, never letting her daughter know she was wasting away, Camille-like, in Carol Lombard's guest house. It's much easier knowing she hadn't been brave, only bored."

Jean made her way through the absurdities of Forest Lawn to the older section where the Halladays' sedate mausoleum sat. A replica of the Pitti Palace was on its left, one of Ludwig's lesser follies on its right.

"It looks as if it belongs in our nation's capital," Jean says. "A smaller, but not much smaller, version of the Jefferson Memorial. A young man with lemon-blond hair, looking like a Disneyland guide, opened the gates for me and escorted me into the wing in which Lorraine Rice Halladay Rank lay. There I was, searching for some emotion to take home with me, some momentous feeling to carry away, and all I could think of was how neat everything was. It was incredibly anticlimactic—a non-experience. There was a slab of marble in between three other slabs of marble. It had her name, her date of birth, her date of death, and that was it. No pithy limerick: 'Here lies Lorraine Rice/had but one child/married twice.' Just the facts. Daddy was above her, and below her were my grandparents Halladay.

"I came away feeling sorry for her. Lorraine would have much rather been buried, or whatever they do to ashes, in the new section, with revolving lights, perpetual music, one of her films playing round the clock."

Jean tried to tip the lemon blond (who wouldn't accept money but asked to be remembered in her prayers) and got into the Ford. She drove through Burbank, waiting for some emotion to rise, and when it didn't, she decided to force the issue. She got onto the Hollywood Freeway, got off at Sunset, and went directly to the Beverly Hills Hotel. If her mother's ghost was going to be haunting any one place, it was certain to be the Polo Lounge. She had some vague idea of getting a room, but there were too many advertising men from New York at the front desk.

"I went right into the Polo Lounge. It's one of the few places in the world that never disappoints me. It always looks exactly as it's supposed to look."

She almost didn't get past the Polo Lounge's equivalent of a velvet rope. The maitre d' didn't recognize her, and he looked as if he were going to ask her to leave. "They're not all that hot about single women hanging out there, as you might imagine.

"But Red Buttons was there, looking for someone, anyone, to say hello to, and he saw me and I smiled and he said, 'No, it can't be. Lorraine's girl.' He bought me a drink and we sat in one of the banquettes and I saw a million people I knew but none of them saw me. I am still persona non grata in Hollywood, I want you to know. I said as much to Red.

" 'They like to think you pulled the trigger,' he said to me.

"I sat there looking at familiar faces, past and present, still waiting for this revelatory feeling, for this burst of understanding and compassion and monumental sense of loss. *Nada. Rien.* I had flown three thousand miles to find out how my mother died, to experience something, anything.

"I needed to get out of the Polo Lounge, to get out of Beverly Hills, to get away from the totally self-involved people but Red had been called to the phone and still hadn't come back and I didn't want to leave without saying good-bye and thank you.

"Johnny of Phillip Morris fame materialized wearing

his little red pageboy outfit. He handed me an envelope. I thanked him and gave him a tip which he gave back to me. He remembered Lorraine. Not to mention Lita. I chatted with him for a few seconds, then he was called away and I opened the envelope. In it was a check from Rank for five thousand dollars.

"Red came back and I said thank you and blah blah blah and then I got into the Ford, thinking I was headed for the airport and the first available flight to New York."

She wasn't. She was on the Hollywood Freeway, and without knowing exactly what she was doing—operating on "gut think" as I once heard Bert Brown describe some unconscious action—she was at Forest Lawn for the second time that day.

She half walked, half ran to the Halladay memorial. She was hysterical by this time, but sane enough to avoid the guards, to pass herself off as a nocturnal mourner.

When she finally reached the mausoleum, it was, of course, locked. She went around to the back, forced herself through some manicured shrubbery, and looked in through the barred arched window.

At that moment, she went absolutely berserk. All of her anger, all of her love for that impossible woman, her mother, came spewing out of her. She was crying and screaming at the same time, attempting to get in through that narrow, barred window, shouting all of the questions she had never asked.

"Why the fuck couldn't you love me? Why couldn't you need me, just once in your shitty life? Why didn't you pick up the goddamned phone and say help me? *I* need you, you egomaniac. You bitch. I need you. Mother!"

It took them a little under ten minutes to find her, and by that time she was over it. The Forest Lawn storm troopers didn't know that, however. They strapped her up, put her in a van, and in a very short time she found herself in the sheriff's office in Burbank. "I felt so dumb," she remembers and shudders. Not that she was treated badly. The sheriff was a master at handling dubious Hollywood types, and if she had been sane enough to come up with some reasonable excuse ("Mother died recently and I'm overcome with grief"—not even a lie), he would have let her go.

She was too catatonic. Someone—a female deputy—slipped her a Valium, which helped, and then they had found Rank's check in her purse. They called him, and an hour later the Filipino arrived and drove her to the airport in a gold-colored Bentley. She gave him the keys to the white Ford, he escorted her to the first seat in first class, said something to the stewardess who nodded sympathetically, and then he disappeared.

When she arrived at Kennedy, she endorsed Rex's check and sent it to Auntie Mae Bonita. It seemed to Jean that Auntie Mae deserved it. "She was the one who kept quiet."

Then she called an all-night locksmith. He was waiting for her when she arrived at the apartment. He made a desultory, obligatory pass, which Jean blocked. He then changed the three locks on her door, asked her for more money than even she would have thought possible, and left.

She locked all three locks, got into her circular bed, set the luminous alarm, and slept the sleep of the mentally undisturbed.

CHAPTER 9

"Amelita Lizzardi tells me you're having an affair with Christopher Meade's wife," Aunt Alice said over the telephone.

"I'm not," I said, though I was.

"Not quite the thing, James. After all, you and Christopher have been friends since St. Paul's. . . ."

"I am not having an affair with Chris's wife, Aunt Alice. She's been decorating my—um—new living space." "Loft" would only cause her to worry.

I was not actually having an affair with Cora Meade. Not my idea of an affair, at any rate. An affair implies stolen weekends in the Catskills, dark corners in Jersey City restaurants, motel rooms in Queens, Tiffany bracelets. Cora Meade and I were having a biological necessity.

"I hear she's done up your—um—new living space and it's all very spiffy and modern."

"It is, rather."

"James, every time you get that English note of reserve in your voice, I begin to worry. Your father used to go all British on me every time he made some disastrous mistake. I remember when he went and enlisted in the Regulars right after Mr. Roosevelt declared his war, and it took Garfield a month to worm him a commission. . . ." Aunt Alice went on for some time with her reminiscences of Mr. Roosevelt's war while I watched Cora Meade put on her raw-silk blouse and her navy-blue cashmere skirt.

Cora Meade's enemies, and she has a great many, call her Corea Medea. But not to her face. She is, as BaBa used to say, one tough lady. She is tall and blond and seamless, like those pneumatic porn dolls that are sold on Forty-second Street or in certain mail-order catalogues.

Appropriately enough, in light of Aunt Alice's conversation, Cora is English. Very English. She pals around with Princess Margaret when that unhappy woman is in New York and her father is a long-standing member of Parliament, a fact which Cora only makes use of when her back is up against the wall, which is not all that often.

She married Chris Meade, my official best friend, when he was doing postgraduate work at the London School of Economics and Cora was posing as a Bright Young Thing. I went over for the wedding, which featured Royalty and tinned salmon. Her parents, Parliament notwithstanding, are what is known as nouveau poor.

A year or so after their marriage, when Chris was making noises about returning to New York, I happened to be in London trying to get a recalcitrant author to complete his contract. Cora invited me to accompany them to Glyndebourne. Glyndebourne is the opera festival that takes place each June on the Sussex Downs. It is madly Upper Crust. Immediately after lunch (more tinned salmon) we all got ourselves into evening dress and then raced to Victoria Station. We could've gone down in comfort in the Meades' Rolls, but Cora and Chris are sticklers for convention.

We took our seats at five thirty and pretended to listen to *The Magic Flute,* but we were all counting the crowd. The men looked wonderfully comfortable in their dinner jackets, while the women, even the beauties, had contrived to look turn-of-the-century dowdy in dusty rose-colored long dresses.

That night, in her London town house, Cora presented herself for my bed. "Chris is a shit in the sex department," she said. I felt a bit of a shit myself, but then I am a person who is easily seduced. Hold out a carrot and I will bite.

After BaBa's well-publicized departure, Cora represented herself, this time in the guise of a modern working woman, yet another interior decorator. "I only do my very good friends," she said, and I believed her.

In no time she had everything in the loft painted a glossy white. She forced me to get my Frank Stella out of storage and had it hung from the ceiling just inside the door. "It's a classy room divider," Dutch said. She got Chris to lend me a Jackson Pollock, which she had hung along the longest wall. She took me up to Stendig, where she chose a couple of dozen sky-blue leather modular seats, which she caused to be placed around the living area in a serpentine motif. She had built-in closets installed, tore out the kitchen and put in a new one ("A galley, James—that's all a man with one servant needs"). In one corner she had a white, round dining table built and had it surrounded with Breuer chairs. In another corner she placed the platform bed. Then she sprinkled white molded plastic tables throughout.

I thought it seemed a bit sparse.

Cora said it was crisp and super.

Dutch said, "It has as much personality, dolls, as B. Altman's lingerie department. Why don't you paint the floor pink and the ceiling turquoise?"

Despite its lack of apparent personality ("The people will add the color, James," Cora said), I was enjoying life in my new "total environment." For one thing, it didn't feel as if it were mine. It felt as if it came out of the pages of *Architectural Digest* or *High-Tech*. And there was all that whiteness. The very lack of color and clutter was particularly soothing then, an antidote to the clutter and color that had been BaBa.

"I have decided, James," Aunt Alice was saying, "that since you're not about to invite me, I will invite myself. It is my duty"—those words again with which Aunt Alice often justified her curiosity—"to see how you are living. I shall be round about four. You might arrange to give me a cup of tea."

I didn't argue, because there was no arguing with Aunt Alice. I got out of bed, wished Cora godspeed, and helped her on with the sort of chinchilla coat I imagine the empresses of Russia used to wear. She patted me on the cheek and went home to play house with Chris and all the other little Meades in the fourteen-room apartment Chris's mother gave him for being a good little Republican boy.

I got into the white plastic modular shower stall Cora had insisted upon and washed away all traces of that indelible woman. I put on some clothes, thinking I was not in the mood to deal with Aunt Alice but neither was I in a condition to put her off. I wondered why she wasn't in that pile of stone she calls a country house in Brewster. For that matter, why wasn't she busy making the staff crazy in her moorish palace in Palm Beach?

"Very modern," she said, as she moved into the loft, Madam Lizzardi in several layers of matte black jersey sailing in behind her like a protective pilot boat. "You remember my nephew, James, don't you, Amelita?"

Amelita admitted she did. She removed one thick leather glove and touched my hand. Her fingers were covered with rings, each set with a gaily colored stone.

"Doesn't all this white hurt your eyes?" Aunt Alice asked, handing her furs to Madam who handed them to Peters, an ageless man who lived in the one room (with bath) Cora had allowed in the far end of the loft.

"How are you, Peters?" Aunt Alice asked. He had worked for a friend of hers, a colonel who had died, before he came to work for me.

"Fine, Mrs. Veneering. Just fine."

"And that wife of yours?"

"Fine. Just fine."

"She still baking those sumptuous pecan pies?"

"Still baking."

"I must get Cook to order some. It is very nice seeing you, Peters."

"Nice seeing you, ma'am."

I have never heard Peters utter a single negative, make a single contradiction. His wife, it turns out, is famous for her peach pies.

Peters went into the galley, while I followed Aunt Alice and Madam Lizzardi as they harumphed their way around the loft. "I shan't ask you how you manage to live here," Aunt Alice said, seating herself on one of the low, modular leather businesses.

"Good," I said, attempting to forestall any conversation about the neighborhood, the furniture, the color of the walls. Aunt Alice can be relentless. "What are you doing in New York at this time of year?" I asked, watching Peters out of the corner of my eye as he brought in the tea and placed it on one of Cora's plastic tables.

"The Settlement has chosen January to plan a big fundraising do and naturally I am honorary chairman, though I'm not honorary enough to miss it. Where do those little cheese things come from? They're superb. Have one, Amelita."

Amelita had already partaken. "I understand," she said, patting her face with the tiny tea napkin Peters had somehow unearthed, "that the charming Mrs. Meade did your apartment." Madam somehow contrived to make that simple statement into an accusation of adultery and worse. She filled her teacup, then her plate, and took a pill from a gold-plated box and swallowed it. "Allergies," she said.

"Nothing wrong with you, Amelita," Aunt Alice said, "that a long weekend with a good psychiatrist wouldn't cure." Aunt Alice was being modern. She let her corn-flower-blue eyes roam around the loft again and then allowed them to settle on me. "I suppose all this is a reaction, James; that eventually you'll move back uptown?"

She poured herself more tea, sipped it noisily, while Madam continued to help herself to cakes.

I was thrashing around for a new conversational gambit when the doorbell rang. Peters silently answered it.

"Darling," I heard Dutch say before I saw him. "Darling, I need your *goyishe* advice." He walked quickly across the sixty feet of white-painted pine to the place where Aunt Alice, Madam Lizzardi, and I were sitting. He was wearing what looked like a silver-and-crimson kimono, high-heeled clogs, and total makeup.

"Darling," he said, "I went to the most divine party last night. Everyone was in Japanese drag. I got home at four in the morning and had an inspiration. What do you think of a Mister Dutch Men's Sleepwear Line, inaugurated with this home lounge robe? The question is, would *you* wear it, James?" He circled around like a high fashion model, holding his arms out so the sleeves could show to full advantage. "The truth, dolls."

I managed to stand up. "Dutch, I'd like you to meet my aunt, Mrs. Veneering, and her friend, Madam Lizzardi. This is my neighbor, Dutch Cohen."

"I'm very pleased to meet you, Mister Cohen," Aunt Alice said, her blue eyes registering Extreme Interest.

"Likewise," Dutch said.

"Perhaps my nephew will offer you a cup of tea. That is a most beautiful robe."

"Divine, isn't it?" Dutch said, sitting between Aunt Alice and Madam Lizzardi, who was holding the tea napkin to her heaving bosom. Her black-lined eyelids, each a half-inch long, were lowered, making her look simultaneously ecstatic and aghast. "Do you think a man would wear this to receive at home?" Dutch appealed to both of them.

"Definitely," Aunt Alice said, as Madam cocked her head to one side to seriously consider the question.

"You are a designer of dresses, Mister Cohen?" Madam asked, going on with her catechism. I could almost hear the conversations she would be having the following day: "My dear, he's living with a dress designer. . . ."

"Dresses, separates, resort wear. I just sold my first little wrap dress to Bloomingdale's, and from all reports, I understand it is doing fabulously well."

"How nice for you," Aunt Alice said. "Tell me, what do you think of my nephew's living arrangements?"

"The pits," Dutch said, putting two tiny cakes into his mouth. "Could you live like this? I couldn't. Not for one split second. I need color and life and action. I need pizazz. This is like living in a Kleenex box. James is a victim of the New Architectural Look."

Madam Lizzardi laughed. Aunt Alice smiled.

"Darling," Dutch said, putting his hand on Aunt Alice's arm, an action no one has taken since Uncle Garfield died, "I wouldn't want you to go away thinking we all live in antiseptic tanks. Come upstairs and I'll show you a real loft in action."

I started to argue, but Aunt Alice told me not to be silly, they would view Mr. Cohen's loft and then they would have to be leaving. As Peters helped them with their coats and agreed to tell Thurmond to bring Aunt Alice's car around, I whispered to Dutch, "Are you crazy?"

"Dolls," Dutch said, pressing my hand—an action noted by Madam and jotted down by the pencil in her mind—"it will do them a world of good. They'll see how the other half lives."

Aunt Alice signaled she was ready, and Dutch led us into the elevator and up to the sixth floor. He threw open the door on what looked like the last scene of World War III.

"Darling," Dutch said later, "what did they expect? It was Sunday. Sunday comes after Saturday Night Fever. We were all dancing and fucking our brains out until five, six in the morning. We had energy to dust? It looked lived in."

Aunt Alice showed a degree of savoir faire, of cool, of which I wouldn't have expected her capable. She walked through the dining area past the Bronx Renaissance table covered with the leftovers of three days of meals as if she were walking through an interesting exhibit at the Metropolitan Museum of Art. She made appropriate comments when Dutch led her across the bolts of fabric and around the cutting tables and sewing machines to the rack where he kept his creations and showed her samples of his successful wrap dress. "Adorable, no?" Dutch asked. "Absolutely," she answered.

She admired the chrome stove in the kitchen and the swan lamp in the first seating area, where two people were sleeping on the daybed.

It was the assumedly worldly Madam Lizzardi who turned pale and had to search through her purse for her pills and be given a glass of water. That crisis occurred after she had peeked behind the four-paneled leatherette screen that separated the sleeping area from the living area. Mercifully, Aunt Alice was being shown Dutch's vintage 1949 TV set at that moment.

"*Cara,*" Madam Lizzardi said, after handing me the empty glass, "I think that perhaps it is time for us to depart. I am not feeling in top form."

As the ladies made their good-byes, I went and looked behind the leatherette screen. Three of the kids were sleeping on a new acquisition, a fragile wrought-iron bed which featured hand-painted flowers along its frame.

One of the kids had kicked off the sheet that covered him and was lying there perfectly nude. He was humming softly as he gently massaged the erection in his right hand.

I turned and found Aunt Alice standing on her toes, looking over my shoulder. "I had to see what made Amelita ill," she said, turning and leading the way to the elevator. In it, she held a handkerchief to her face. I wondered if she had taken to imitating Madam, who also held a handkerchief to her face and looked as if she had been electrocuted.

But when Aunt Alice took the piece of silk away and put it in her purse, I realized she had been laughing. Suddenly, I started to laugh, too, and by the time we reached the ground floor, Aunt Alice and I were trying, without success, to control ourselves.

"Really, *cara*," Madam said. "I do not think that that little display was amusing."

"Oh, Amelita," Aunt Alice managed to get out, "*la vie bohème.*"

"*La vie pédéraste*," Amelita said dramatically, leading the way out the door.

Thurmond and I put the ladies in the backseat of the old Caddy, and I kissed Aunt Alice good-bye. She was still smiling, which made me feel especially warm toward her.

A taxi had pulled up in front of the car, keeping Thurmond from moving away from the curb. I stood waiting for them to leave. I could hear Madam saying, almost hysterically, "That's what happens to some men when their wives leave them. I remember the Armstrong-Page boy, Teddy . . ."

She stopped speaking in mid-sentence as she saw who

was getting out of the taxi. "Really," Madam said, for once at a loss for words or conclusions.

Jean Rice said "hello" to me without smiling, and we walked into the building together. "I've come to take Dutch tea dancing," she said.

"I suspect he's had enough of both," I told her as I got out of the elevator at the fifth floor. I went to the window and looked down at the street. Aunt Alice's limousine was just pulling away.

CHAPTER 10

It is a tradition among the people I grew up with that one leaves New York sometime during the period between January fifteenth and April first. BaBa, it was reported to me, had taken a house on St. Bart's, "with a friend." Bert and Catherine Brown had borrowed Catherine's mother's house, which is on the desirable side of Barbados, and took Buddy Ruben with them. (New York managed to function.) Everyone else was in Palm Beach.

The afternoon before I was to leave, in early February, Dutch telephoned and asked if he could have dinner with me. This was unusual in that Dutch rarely made plans for a meal that many hours in advance (four). More alarming, he agreed to dine at eight when he rarely thought seriously about his evening meal until the early hours of the morning.

His eyes, especially poignant that evening, watched Peters pack my bag. "Darling, you do have the woist possible taste," was his only comment during that speedy operation. He was being withdrawn and silent. I found myself, for the first time since we had met, having to make conversation.

Only after Peters had tidied up and left, while he was drinking his after-dinner brandy and smoking his second joint of the evening, did Dutch turn those doleful, heavily mascaraed eyes on me. It was like being illuminated by two giant black searchlights. "Where are the kids tonight?" I asked him, wondering what on earth was the matter and a bit afraid to ask.

"They're all upstairs, dolls, perming their hair. Every single one of those kids is a fashion victim." He took a sip of brandy, a toke from his joint, a puff from his cigarette, and gave out with a heartfelt sigh.

"Dutchy," I finally asked, "what's the matter?"

"Darling, you are the most obtuse person I have ever met in my entire life. You are leaving. Me. You are going away. From me. I'm bereft."

"What?"

"Darling! You must know that I'm mad for you."

I didn't know. I had assumed that he felt about me more or less the way he felt about the kids or Bunny or any of his adopted friends: with indiscriminate affection.

"James," he said, taking my hand in his, beaming those eyes on mine. "Do you think I take this much trouble with every *shagitz* I get trapped in the elevator with? Darling, I'm telling you: I can't live without you."

"You're going to have to, Dutch," I said, after a moment, disengaging my hand. "For at least six weeks."

"Someday, darling, you're going to realize what you missed and you're going to be extremely, extremely sorry." I followed him to the door. His big arms in their kimono sleeves went around me, and for a moment, while he held me, I allowed myself to take comfort from that all-enveloping odor of Gitanes, musk, liquor, and his own special scent. "Bon voyage, dolls," he said, going up the stairs. "And don't think I've given up by any means."

"And are you?" Jean asked, centuries later.

"Am I what?"

"Extremely, extremely sorry."

I said, quite honestly, that I was.

Aunt Alice's Palm Beach residence features twenty-three royal palms, an early and ornate swimming pool, and a pervasive air of faded pleasure. "I always feel so European here," Aunt Alice likes to say as she breakfasts off Special K, skim milk, and an overripe banana. Her father-in-law had the breakfast room transported from a villa in Tuscany. Aunt Alice sits on a thronelike construction, said to be a seventeenth-century Pope's gestatorial chair, in which she looks like a child in a high chair.

Cora and Chris Meade were also in Palm Beach, living at the genuinely palatial Meade family home, Casa Verde. Chris, fatter and balder and more eccentric than ever, had invited a group of Establishment economists to join him there. Bearded, dressed in heavy winter clothes, they met in the rotunda room for the greater part of every day, discussing, presumably, theories of the leisure class.

I would see them earnestly shaking their heads at each other as I entered the enormous rococo gates of Casa Verde and took the pebbled path down into the stuccoed tunnel that went under the road and ended on the beach at the door of the folly Chris's grandfather had caused to be built early in the century.

Its walls are covered with shells that form satyrs and nymphs who leer down upon the bath, which takes up most of its center and has been designed to resemble a natural grotto. There are several dressing rooms, all with the shell motif, all supplied with tables, chairs, and fainting couches.

It was cold and dark and damp, and Cora enjoyed it immensely. Under her hard, perfect veneer, there beats the heart of a soft romantic.

"How much money do you have, James?" Cora wanted to know as we lay in the bath/pool, having just uncoupled.

I told her.

"Before or *après* the divorce?"

"I know of no divorce, as yet. Even if there is one, BaBa has her own money. She won't need mine."

"She'll want it, though," Cora said, tapping one heavily red-polished nail against my chest. "Hell hath no fury like a woman who scorns."

"You should never attempt wit, Cora."

"We could live quite nicely on what you have. And certainly Chris would give us something. How do you feel about the children?"

I spent a great deal of time with Aunt Alice during my visit, escorting her to dinner parties and charity balls, where the men wore pastel evening jackets over Lilly Pulitzer trousers and pushed ladies with lifted faces and drooping diamonds around the dance floors.

Occasionally there would be an elaborate luncheon with bridge to follow. My bridge being what it is, I was allowed after the dessert to go off and amuse myself.

After one such event I left the other guests, who were headed to the card room, and made my own way down a spectacularly curved staircase. Jean Rice Halladay was sitting in a small room off the foyer wearing a yellow dress and a yellow hat and looking ineffably lovely.

"You didn't bring Mister Dutch with you?" I asked, entering, seating myself across from her in a gray, upholstered chair.

"I wish to hell I had. I hate traveling alone."

"How long are you staying?"

"For as long as it takes to show Lilli the plans for Wilma Lyons's drawing room, get her approval, and drive back to the airport." She pointed to a large leather envelope at the side of her chair. "Wilma refused to approve them unless Lilli saw them and signed them first. So I got on an airplane."

"Look, there's dozens of unoccupied bedrooms at my aunt's, and I'm sure she'd be more than happy . . ."

"Thanks, James. But I'm a working girl." Not bothering to hide her impatience, she turned and looked at the enameled clock sitting on a desk behind her.

Lilli chose that moment to enter. She was a guest of the house and seemed very much in control. We said hello (we had been sitting at separate tables during the luncheon), what a nice party it had been, wasn't Palm Beach fun and the weather glorious. Then I left them alone. I turned back for a moment to see Jean poised over the plans, her hat left on a chair, her hair falling in her eyes. Lilli was looking at me speculatively. I smiled and allowed the butler to open the door for me.

Of all the parties, the masquerade balls were the most amusing if the least fun. The getups the winter denizens managed to get themselves into in the name of charity might even have won a nod of approval from Dutch.

Cora gave the grandest, a fin de siècle afternoon party at Casa Verde in aid of that old standby, the March of Dimes.

Somewhere she had found an old surrey, borrowed two of Tony Kiernan's dappled ponies, and came round in it to pick me up. She was wearing a long, pale Edwardian gown and a hugely brimmed white hat and looked the epitome of Gainsborough good looks. She is very beautiful in a way that has nothing to do with the American concept of beauty.

I had put on one of Uncle Garfield's well-preserved ice cream suits, which dated from the twenties but was indefinitely antique enough to pass as period. As the surrey rode through the streets of Palm Beach, the warm afternoon sunlight surrounding us, as Cora gazed at me from under restrained and new eyelashes, I wondered—for a moment—whether or not I shouldn't marry her. She is so very good at arranging things.

We were driven up to the gold-veined marble steps that lead into Casa Verde, and Cora left me at the door.

The center hall, with its dozens of columns and pilasters, with its faux marble floor and its blue-sky-cum-fluffy-clouds ceiling, was filled with what is known as Palm Beach society.

Major Whitney Louis White screwed in his monocle, bowed to me, and held out his Baccarat glass for more Dom Perignon 1970, which was being poured from magnums. A tiny French dress designer named Madeleine popped Beluga caviar canapes into her round, lipsticked mouth. A Texas zillionaire couple whose name was never mentioned nibbled lobster claws and fraises des bois.

The center hall ends in a closed-in and now air-conditioned court which is predominantly pastel. I escaped into it. It is a very simple place (compared to what's going on in the other parts of the house), reminiscent of a good hotel's conference room. Chris was sitting at a circular table, a book propped up in front of him, a half-eaten sandwich in his hand.

"Cora's giving herself quite a do," he said, looking up at me.

"She's outdone herself. And most everyone else."

I hadn't found myself alone with Chris in a fairly long time. I felt so guilty and miserable in my white ice cream suit that I wanted to cry.

We looked at each other for a few minutes and I said, "I'm sorry, Christopher."

"You shouldn't be, J.J. If I didn't want it this way, I would have it changed."

A servant in old-fashioned livery came into the room. "Mrs. Meade has been looking everywhere for you, Mister Grant."

I found her in the Verde Court, an oval room of green marble, dominated by a malachite fountain with a tenfoot-high nude in its center.

"Where have you been?" Cora asked, seating me at her table next to a woman in a black gown whose head was covered with an enormous black-velvet picture hat fringed with white ostrich plumes. It was Lilli Ruben.

Her decidedly ugly face was oddly attractive under the white plumes. It is a European–New York face, and it gave me pleasure to see it. "So you and I have a friend in common, James," she said.

"Actually, Jean's a friend of a friend."

"What do you think of her?"

"Wonderfully good looking."

"I didn't mean that, my dear."

"She seems to have her problems," I ventured. "Like most everyone else."

"I want her to marry Buddy."

"Really." I watched Lilli dig into her sorbet with enthusiasm. "I would have thought you would have wanted something else for your son," I said, since we were both being brutal and frank or as brutal and frank as one could be at that table in that situation.

"Buddy couldn't get himself a first-rate society girl, and the second-rate ones are too mean. Besides," she said, almost echoing Dutch's words to me, "he's mad for her."

Lord Something-or-Other took that moment to compliment Lilli on her hat, and I turned to answer some question of Cora's. I've forgotten the question, but the answer was no.

I wonder now if Lilli remembers that conversation, if she is appalled or unhappy or even aware of the unconscious irony that underlay that belief of hers: "Besides, he's mad for her."

CHAPTER 11

I was on a plane for New York the following morning, as was Lilli. She was sitting in the first-class smoking section, talking to a woman I didn't want to know. We smiled and nodded, and she went back to her presumably prospective client and I went back to the manuscript I was attempting to read without much success.

Though I had a great many things to think about, I found myself wondering why Lilli had been so transparently open with me. Lilli is not a woman given to private confidences with anyone, especially not with a man she hardly knows.

"She thought we were lovers, you dope," Jean told me later. "She was gauging your reaction to the plot she was just then hatching. She thought I would have the strength Buddy didn't, that you would return to New York and, in the privacy of your boudoir, tell me what she had said. Then it would be up to me."

"Why on earth would she think we were lovers?"

"A great many people did. No one thought I was schlepping down to Twentieth Street every day to have tea with a fag dress designer."

"They thought Dutch was the beard?"

"*Exactement.*"

"What about Cora?"

"Good old Corea Medea. Yes, everyone knew. What Lilli was suggesting—you are thick—was that you should stick to Cora and let go of me so that I could improve myself by having a *mariage de convenance* with Buddy."

"I must have had some reputation," I said, not displeased.

"They should have known."

As we left the plane on that cool day in early April (the third), Lilli offered to drive me into the city. But Aunt Alice had arranged for Thurmond to come, so I declined. She pecked me on the cheek, gave her driver her luggage receipts, and stepped into her Mercedes.

Forty-five minutes later she was walking into her office, which takes up an entire floor of the Decorator and Design Building on Third Avenue and Fifty-ninth Street. She gave her secretary, Sophie, her coat and strode through the showroom into the cubicle where Jean sat, drowning in wallpaper and carpet samples.

I have been in Lilli Ruben's showroom. It is a beautiful blend of the antiques she acquired from Rose Cummings's Park Avenue shop, of the reproductions her manufacturing company turns out, and of pricey, contemporary furniture that she has designed. All of her signatures—the tortoise blinds, the tile floor, the Imari bowls—are there to make clients happy.

The cubicles where her staff works are somewhat more austere, windowless spaces defined by white plastic room dividers. She pays the decorators who work for her very little, but all of them working there realize Lilli Ruben's is the best place from which to be launched.

She stood in Jean's office, studying the birds of paradise that were stuck in a white vase on Jean's desk. "Ugly creatures," she decided. "But expensive. Bert's getting extravagant."

"Bert wouldn't send flowers to my funeral," Jean said.

"New man in your life?" Lilli asked, sitting down in the one chair, lighting one of her thin brown cigarettes.

"Not exactly."

"You look very well, Jean."

"You're looking tan and tired."

"Palm Beach is all work and no play. How is Babs Raymer?"

"Not good. Everything is set for the installation but the goddamned mantle. She infests my dreams."

"You've taken her to Chez Thomas?"

"On any number of occasions."

"You'd better take her down to Cunningham. Let him come out of his workroom in those blue jeans, smelling of sweat. Sex has always been Babs Raymer's downfall. She'll buy something fake and overpriced."

"I should have thought of Cunningham, but he always stands so close when he talks to me."

"Put the Raymer in the way." Lilli stood up, removed her lynx hat, and started for her own office. "Have you seen Buddy?" she asked, stopping at the door.

"He's back from Barbados. I said I would have dinner with him tonight."

"And Bert?"

"Still in Barbados."

"When he returns, I wonder how long it will take for you to resume."

"I've changed the locks, Lilli."

Lilli laughed. "You won't go through with it, my dear. He won't allow it."

"I'll get Buddy to challenge him to a duel."

"Buddy and I would go out to dinner two, three, four times a week," Jean says. "Lutèce or Christopher's or The Four Seasons. A place where someone would be certain to spot us."

"Did you sleep with him?"

"I didn't even fuck him."

"Why not?"

"He didn't ask. And I don't think he wanted to. I thought he was a gentleman from the old school. He'd take my arm when we got in and out of Lilli's car. He'd kiss me good night when he dropped me off at the apartment. He was consistently sweet and earnest and dead set on doing what he thought was the right thing. He was acting as Bert's stand-in, the knight's chivalrous friend protecting the virtuous lady. I couldn't figure out whether he was acting on Bert's orders or on his own misguided impulse. There was also the possibility that Lilli put him up to his squire number. And all the time we were going in and out of those restaurants, I was wondering how Bert would react to the lock changes."

"What made you think he would react at all?"

"Bert wasn't going to let *me* lock *him* out. Buddy and I were eating our way through Manhattan's three-star restaurants waiting for Bert to come back. With orders."

After those dinners with Buddy, she would go home to that apartment, change, and take a taxi downtown to Dutch's loft. Sometimes they would sit up all night, smoking marijuana, drinking scotch, talking. More often, they would go to Studio 54.

Studio 54 was the discotheque of that season. Far hipper than Régine's, which was on Park Avenue and catered to an aging international set, Studio 54 had a very long run by Manhattan standards before it became a gathering place for the BQN (Brooklyn–Queens–New Jersey) crowd, as Dutch would have put it.

Its policy of allowing its doorman to decide who could go in and who would have to stand on the street and watch others go in was the basis, according to Dutch, of Studio 54's success. Dutch himself was occasionally denied entry.

"Why would you go if you're not certain to get in?" I asked.

"Darling, you'll never know until you're there."

I was spending my evenings dining at the Meades'. They have a long, narrow dining room upholstered in shirred silk. It is like the inside of a prom queen's dress. Chris always sits at the north end of the table, which is supposed to have come from a sixteenth-century Inquisitorial investigative chamber and has room for thirty-six, seats for twenty. At Chris's end were the bearded economists from Columbia University, Harvard, the London School of Economics. The children, two overbehaved New York children, would say "may I" and "please, sir" each time they reached for the béarnaise sauce. They and I cordially detested each other.

Cora and I would sit at the end of the table closest to the kitchen because Cora, having grown up in Sussex where everything is served cold, likes her food hot. "Piping hot," she would say, as if she were advertising soup on television.

Chris and his cohorts didn't care what they ate as long as they were free to fight over Veblen, Galbraith, and Marx. It occurred to me on more than one occasion that Chris and his pals, with their balding heads and protruding bellies and economia, were a lot happier than Cora and I with our knee-touching, openhanded adultery.

"Whatever did you see in her?" Jean has asked.

"Probably the same thing you saw in Bert."

After Palm Beach, Chris was more jovial and back-slapping and less of a friend than ever. Cora seemed uninterested in any further discussion of a more permanent, disciplined arrangement. They were both afraid, I think, that I was about to bow out. They needed me for stability.

It was understood that after dinner Chris would move on into the John Jacob Meade Library which took up an entire floor while Cora and I would descend to her sitting room and get on with it. I'm not sure what happened to the children. A woman in a blue dress would come and take them away after dessert.

It was also understood that I would act as a stand-in for Chris whenever a social obligation cropped up, which was virtually every other evening. Thus I found myself once again making the rounds: charity balls with Aunt Alice sitting at neighboring tables, glowering; theater benefits, plays no one outside of BQN had any interest in unless they happened to have written them; parties in penthouses and regular houses and museum cafeterias and once in the Sixth Avenue Subway station.

It was much like being married to BaBa, but less expensive in a number of ways. I made it a point to return to my loft each evening, though none of the Meades—with the possible exception of the woman in the blue dress—would have been thrown by finding me at the breakfast table in one of Chris's robes. "Uncle James has come to live with us, dears."

In mid-April, the fifteenth according to my diary, Cora was to dine with her in-laws in their Edward Durell Stone house on East Sixty-fourth Street. It was an annual event of some kind, someone's anniversary, and it made Cora anxious. "I wish you were coming," she said.

"I think Harrison Meade might notice that I was not his son."

"They're so bloody Episcopalian. They always sit Bishop Potter on my right. What on earth am I to wear, James?"

I went home to my loft. Peters had been instructed to prepare a meal, which he did with almost too intense a degree of gratitude, as if I had given him his indenture papers. I sat chewing the steak, which was tough and overdone, wondering why everyone I knew was so out of touch with reality. Not excepting myself. I managed to get down a slice of Peters's wife's famous peach pie, which had suffered from the freezing process. I sent Peters home and went up to Dutch's loft, which for all of its chaos seemed an oasis of sanity.

"Darling," Dutch said, kissing me. "Darling! Two more dresses this morning. One to Bendel's and one to Ohrbach's. That little yellow-and-white pinafore and a slinky, sexy backless extravaganza I always knew was exactly right for Ohrbach's. Darling, have some pink champagne and gin. I'm celebrating."

He sat himself down at a taffeta-skirted dressing table that his friend Bunny had given him as a housewarming present. A green sheet was wrapped around him. He studied his face in the three-paneled mirror. When I asked him what he was doing, he said, "Dolls, what does it look like I'm doing? I'm giving myself a facial." He tweezed his eyebrows carefully and thoroughly. He dabbed tufts of cotton, immersed in a pale ointment, across the surface of his face. He sprayed another liquid on top of the ointment with a glass atomizer, the sort women used to perfume themselves with. He pinched and pulled and applied. He shaded and colored and powdered. And through it all he kept up a stream of autobiographical monologue.

I avoided the champagne and gin and poured myself a glass of Mexican beer. Dutch's bar ran to the exotic. I drank a toast to his new success and lay down on the pink couch, nursing the beer. I felt very comfortable, more at ease there than anywhere else, a child in his crib. Indeed, the situation reminded me of evenings when my mother would allow me into her dressing room as she prepared to go out to dinner.

"And I'm making the announcement now, James, so that there'll be no surprises mañana: I am out of mourning for Angel. Finished with celibacy. Enough is enough, already. I am officially in the market for a new lovette. If there is anyone at your office or in your clubs who would like to learn about downtown love, feel free to give them my number. Unless you, of course, have decided you're available?"

I disregarded his last question. "Every male I know is over thirty and presumably heterosexual."

"Then don't bother. I want a boy."

"As long as he doesn't try to kick your head in and force me to go to Jersey City to retrieve your body, that's fine with me."

"Has anyone ever told you, James, that you can be

extremely, extremely negative? Hand me that turquoise eyebrow-liner sitting on the little bamboo table next to you, darling. Thank you. Maybe, on second thought, I should consider one of your friends. A little stockbroker with thick calves . . ."

I would have stayed all night, watching Dutch prepare himself, listening to his fantasies and his stories and his ideas about Life, but Jean arrived soon after midnight.

She was wearing a dress of no particular color. It fitted her loosely, making her seem Scandinavian and aristocratic, like the Snow Queen in the Andersen story. Her hair had been rolled into a French knot, the way it had been when I first saw her, and, as usual at that time, she wore little makeup. And as usual at that time, she was out of sympathy with me.

"Darling," Dutch said, taking her in his arms, announcing his dress coup, "you and I are going stepping. I've ordered a limo complete with champagne, poppers, and two spoons of coke. James," he said, looking at my three-piece suit and what he called my 'clunky' shoes, "you are invited if you would like to get out of that outfit. . . ."

Jean seemed distinctly unhappy at the possibility of my going with them. I got off the couch, said it was past my bedtime, and went down to my loft and felt disconsolate. I had wanted to go.

"It wasn't so much you, James. But you look like Bert. I don't mean that. You're blond, he's dark. You've got muscles and he's got sinews. But you were wearing one of those suits. Uptown suits. You belonged uptown. I had come downtown. To get high, to get off on being with the only man who accepted me unequivocally. There were no threats in Dutch's loft."

"Excepting me."

"Excepting you."

They had the hired limo drive them round and round Central Park as they smoked marijuana, drank champagne, snorted cocaine through a tightly wrapped fifty-dollar bill.

"What did you two find to talk about?" I asked Dutch.

"Life, dolls. We would talk about life." He was fascinated by her California stories: the Bel-Air house, the studio, Cary Grant, DeMille, her grandmother, her mother, the cars, the chauffeurs, the men she had been to bed with. She told him about Bert and Catherine.

That night, after the limousine had made its tenth tour of the park, logging in some sixty miles, he took her hand and said, "If I were straight, darling. If only I were straight. I could teach you a thing or two about love. Not to mention sex."

"Somehow I'm glad you're not, Mister Dutch."

They arrived at 54 at two in the morning. The owner/manager, Steve Rubell, was standing at the door, and waved them in. He kissed Jean and smiled at Dutch. "Is she famous?" someone in the crowd that flanked the entry called out.

They went through the dim first room, past the coat check, and into the cavernous ex–television studio for which the discotheque is named. The music was rock and loud, but not ear-splitting. The lights were dim, reminiscent of a theater's when a play is in progress. The room smelled of air-conditioning and expensive sweat. Men in jock straps stood at the bar, drinking scotch. Boys in cotton undershorts served drinks. Studio 54 was then at its height, and Society was well represented. Kate Paley and Amanda Burden and Betsey Whitney and Dorothy

Hirshon wore their Valentinos, Galitzines, and Given-chys, having just come from one of Babe Paley's benefit parties for her North Shore University Hospital. Truman Capote and his coterie were ignored by Gloria Vander-bilt and hers. Caroline Kennedy and a friend were seated to the right of the dance floor on low chairs.

The dance floor itself, located where there once was a stage, is perpetually bathed in soft pastel lights, like a Forest Lawn monument. Neon fixtures, penis shaped, descend and ascend over the dance floor, seemingly at will, giving off purple and black light.

"Nonthreatening Sex is the theme," Dutch said. "That's why we all get off on it. That and the fact some people can't get in. Everybody loves a monarchy."

He and Jean danced for hours. With the kids who had been allowed in for atmosphere. With men Jean knew. With two women in matching Stephen Burrows gowns.

"Heaven, isn't it?" Dutch asked Jean, passing her a joint one of the Stephen Burrowses had passed to him.

"It was," she says. "So mindless. So bodyless. The drugs and the atmosphere combined to make one feel weightless. I floated through the music and the neon lights. I was one-dimensional. I had no body. The music passed through me."

"Far out," I said.

"Fuck you."

Later, Dutch took Jean home in the limousine. "Come up," she told him. "We'll have jasmine tea and apricot cookies."

"I didn't want him to go. I thought, in the back of my mind, that we might sleep together. Not sex. Sleep. I felt so close to him."

"Dolls," he said, kissing her goodnight, "there's a little

117

hustler bar in my neighborhood that I've been dying to try, and something tells me tonight is the night."

"You're not going to find true romance in a hustler bar," Jean told him.

"Darling, where do you think I found the Angel?"

CHAPTER 12

". . . a little hustler bar in my neighborhood that I've been dying to try . . ."

The little hustler bar was Le Dirt, and he hadn't tried it since that night in January when he had allowed himself to be taken to Jersey City and nearly blinded.

At Dutch's invitation—now that I think of it, it was more of a request, the asking of a favor—I once went with him to Le Dirt. I remember asking if the name were intentionally ironic. "Darling, do you think I have any idea what goes on in the minds of the Mafia when they name bars?" Dutch asked as we walked into the establishment in question. It was a late spring Saturday afternoon (May the twentieth), and I was putting off the decision of what to do with the Southampton house (rent? sell? occupy?). Dutch was nervous, though he denied it.

"The Mafia?" I asked as we approached Le Dirt, which looked like any other bar on Sixth Avenue: stenciled gold letters on a glass window spelling out the name, a black painted door that looked unwelcoming. "The Mafia?"

"Mister James, the Mafia owns every gay bar in the city. The Sewer. The Toilet. The Hole."

"One of the capos must be a psychologist."

We went in through the black door. The change from daylight to cocktail-lounge dim was disconcerting. There was a long, narrow entrance along which ran a vinyl upholstered bar. Behind the bar were bottles of liquor that appeared virgin and men in wash-and-wear short-sleeve shirts who appeared unhealthy in a nonspecific way. At the end of the bar was a large, dark room with a pool table and an old-fashioned Wurlitzer juke box. A wooden floor covered with sawdust and a pressed tin ceiling painted black ran throughout. One could imagine Le Dirt one day being restored, being turned into a restaurant for professionals moving into Chelsea, all clean and butcher-blocked and antiseptic, green plants hanging under newly installed skylights.

The atmosphere that afternoon was heavy and unpleasant, filled with the smells of tobacco, beer, cheap liquor.

"It's hot with fashion," Dutch told me, looking around.

"Why are you so nervous, Dutch?"

"Darling, I'm the calmest I've ever been in my entire life."

Three or four men of indeterminate age, wearing blue jeans and tight T-shirts, stood at the bar, holding sweating bottles of beer. Two others were playing pool. A thin man in a brown suit, indefinably but definitely menacing, was sitting at the far end of the bar, on what appeared to be the only bar stool. He nodded at Dutch. "Have a drink, darling. I have to talk to someone. I'll be right back."

I went to the bar, ordered a beer, and tried not to feel

as uncomfortable as I was feeling. The man closest to me looked my way every few moments. I tried to decide whether he was hostile or amorous. It was very quiet; only the muted sounds of Dutch and his friend in the brown suit talking disturbed the silence. Suddenly the juke box came to life like a corpse sitting up. It played "Macho Man," a song I had heard several times on Dutch's elaborate stereo system. I tried concentrating on the words.

"Ready, dolls?" Dutch asked. I put my unfinished beer down on the bar and followed him out. In the cool sunshine, I saw he was sweating.

"What's the matter with you?" I asked.

"Darling," Dutch said, wiping his face with a huge green handkerchief, "that was Eddie Rabinado."

"That doesn't enlighten me. What're you so scared about?"

"James, darling, I have a few business problems. Eddie is going to help me."

"What kind of business problems? What about all those orders? Maybe I could help."

"Very sweet of you, Mister James, but Cardinal Rule Number Three Hundred and Twelve says 'Never let friends get involved in your business on a monetary basis.' If you'd like to come up and sew a little, that would be much appreciated. Sylvia Einhorn is giving me terrible trouble."

He went on to elaborate about Sylvia, his head seamstress, for several minutes before I was able to bring the conversation back to Eddie Rabinado and Dutch's business problems.

"James, it's much too complicated to explain right now. You don't know the first thing about the garment business. You can have a million orders but there are all sorts of aggravating complications that can keep you from turning over a profit."

"Such as?"

"Such as if the fabric isn't delivered on time and there's not enough capital on hand to pay for it when it is. That's the kind of complication I'm having right now. Eddie Rabinado is going to help me out."

"He looks like a loan shark. Listen, Dutch, maybe my bank could advance you—"

"Darling, believe me, Eddie Rabinado is on the up and up. Maybe a little threatening, but in the long run he's strictly legit. Besides, he adores me. James, not another word. Everything, I swear on my mother's Jewish heart, is going to work out."

"You could have insisted," Jean says, which we both know isn't a fair thing to say, but nonetheless, she says it.

The morning Dutch left Jean to try his luck at Le Dirt, it was "packed to the rafters. Every john in town was there," Dutch told me. "I'd love to know where they get all their money. Can I compete with Lincoln Continentals with moon roofs? Hookers love fancy cars. I knew the second I walked through that *fashtunkanah* door that I was wasting my time. I stood at the bar toward the front, kibitzing with Bunny, and decided to get really drunk."

Bunny is black, somewhere between eighteen and forty, and quintessentially New York. He peppers his speech with Yiddishisms and wears his hair elaborately plaited in what is called corn rows, leaving narrow aisles of naked, oily scalp between the braids.

They schmoozed as Dutch eyed the crowd, Dutch wanting to know who had done Bunny's hair ("Seth, in the Village, that stutterer who lives over Orange Julius on Eighth Street with that divine boy") and Bunny wanting to know who was at 54 ("everyone").

The hustlers stood at the far end of the bar, drinking their one beer for the night, talking to one another about their heterosexual prowess or standing by themselves, striking loner poses. They ignored the potential johns.

"Darling," Dutch explained, "it's all part of the attraction. Unattainability. That's what each and every one of them is striving for. The dopiest little hooker from the Bronx knows that once he's unattainable, he's got it made."

"The same principle as Studio 54."

Exactly.

A Puerto Rican kid in his early twenties came in and stood next to Dutch. He ordered a Piels and, as soon as it was in his hands, began peeling the label from the bottle. "That's a sign of suppressed masturbation," Dutch said to him.

"I don't suppress it, man." He wore a leather jacket over a black T-shirt, blue jeans, and sneakers.

Dutch gave Bunny his "get lost" look and turned to the kid and asked if he could buy him another drink.

"Just got this one, man."

"You're not drinking it."

"I don't dig beer."

The kid studied his label-less bottle for a while as Dutch studied him. "The barracudas with their moon roofs were getting ready to attack so I tried the direct approach. I asked him if he wanted to 'get together.' "

The kid said, "Sure."

"I knew he was new," Dutch told me. "First of all, James, we never said a word about money. No hustler in his right mind wouldn't set up a price, even if it's only a bargaining position, right from the top. Second of all, he walked out with me. A hustler and his trick *never* leave together."

He wasn't about to take him back to the loft. "Not on the first date, anyway. Think of Ramon Navarro. Think of Sal Mineo. Think of Michael Greer. Once you let a hustler cross your threshold, something happens. A miniature class struggle takes place and you're the one that gets beheaded."

Dutch took the boy, Louie, to a hotel he patronized on Twenty-third and Lexington. It was called the Monte Excelsior and had once been a tenement. They sat on the narrow cot under the honest forty-watt light bulb, listening to sounds coming from the next room, half an inch of wallboard away.

"Man," Louie said, "I got to tell you something."

"Lay it on me, dolls," Dutch said, smoking a Gitane with one hand, a joint with the other.

"I ain't no hustler."

This, according to Dutch, is Standard Hustler Denial Number One.

"Whoever said you were, darling?"

"Come off it, man. You were in that hole. I was in that hole. And now we're both in this hole listening to the whore in the next room pretend she's coming. There ain't no TV, so what are we doing here?"

This was not expected john/trick repartee. "So what *are* we doing here?" Dutch asked.

"You're here because you want to make it. I'm here

because I thought like maybe hustling might not be such a bad gig. I could make a couple of dollars. But I got to tell you, man—I can't do it. I mean I *could*. I could let you blow me and give me twenty bucks. It's no big deal for me to get a hard-on. But I'm looking at you with that homely face and you're a little fat and you seem like this very nice person and I'm saying to myself, Louie, what're you doing? Louie, go home. Louie, you're keeping three people up—this cat, you, and your mother.

"You know what I'm trying to tell you, man?"

"You mean you've never done it with a boy, dolls?" A standard Dutch gambit.

"Did I say that? Shit, man, I have fucked with girls, women, boys, men, my big sister Carmen. What's that got to do with it?"

"Louie," Dutch said, "I didn't necessarily pick you up to blow you. I picked you up because you're cute and I wanted to be with you. If we do a little something, well, I wouldn't say no. If we don't, that's cool, too."

Louie refused the joint Dutch was smoking, consulted the imitation gold watch on his wrist, looked at Dutch and then away again. "What would you say if I asked you to lay fifteen bucks on me till Thursday?"

"Just like that?"

"Just like that."

"You're not going to tell me what it's for or why you need it. You just want me to hand you fifteen bucks, right?"

"That's it, man." Louie stood up. He was an inch taller than Dutch, an inch broader across the shoulders, several inches smaller around the waist. He had oiled and slicked back his jet black hair. He had big black eyes, big feet, big hands, and a cleft in his chin. He had a bulge in his trousers that looked as if he had stuffed a meatball hero behind his fly.

"I'll give you twenty-five," Dutch said, "and you let me do you."

"Man, all I want is a loan. Fifteen bucks. I need the bread. I will repay you come Thursday," Louie said, slowly, as if he were talking to a backward child. "And I will tell you a secret, man—you will never get my ass with money. I only ball people I dig. And when I do ball, it's a two-way street for me. No blow jobs. But I can see where your head is at, man. Nice meeting you. No hard feelings, right?" He walked out of the room and out of the Monte Excelsior.

"It was certainly a novel hustler approach," Dutch said. "Either that Louie is a genius or so innocent and sweet and naive you could *plotz*."

"So what did you do?"

"Darling, what do you think I did?"

Dutch followed him down and out onto the street. Louie was standing on the corner, pretending to eye the lady hookers in their purple wigs strutting up and down Lexington Avenue. Dutch came up behind him and put two tens in Louie's jacket pocket.

"I'll call you on Thursday, man," Louie said, thanking Dutch, getting into a taxi.

CHAPTER 13

I had a bad time of it on that promised Thursday. I was lunching with my sister, Bernice, at her club. It is gray and white and stiff, like the cardboard they used to wrap laundered shirts around. It is called the Cosmopolitan by its older members and the Coz by the younger, peppier crowd of women who make a great deal of fun of it but still belong.

Bernice falls somewhere between the two generations in age and simply calls it The Club. Bernice has the odd ability of making me empathize with the food we eat when we lunch together. It started when I was a child and she was a teenager going through an antivivisectionist stage. The children in my father's house—Bernice and I—dined alone until a fairly late age in a room set aside for that purpose. The kitchen was to the left, and beyond that was the grown-up dining room. I would try to hear what the adults were saying—a fairly impossible task given the noise Cook made in the kitchen—while Bernice would treat each item on her plate as if it were once alive. "To think," she would say, "that this lamb chop was once a sheep, baaing its way happily through the fields. To think that this potato was once a bud that grew its way . . ."

That Thursday we had ordered smoked fish and wilted vegetables.

Isobel Barnard was at the next table with her decorator, a shining bald man in a tight blue blazer whom I had met at a party Dutch had taken me to. He waved.

"Who on earth is that?" Bernice asked, though I don't suppose she really wanted to know. Bernice is a woman capable of following only her own limited interests in a luncheon conversation.

Forking little round potatoes flecked with packaged parsley into her mouth, she told me that she had been in touch with Barrett. She has always refused to call Barrett BaBa, which is, I think, a definite point in Bernice's favor. "Barrett," she said between mouthfuls of overcooked peas, "is very, very tired of England."

"So am I. Do you suppose I could have my coffee now?"

"You haven't finished your fish. She wants to come back to New York, J.J."

I concentrated on attempting to attract the octogenarian waitress's misty attention without upsetting any of the octogenarian diners.

"I believe, J.J., that Barrett wants to come back to you."

"And give up her dalliance with the thirteen-year-old rock star?"

"He's closer to thirty, and I gather, from what Barrett did *not* say, that it's over. She wants you back again, J.J."

There was a small hiatus in the conversation while

Bernice said hello, how are you, yes, we are going to Maine for the summer and no, I think we're going to try and avoid Newport this year, to two women built very much like her. I managed to get the waitress to bring coffee and the house dessert, which had been billed as bread pudding.

"She is still your wife, J.J."

I added cream and sugar to the pudding while Bernice watched disapprovingly. "All that sugar can't be good for you," she said.

"It's doing wonders for the bread pudding."

"If you won't talk about Barrett," Bernice said, thoughtfully digesting a large gray lump of the matter in front of her, "you might wish to talk about the life you appear to be leading. Aunt Alice won't say it, but I happen to know she is very disappointed. I'm sure it's all very fashionable for young unmarried couples to take lofts in places in Manhattan one has never heard of, but J.J., you are on the windy side of thirty-five. . . ."

"In light of that fact, Bernice, don't you think it's time you allowed me to choose my own route to destruction?"

"I won't even begin to think of what Father would have thought," Bernice said, belatedly wiping her face, missing the moist crumb that had lodged itself in her right laugh line. "He left you a great name, a great deal of money, and an example of a truly patrician way to live one's life. He was so very, very generous to you. He allowed you the time you requested. He helped to have the thing published. Everyone including you agreed it was a terrible failure. As Father said, 'People like us do not write or paint or compose. We assist others to write and paint and compose.'

"You have enough money, James, to do whatever you wish with it. I know you give a great deal away. I also know you refuse to sit on any board or fund-giving committee, that you have even refused a place on Father's foundation. You agreed that if your book was not a success you would come back to New York, give up your artistic ideas, and work with Uncle Elwyn. Well, you did, and that seems to have panned out quite nicely. Your marriage, on the other hand—"

I reached across the table and cupped my right hand around the back of Bernice's graying head and clasped my left hand across her mouth. After a few moments I let her go. She looked up at me—I was standing by this time—like a goldfish deprived of air. "Father would say," she said in the low, measured tones of that man, "that you're a failure, J.J."

"Fuck you," I said so loudly that the main dining hall in the Cosmopolitan Club—with all its attendant members and guests and servants—became pin-drop silent. "And fuck Father."

"J.J.," Bernice said, realizing too late she had gone too far, putting her gloved hand on my arm. "Please. Sit down. And lower your voice."

"Fuck," I shouted as loud as I could. "Fuck all of you," I went on, watching the words reverberate around the room, faces freezing in mid-bite. "You're all fucking hypocrites, preserved mummies, judgmental sideliners. I'm getting out of this mausoleum." Fairly berserk, I pushed my way past the startled waitress, past the club secretary and other officials who had been summoned to handle the disturbance, and went out of the Coz Club onto Sixty-fifth Street, where I got into a taxi and told him to take me to Twentieth Street. I felt like a watermelon that had just burst—a not overly pleasant feeling, but not entirely unrewarding.

Not too long ago I ran into Isobel Barnard, and we reminisced about that Thursday lunch. Isobel told me that Bernice, with enviable sangfroid, had opened her purse, swiped her nose with the mustard-colored powder she favors, signed for the check, and exited, nodding at acquaintances as if she had not just been part of what would be known for the next fifty years or so as THE TIME J.J. GRANT GOT DRUNK AND SHOUTED DIRTY WORDS IN THE COZ CLUB DINING ROOM.

Jean's Thursday was also not of the brightest. Babs Raymer was in her office arguing all by herself the pros and cons of the proposed wallpaper for the servants' bath. Jean had read in Lee Dembart's column in the *Times* that Bert Brown was back from his extended leave. that the rumors of a feud with the mayor were just that, and that Bert was being considered as the Democratic contender in the next senatorial race.

Catherine had had all of New York's power brokers as guests on Barbados at one time or another, and she was getting ready to launch Bert into the national spotlight. She was managing him like a very good horse trainer: with careful and perfect timing.

The telephone rang. It was Bert, as she knew it would be. She excused herself and went into an adjoining office that had a door, a telephone, and an interior window. Through the window she could watch Babs light a cigarette, tap the tocs of her three-hundred-dollar lizard shoes on the twelve-dollar-a-yard industrial carpeting, and otherwise express impatience.

"She changed the locks," Bert said.

"Bert, I don't want to know you. I don't know how else to say it. I want you to leave me alone."

"Mummy's dead. Baby doesn't need Bertie anymore."

"That's a perfectly adequate analysis, Bert."

"She doesn't have to worry about threesomes anymore. Not if she doesn't want to."

It sounded as if Bert was begging, and that scared her.

"I'm not worried about threesomes, Bert."

They listened to the sounds of the New York City telephone system at work for a while, and then he said, "I'll come by for a drink later. We'll talk."

"No drink, Bert. No talk. No *nada*. I don't want to know you anymore." She placed the receiver back on its base gingerly, as if it would explode, and, not very steadily, went back to Babs Raymer's harmless sadism.

She couldn't risk seeing him. And she couldn't risk going home to that sex doll's apartment with its claustrophobic walls and its gigantic bed. She called Dutch, who said, "I'm not up for going out, dolls, but if you'd like to come down for a quiet schmooze, I'll get the Chinks around the corner to deliver."

I stopped by on my way to the Meades', but even Dutch seemed depressed. "I'm waiting for fabric for a dress I promised Gimbels two weeks from yesterday. If you were in my boots, darling, you wouldn't be slightly nervous and anxious?" He put his fist to his ear and pantomimed receiving a phone call. "Good morning, Nervous and Anxious."

Jean looked up from the sketch pad she was drawing on and laughed. "Good morning," she said, "Trapped and Helpless."

I felt left out of the game, out of their mutual sympathy, so I went uptown to play with Cora. Jean fed Dutch a couple of joints, and he regaled her with the story of his life again over roast pork lo mein.

He was born in "high middle Brooklyn," right after the War, to a young mother and a father solely interested in his business, the manufacture of paper bags. The business thrived; the marriage did not. When Dutch was five, his mother left for Reno, where she secured a divorce and a cowboy boyfriend.

"She's quite a character, dolls. But Faye has style. Campy, ditzy, destructive, nuts. But style, nevertheless. Julius had chopped liver."

Julius married his bookkeeper, a *"glatt* kosher woman who patronized the *mikvah* and actually threw every crust of bread—even frozen—out of the house come Passover."

She was good to Dutch, but his father wasn't. "All he was interested in was his sons. He didn't consider me his son. I belonged to Faye."

Dutch lived for the annual two weeks (paid for by Julius) he would spend with her in resort hotels around the country. He memorized the details of her wardrobe. "I wanted to be just like her. You think *he* was a role model? When he died, do you know what that cocksucker had the nerve to do? He left the boys, the *schlemiels*, everything. Me, I got ten thousand dollars and a reminder not to spend it all in one place."

His stepmother died soon after. "Faye survived them all. Darling, she's the funniest, campiest lady you'll ever meet. She's a glove buyer living on Thirty-fourth Street with her boss, a *chazer* named Sidney Sheldon Cohen."

In the middle of the story of his first crush (Anthony

Perkins), he stopped and asked Jean to dial WE 6–1616 and find out the time. It was after midnight. "There goes my twenty bucks," he said, sighing.

"What twenty bucks?"

"I met a boy the other night. A genuine sulky beauty. The cutest, toughest, sweetest bowlegged boy—you know how crazy I am for bow legs—with the most fabulous, fabulous hands. Broad and thick, with adorable chewed-down fingernails . . ."

"A hustler?" Jean asked.

"I wouldn't go so far as to say he's a hustler, exactly."

"How much does he charge?"

"Whatever the traffic will allow, dolls, I imagine. I'm not absolutely positive sure he's a hustler. He might only be a swindler. But you should have seen him. The blackest, curliest, greasiest, Puerto Ricanest hair you've ever seen in your life, with a basket halfway down his leg and lashes four inches long . . ."

The telephone rang. It was Louie. He wanted to return the money and suggested they meet at a coffee shop. Dutch invited him to the loft.

"What happened to 'No Hustlers in the Home'?" Jean asked, getting up from the pink sofa, preparing to leave.

"This is our second date, darling. Besides, as I've said, I'm not absolutely sure he's a hustler."

Louie arrived. "Hey, man," he held out his hand and slapped Dutch's. "I got your bread." He gave Dutch twenty dollars, all in singles, unzipped his leather jacket, and took Jean's place on the pink sofa. He refused the joint Dutch offered him, taking one from the pocket of his jacket. "No, man. Always do my own dope. You never know what they put in that downtown shit."

Jean went home to her apartment. One of the black limousines the mayor allowed his favorites to use was parked in front of the building. She ignored it and went inside. A few minutes later, the bell in her apartment began to ring. She ignored that, too, and went to sleep.

CHAPTER 14

Babs Raymer's installation was scheduled to begin on May the fifteenth. In decorating-ese, *installation* means that all plans have been worked out and approved on paper, that they are about to be translated into reality. Installation—the days when the hall is mirrored and the dining room is lacquered—is the big moment for both client and decorator.

"Babs Raymer was like a lot of my clients," Jean says. "She thought that because I was decorating her house, I was decorating her personality. She wanted the settee in the drawing room to be a reflection of her innermost self. Unfortunately, her innermost self didn't exist—it was an amalgam of rich-people characterizations in B films—and the settee was a fake with trumped up ormolu hiding contemporary wooden pegs."

"I didn't know you hated Babs Raymer."

"She put me down constantly, at the same time hoping some of what she called my 'Hollywood tinsel' would rub off on her. She was typical of a lot of society broads I have met in New York. I did hate her."

During those last two weeks of April and the first two

in May, while Babs was suffering decorator separation anxiety, Jean was being, for want of a better word, harassed. At unexpected moments, on a fairly regular basis a black mayoral limousine would suddenly turn up, its back shades drawn, its presence menacing and theatrical, but still frightening. "It was as if a funeral hearse was constantly at my heels." The weather had turned warmer and the days were longer. Jean liked to walk up Madison Avenue after work, looking in the windows of the expensive Italian shops. "I'd see the goddamn car reflected in the plate glass. No one ever got out. There was never any invitation for me to get in. Just the car.

"Then there were the midnight phone calls with no one on the other end. My bell suddenly being rung at four or five in the morning. I finally called the police who said they'd keep an eye on the building, but of course they couldn't and didn't. New York Telephone told me it would take weeks to change my phone. It was all an old melodrama, an almost comic war waged, I thought, by Bert, to break me down. I knew that, but still I began to be frightened. I imagined *he* was having some sort of breakdown, that he had become genuinely dangerous. I had fantasies of lye being thrown in my face."

"Why didn't you tell Dutch or me or Lilli?"

"I was being brave, hoping it would all pass over. I sat through a lot of my mother's old films, you know."

Catherine was evidently worried by Bert's behavior, as well.

My uncle, my mother's brother, Elwyn Lawrence, is nominal head of the gentlemanly literary agency for which I nominally worked. Its name is Grant, Grant, and Lawrence, and it was begun by my father to give mother's brother both a livelihood and a means of using up his allotted time on God's earth. After a series of contests in which my father attempted to bend my will, as he was wont to say, it was broken, and I allowed myself to be installed as a partner in the enterprise, pursuing my father's Protestant Ethic.

He was close to death when I promised I would not write another novel; I would not degenerate into a philanthropist or any other kind of do-gooder; I would play out my role as a twentieth-century patron of the arts by helping others get their words into print.

My father, whose full name was James Fenimore Cooper Grant, was something of an anachronism. And, as Jean has pointed out, so am I.

It was perhaps our one family joke that Grant, Grant, and Lawrence is a nonprofit organization. For several years that held true, but after Father died, Uncle Elwyn sought to change that by signing up a series of writers Father wouldn't have allowed in the office.

Elwyn specializes in authors who specialize in nonbooks, how-to books, novels based on celebrities' lives. In short, the best-sellers. Elwyn gives parties. He arranges and gives interviews. He is almost as well publicized as his authors, often on talk shows, occasionally writing a piece for *New York* or *Esquire* on office politics or the pleasures of young flesh. He is famous for selling books to motion pictures and television networks. Elwyn has done exactly what my father hoped he would not do. He has turned Grant, Grant, and Lawrence into a profitable business. Both Bernice and Aunt Alice sniff when his name is mentioned, yet in their own respective ways they admire him.

Most people do admire Elwyn. They enjoy his bourgeois pleasure in success, his patrician lack of modesty. "Your father," he has said once or twice too often, "must be spinning in his grave."

I do not admire Elwyn. However, I seldom come into contact with him. I handled "serious" novels that received two-thousand-five-hundred-dollar advances from publishing houses who were anxious for our other authors and were never heard of again.

That was why I thought it was odd when Elwyn personally came into my office and asked me to attend a publication party for a book of reminiscences of the Harry Truman days written by a Washington, D.C., hostess named Maggie Drew. The book, entitled *The Party Has Just Begun*, was three hundred and twenty-two pages of correctly spelled names, most of which belong to people who were long dead.

For some reason, Elwyn knew that the book was going to be a major best-seller (one indication was that he had already sold the movie rights to Warner Brothers) and arranged the party. He invited as many political society people as he could muster, along with the usual array of media men and women who are forced to attend such functions. He made a point of asking me if I would make a special effort to be there, and since he very rarely called on me for such service, I said I would go.

Elwyn had taken one of the suites at the St. Regis and filled it with champagne and caviar and flowers of a suspiciously vibrant hue. Balding men in dark red Eisenhower jackets circulated, offering trays of tiny crackers and sodden meatballs to the guests. "The author is paying," Elwyn assured me as I examined the champagne's label before the doors opened.

I played cohost, introducing the guests who needed introducing and occasionally holding the wrinkled, beringed hand of the author.

A short time before the party was due to break up, I was surprised to see Catherine Brown in the room, standing against one of the gilt pillars, talking to Irwin Shaw and James Jones's widow. The three of them had somehow managed to get genuine whiskey. She looked up as I saw her and smiled. Shaw and Mrs. Jones moved on and I went to where she was standing.

Catherine Brown is a great beauty, but not my sort. She has too much cheekbone and too little warmth. "I didn't know your social life included parties of this sort," I said, giving her an obligatory kiss. "I must put you on our permanent list."

"I virtually grew up in Maggie's house," Catherine said. "She taught me a great deal."

That did not seem to call for comment, so I turned to look at Maggie, who had removed her big picture hat and was talking to Eric Pace who sometimes writes about books for the *Times*. I prepared to join them in the event she was saying something libelous.

But Catherine put her hand on my arm, detaining me. "I have a question," she said in a voice I didn't like. "It's going to appear rude, but the answer is important to me." She stopped and looked into my eyes with her transparent green ones.

"Shoot," I said.

"Do you have any intention of formalizing your relationship with Jean Rice Halladay? Through marriage? Through a permanent sort of arrangement?"

"I barely know her," I said, surprised. "She's a friend of a friend."

She knocked down a good two fingers of scotch and tied the belt of the silk raincoat she was wearing as if my neck were in its center. "Knowing your background, one would never think it."

"Think what?"

"That you'd be interested in carrying on simultaneous affairs with Cora Meade and Lorraine Rice's daughter."

Uncle Elwyn picked that moment to introduce me to Harold Robbins. The next time I looked at the corner where Catherine had been standing, all I saw was the empty scotch glass sitting on an ornate radiator cover.

"She was scared shitless," Jean said, a long time after.

"A pleasant visual."

"There was Bert, not only behaving like a rejected sixteen-year-old—he seemed to be actually begging for the sort of publicity that slaughters political careers. Catherine must have known about the cars and the wee-hour phone calls from Lilli. Catherine's life was devoted to getting Bert as high up in political office as possible. And there he was, on the verge of taking his first big step—the senate nomination was all sewn up that winter —and, at the same time, acting like a two-reeler villain, tormenting a fickle girl."

"But why come to me?"

"She was holding very few cards at that point. She wanted to find out if you could be depended upon to remove me from the immediate vicinity. The answer you gave her—whether or not she believed it—told her you were not going to be of any assistance."

"It's a wonder she didn't have you killed," I said, as a kind of joke.

"Everyone would have thought Bert had arranged it."

Dutch was having a great time that spring. He was selling dress designs at the rate of one or two a week and issuing daily bulletins as to his progress with Louie.

"We're in the wooing stages, dolls."

"Have you been to bed?"

"Darling! Naturally we've been to bed. However, nothing has happened except a little wrestling. He says he has to get to know me better. It's the longest cock tease in history."

I said something about the game not being worth the candle, and Dutch gave me his pitying look. "James, darling. When the day ever comes on which you really fall, head over heels, like a ton of bricks, when all you can think about is doing it with that person, then I'll know you're not a mannequin from Brooks Brothers who happened to rent the loft below mine."

It was the week of the promised Raymer installation. For no reason Cora could come up with, Chris had suddenly demanded her presence at his mother's house in Lyford Cay. "I hate Nassau," Cora said.

"Perhaps he wants a second honeymoon," I said.

That evening I was invited by Dutch to have dinner in his loft. Dinner was pizza delivered by a kid in a white apron who was offered a joint and ended up spending the evening. Bunny was attempting to seduce him with little success. Jean came in looking tired and announced that there had been a bomb scare in the Decorator and Design Building and everyone had to leave except Lilli, who refused.

"That must have been some sight," Bunny said, looking at the delivery boy who was looking at Jean. "All those flamers screaming out of the D and D Building, clutching their favorite pieces of chintz."

After the pizza and assorted drugs and visitors, I asked Jean if she wanted me to take her home. She looked ill. She shook her head, said she was only tired, and left. When she reached her apartment, she put the key in the lock. The lock wouldn't turn. She tried another, which also didn't work, and then went back to the original when the door opened from the inside.

Bert stood in the doorway. "She didn't think a changed lock would keep me out, did she?" Jean stood against the wall as he explained how he had arranged with the Seventeenth Precinct's Felony Division to gain entry. "I told them a suspicious character lived here."

"Get out, Bert," she said. "Get out."

"Losing control?"

"Bert . . ."

"I've got all the keys."

He reached for her, grabbing her arms and, at the same time, attempting to pull her into the apartment. But she held onto the doorjamb, trying to kick him. He slammed her across the face with an open hand and dragged her in.

There was a discreet cough at the still open door.

The short intern with the big nose from Lenox Hill Hospital who lived in the next apartment stood in the doorway with his pant-suited girl friend behind him, chewing gum, peering over his shoulder. "Mister," the intern said, going in, "why don't you lay off her?"

"Would you put this man in office, doctor?" Jean, a little hysterical, asked. Bert slammed her again. The doctor went for him while his girl friend ran for the door, saying, "I'm calling the cops."

Bert pushed the doctor out of his way without too much trouble, took a last, long look at Jean, and left.

"He didn't have an exit line," Jean said. "Somehow that scared me more than anything else."

The girl friend came back, saying 911 was busy. Jean told her not to bother. She made Jean a cup of tea, the doctor gave her a Valium, and then they left her alone with her satin teddy bear.

When she left the apartment the next morning, the black limousine was parked across the street, in front of the French tailor's.

Jean made Lilli nervous by being late for the final preinstallation session with Babs Raymer and by looking paler than she had been. Lilli was having second thoughts about the way she was treating the Raymer: Babs does have a certain amount of clout in this city.

Lilli sat in on the meeting, smoking half a pack of cigarettes through her jade holder. Babs was being especially cranky. She didn't like Lilli's new obsequiousness any more than Jean did.

After a full day of Babs and Lilli, when she arrived home without seeing the limousine, all she wanted to do was get into her bed and sleep. At her door, she found she didn't need a key. "I was too afraid to go in. It wasn't exactly opened. It was more ajar. Like in a Hitchcock film. I could hear the doctor and his girl friend arguing and I thought I would go and ask him to come in with me and then, suddenly, their voices stopped and I got crazy scared. I ran down the stairs, found a taxi and told the driver to take me to JFK. I wanted to get out."

As soon as they reached the other side of the Queens-Midtown Tunnel, she told him to turn around and take her to Twentieth Street.

Louie was trying to teach Dutch and me, without much success, a card game called Spit when she walked in.

The three of us got into another taxi with Jean and went uptown to that apartment.

Bert was not inside.

Everything that was had been slashed or otherwise mutilated. The carpet, the framed photographs, the wallpaper, the mirrors. Hacked up like so many pieces of chopped meat. A bottle of perfume had been broken. The apartment looked like a slaughterhouse and smelled like the cosmetics department of Bloomingdale's.

Jean opened the closet door. Her clothes hadn't escaped. Bits of white satin and silk clung to the quilted hangers like skin on overcooked chickens.

What was most upsetting was that none of it seemed as if it had been done in passion. Lunatic frenzy one might forgive. This seemed methodical, neat, destroyed according to computer plan.

Dutch put his arms around Jean who was holding on to what was left of the teddy bear. Tears filled those incredible silver eyes but didn't spill over. "You didn't need any of this *chazerai*, darling. And you want to know something?" He went on leading her down the stairs, taking the teddy bear, whose guts were spilling out, and dropping it on the floor. "You're an extremely lucky lady. You got an in in the garment business second to none. It's like being Coco Chanel's best friend, only better."

Louie and I stayed behind, poking helplessly through the debris. "We gotta do something about that fucker," Louie said.

I picked up the top half of a photograph of Lorraine Rice. She was all dressed up in late 1950s Hollywood, her usual black satin dress, a starry, sultry I-Love-All-My-Fans gaze in her eyes. I dropped it next to the teddy bear. "I don't think there's much we can do about him," I said to Louie.

CHAPTER 15

Jean became a resident of 120 West Twentieth Street. Dutch set up a bamboo screen at the far end of the living area, as far as possible from the sofas where the kids used to crash and where Dutch and Louie now slept in the connubial wrought-iron bed.

"No more crashees?" I asked Dutch.

"Darling, when you're in love, who needs house guests?"

Behind the bamboo screen he placed a wicker daybed that looked as if it came from my grandmother's summer house in Newport.

"Don't be silly, James. It comes from the Salvation Army."

Next to it was a small, squat mission-style table with an ugly black ink stain hidden by a wrought-iron reading lamp Dutch had found in a garbage can on Nineteenth Street. Facing the bed was an upholstered boudoir chair Bunny had "schlepped from One Hundred and Twenty-fifth Street where those dumb *schvartzas* don't know quality from trash" as a welcome present for Jean.

"I can't stay here forever," Jean said, on the fifth morning of her residence.

"*Pourquoi pas,* darling?" Dutch asked, shaving his sideburns off in the bathroom, which was located a few feet from Jean's bedroom. "You have plenty of privacy —feel perfectly free to have gentlemen callers—and I don't suppose that lunatic is going to try to break in. Besides, you can be a big help to me with the business. Just this week I've been thinking and working and thinking and working and I've come up with a little wrap dress that will make every *schlumpadikah* buyer in town sit up and salivate. I've decided, dolls, to call it My Jean Dress in your honor. Just a simple little wrap like my pale blue pinafore, only with two tiny tucks at the waist and a touch more tit. Nothing sells better this season than transparent innocence."

Jean got out of the daybed, put on a polka-dot silk robe with deep red lapels that Dutch had had in his robe repertoire, and stood over him while he sketched the My Jean Dress.

"A touch less tit, Mister Dutch."

"I'm going to feature it," Dutch said, studying the sketch, "in my fashion show."

"Fashion show?" Jean asked, picking up the telephone, dialing WE 6–1616. "What fashion show?"

"Darling! I didn't tell you about the fashion show?" He turned and, seeing her expression, asked her what was the matter.

"It's eleven o'clock in the morning."

"It seems later. You must be starved. I think there's some chicken salad in the fridge. . . ."

"I have a terrible feeling," Jean said, getting into one of the dresses Dutch had given her, "that I've just been

150

fired from my first job. I've missed the Raymer installation."

Missing the Raymer installation was an act akin to Lindbergh missing his airplane.

Lilli was in her office when Jean arrived a few seconds after noon. She kept Jean waiting only fifteen minutes. She smiled her polite smile when Jean was shown in by the woman who had been her secretary for over thirty years.

Lilli took the jade holder from between her tiny teeth. She stood up and paced the floor as Jean sat in the dark velvet visitor's chair—everything in Lilli's office that season was velvet.

"Don't worry about the Raymer, my dear," Lilli began, pausing in front of the Chamberlain portrait of her. "Lonnie Spangler's in charge." She resumed her pacing. She was wearing yards of gray-green silk which made an unpleasant swishing sound as she walked.

Eventually she sat down and looked at Jean. "Of course I have to let you go. There's no excuse for—"

"I'm not offering any."

"So you're not. But I do care about you. I'm wondering how on earth you're going to live."

"I'll manage."

Lilli took a long puff on the holder, removed the cigarette, and stumped it out in an ashtray that bore her initials. "I daresay you will. A woman like you can always get her hands on money. But aside from money, dear, permit me to make a suggestion. You're much too old to be hanging about with the boys. You do know what happens to women who spend their lives dancing with them every night, going home alone, don't you?"

"As a matter of fact, I don't."

"Not much, my dear. Not much at all." Lilli stood up, signifying the interview was at an end. "You might try marriage, Jean," she said, fitting a new cigarette into her holder.

"I wasn't nearly as devastated as I thought I was going to be," Jean said, later. "I knew I was going to be fired when I walked in there."

"Then, darling, why did you bother to go?" Dutch asked.

"It would've been too easy, too cowardly not to. Anyway, it was worth it. I felt very free and ridiculously happy when I left Lilli. All I could think about was the new wrap dress and how on earth I was going to break the news to Victoria DeVine."

Buddy Ruben was standing in the outer office as Jean left. He smiled at her, she said hello, but Jean says, "I never did see Buddy. I'm all too aware of that now. In my fantasies, I cast him as a 'good husband.' But in reality, he was like someone else's ghost. His mother's. Bert's. I suppose it ended up the way it did because he wanted me to see him."

I ran into Buddy Ruben and Bert Brown around that time in the steam room of the Athletic Club. They were wrapped in thick white towels, sitting side by side like transatlantic passengers bored with the voyage. I had been up half the night with Dutch and Jean, attempting to learn to smoke marijuana and ending up getting drunk on tequila.

Inadvertently, I sat next to Bert, who unwrapped his head towel just enough to be identifiable.

"How are you, Grant?" he asked.

"Terrible head, Bert. Hello, Buddy."

Bert and I talked for a few minutes about mutual acquaintances and social events, and I left him with Buddy, who hadn't said more than hello. Bert didn't seem to me like a man who would systematically destroy his mistress's clothing and personal effects. He seemed more like a man who would try to get ten cents on the dollar for them.

I didn't mention the meeting to Jean. By early June there was no question—not in anyone's mind—of her living anywhere else but in Dutch's loft.

"She's a tremendous, tremendous help, dolls," Dutch told me. "With the business."

I didn't comment, and Dutch asked me if perhaps I weren't a little jealous. I said I doubted it, and he said, "Not to worry, darling. There's room in my heart and my life for both of you. Not, of course, to mention Mister Louie."

Working and living with Dutch, never going above Thirty-fourth Street "if I can help it," seemed to agree with her. She was happier then than at any other time that I have known her.

She was totally involved in the fashion show. Dutch and two other Off-Off–Fashion Avenue designers had been offered a small grant by the Fashion Foundation to present their summer collections in a three-part show.

"It sounds to me like a prestigious opportunity," I told him.

"Believe me, darling, it is not a prestigious opportunity. First of all, as far as fashion is concerned, the summer was over last December. If I show anything, it will be for next year's Cruise Wear line. Secondly, all the stores send their third assistant buyer who has about as much decision-making power as Pat Nixon. Thirdly, the two faggots I have to show with both think they're Saint

Laurent. Dollars to doughnuts they gussie up their presentations with Muzak and what those ditzes think are 'haute' garments. It is not prestigious, James darling. It's only a lot of work."

"Then why do it?"

He looked at Jean, who was applying all her concentration to putting two pieces of material back to back at the long cutting table, and said, "What can I tell you, dolls? I'm a masochist."

I was being especially conscientious about my work, rather the way I was when, as a child, I would be especially good about studying, hoping that my efforts would ward off the impending storm that gray clouds made almost a certainty. I was breakfasting with authors and editors if I wasn't too fond of them, lunching them at the University Club if I was. There's no greater snob than an author.

Uncle Elwyn, more involved than ever with movie and television tie-ins, had taken to speaking with a Yiddish inflection that reminded me of Bunny. "That's some package," Elwyn would say about a particular novel. "Some beautiful package." It made me thankful that I handled the books.

The clouds began to break about then.

Cora had returned from Lyford Cay and, with the exception of one telephone call during which she complained of ptomaine from lobster salad, had remained silent.

When Chris called and asked me to lunch, I accepted, though I had a suspicion it was not going to be pleasant. When his secretary told my secretary that I was to meet him at '21,' I was definitely worried. The only reason

Chris could have possibly chosen '21' was because he thought it was the sort of place where I habitually dine. I almost never do.

'21' is where Uncle Elwyn likes to have his lunch, surrounded by what he chooses to call "movers." As I walked in, I wondered where we were going to be seated, assuming it would be in the back end of the upstairs dining room where they stuff the forever anonymous. Someone must have recognized Chris's name and tipped off the maitre d', because I was immediately shown to the prime seating area in the downstairs bar. It was filled with red-checkered tablecloths and Frank Sinatra, Otto Preminger, Howard Johnson the third, Dan Rather, and former Governor Nelson A. Rockefeller.

Chris was at a back table, mooning over a copy of *Barron's*, looking like a Christmas child under the hanging toy models of products made by the companies whose honchos like to eat at '21.' He was drinking a glass of 1966 Chateau Calon-Ségur, a bottle of which was on the table in front of him. I asked how Lyford Cay was and he said fine, considering, and why don't we order. A waiter was immediately at our table—Chris has always had that kind of magnetic attraction for service people—and he asked for some sort of messy veal dish while I chose the hamburger, which came dry and indigestible and exactly the way I like it.

Chris was well into his berries and cream and I was on my third cup of coffee when I noticed Buddy Ruben in the far corner, lunching with a few politicos, including Perry Duryea. They were both talking earnestly, but Buddy's eyes were on me. I smiled, amused at how often we were suddenly running into one another, and he nodded; and the next time I looked, his table was empty.

A good many other diners had also left, so that it was now more possible for us to talk to one another. Chris seemed to recognize that fact, for he poured himself the last of the Calon-Ségur and said, "Do you want to marry Cora, J.J.?"

I said no, unhesitatingly.

"Then I wish you'd get off her, old man. I want her back again. Not good for the children, Mother says. Scandal." Chris tends to speak like a British Western Union telegram when he's nervous. My voice goes very low, like a serious radio announcer's. I knew how difficult it had been for him to say those words, and I suddenly felt very ashamed and cheap and ugly. I began to apologize in my low voice, saying something to the effect that I had thought he approved of the situation, but he cut me short.

"No need to get into that, J.J. I want her back. Cora's willing." He paid the check, retrieved his *Barron's*, and I followed him out into the bleak New York sunshine. The jockeys in front of '21' were not smiling at me. Chris got into one of the chauffeured limousines forever double-parked in front of '21' and asked me if he could drop me anywhere. I said he couldn't.

"Come to dinner soon, J.J.," he said before the car drove off. I believe he meant it.

It had been the kind of scene of which farce is made, yet I went back to my office feeling fragile and useless, like an empty eggshell. It was as if I had lost someone very dear to me. It didn't take me long to realize that I wasn't mourning Cora, I was regretting Chris.

It was the following afternoon when Bernice called at Grant, Grant, and Lawrence. Bernice is not a person who ever looks well during the summer. Her skin takes on an unpleasant shrimp color, and her body's lack of definition —despite the girdles and other undergarments one can see the ribs of through the cotton dresses she wears—is all too apparent. Bernice looks her best in late March when she is wearing stone martens and thick gold earrings.

"Barrett's in New York," she said. "She wants to see you, J.J." It occurred to me that the only two people in the world who called me J.J. were my sister and Christopher Meade.

"I very much do not want to see her," I said, offering Bernice a chair, which she didn't take. Instead, she chose to stand by the window and look down at the traffic on Fifth Avenue, twelve floors below.

"I suppose you're still miffed."

"Miffed? Bernice, I've barely stopped hating her. I'm only now coming to the point where I can even think about her. After seven years, my wife one day announces she wants what she calls an 'open marriage.' Which meant that she could climb into anyone's trousers she chose. The fact that she ended up with that little media monster shows how serious she was about 'feeling out new directions,' about 'trying her own wings.' She can fly off the fucking Empire State Building for all I—"

"J.J.! If you're to keep on using that word in that tone of voice—as you did that day at my club—I am afraid I shall have to leave."

"Sorry, Bernice."

"I'm only suggesting that you see Barrett, not that you resume your marriage. I think you'll find that she has changed in certain ways." She touched me with her ungloved hand, a rare gesture. "You know I'm right, J.J."

"You're always right, Bernice. Remember the mulberry tree we had in the Southampton house? You found me standing under it one day, picking each berry, one by one, popping them into my mouth, having a wonderful time. You ran into the house, got an old sheet from Nanny, spread it under the tree, and shook the trunk. All the ripe fruit came down quickly, efficiently. You were right, of course. But it wasn't the fruit I enjoyed so much as the picking of it."

I looked at the face that was so reminiscent of my father's and heard her give an answer worthy of him. "J.J., if you're going to go all existential on me, I'm going to have to cut this conversation short."

"You knew she was immature, James," Uncle Elwyn accused, later, when he had joined the conspiracy to get BaBa and me back together again "for the first time" as Dutch said. It was a belief held by Elwyn and Bernice and possibly by BaBa herself that once I saw her, I would be so overwhelmed with regret, I would drop to my knees and beg her to take me back again.

"I didn't know immaturity went hand in hand with indiscriminate adultery," I said to Uncle Elwyn.

"Why do you always sound exactly like your father when you're angry?" he wanted to know.

I concentrated on the air conditioner behind him. It was a big, handsome, old-fashioned machine, and it was sending out blast after blast of frozen air. New York had turned hot and dirty and unbreathable for the summer.

"You can't expect not to meet her when you're both in New York, you know. Certainly if you plan to spend any time in Southampton . . ."

I said I didn't, that I had instructed the lawyers BaBa could have the house for the summer, that if she needed more money, I would certainly be prepared to up the amount she was getting, that on no account was I prepared to see her again.

Elwyn gave me his I-despair-of-you shrug and went on to talk about moving our offices to a new building like General Motors where they had central air conditioning. I said I felt nostalgic about early air conditioners.

"You really are your father's son," he said, leaving, but not slamming the door, since father did will me the controlling interest of Grant, Grant, and Lawrence.

I packed up my briefcase and put it in the lower drawer of my desk, one my great-grandfather had caused to be built in 1842. It was heavy and ugly and filled with manuscripts I liked but couldn't sell, which included one of mine. I locked it and went downtown to see how Dutch was getting on with his fashion show.

CHAPTER 16

"Jean Sings" is one entry for my diary during the period in early June just before preparation for the fashion show reached fever pitch.

"Only the family," as Dutch would say, was gathered in the loft that night. Dutch, Jean, Louie, Bunny, Sylvia Einhorn, the fifty-year-old seamstress who hated her home, husband, and children in Rego Park, Queens, and had taken to spending as much time at the loft as she could.

An old upright piano was the stimulus for Jean's song. Louie had found it on the street, put a rope around it, wheels under it, and had hauled it into the loft. "A present for Mister Dutch," he said.

"Darling!" Dutch beamed, unused to presents from his boyfriends. "I'll have to take lessons." It had been painted the shade of green I associate with country kitchens and was missing two white keys at the far end of the board.

Bunny, a joint clenched between his dazzlingly white teeth, sat down at the piano and began to play a Scott

Joplin song with, considering the instrument, amazing virtuosity. "You are some smart *schvartza*," Dutch told him.

"A regular Paderewski," Bunny said, continuing to play a piano roll kind of music. "My granddaddy worked in a New Orleans whorehouse."

"I thought your grandfather came from San Juan, man," Louie said, looking down at Bunny with his big, trusting/skeptical New York eyes. He didn't like Bunny's claim to "Rican" blood.

"Does that mean he couldn't play piano in a New Orleans chop house, you *schlimazel?*" Bunny said, still playing, his face assuming a remarkably droll, whorehouse-piano-player expression, all teeth, like the piano.

"That's the song," Jean said, "my grandmother used to try to break into talkies. They all *had* to sing when sound came in. Every one of them—from Swanson to Clara Bow—cut a record. Lita's first cut, unfortunately, was the deepest. Louie Mayer heard it and ripped up her contract."

"Sing it, Lita," Bunny said, banging away at the keys.

Dutch switched off all the lights except for the naked bulb over the sewing machine next to the piano. Jean was spotlit in its glare, wearing a new Dutch design modeled on the blue bloomer gym suits girls in my day wore to exercise class. Her platinum hair seemed white and was tucked up on top of her head so that several strands hung loose.

She put her hands on her hips in a pose wonderfully evocative of the period and began to sing, to Bunny's accompaniment, in a high, tinny voice that was especially affecting.

MIDNIGHT MOVIES

All dressed up
in a long red gown/
diamonds and rubies
and a sad little frown.
They call me Lonesome Sal
(a swell little gal).

If you see him
tell him I'm fine.
Singing and dancing/
drinking my wine.
Don't tell him I'm Lonesome Sal
(a swell little gal).

She did a sort of fast two-step and fell into one of the chairs, laughing. "It was a lovely time," Jean says, when speaking of early summer at Dutch's loft. "No one was serious, leastways not about the fashion show."

When asked to "do" her mother, to sing one of Lorraine's songs, Jean refused, claiming she didn't have the voice. But occasionally someone would play a reissued album on one of the various stereo systems that would turn up at the loft, and Lorraine's sexy, mindless voice would fill the space with lazy irony. "*Was I gay/till today?*"

"That early summer at the loft," Jean says, "was a wonderful time for me. I refused to think about anything or anyone: Bert or Lilli or even me. I was being entertained, fed, loved. It was like the times when Lorraine would suddenly disappear from the Bel-Air house for days at a time.

"She'd take the red car—there was always one red car

in the garage—scream something at the servants and take off for Auntie Mae Bonita's hideous bungalow way out in the Valley. She'd hole up there for weeks at a time, letting Auntie Mae fuss over her, read her cards, play with her hair.

"After a while the studio would make noises—lawsuit threats were always being hurled at her—and she'd come back, looking years younger. For a few days she'd laugh a lot and be nice to everyone, and then she'd get caught up again. Pills in the morning to get her going, pills at night to put her to sleep, and in between those eighteen-hour days on the set. Lorraine had a shitty life."

"But, darling," Dutch said, "think of the high living. The cars, the clothes, the glamour. Think of the glamour . . ."

"Dutch never heard a word of what I said. He was hooked on the stuff he'd read in the movie magazines on the way to visit his mother in hotels in Reno and Tahoe. Just like Auntie Mae, he had swallowed whole the entire Hollywood wet dream. His life was fantasy stuff. Louie was his Gary Cooper. I was his Monroe. Bunny played Miriam Hopkins to Dutch's Bette Davis. Even Sylvia Einhorn had a role—Thelma Ritter."

"And me?"

"You? You, James, were a double fantasy. The first was the high-society polo-playing playboy."

"I didn't play polo."

"And I never made a film and Louie never saw a horse. We were the best Dutchie could do," she says, looking unhappy, as if we should have done better.

"What was my second role?"

"The frustrated writer. He knew about the novel in the

desk. He decided he was going to be your inspiration, your Holly Golightly. You're such a dope, James. Didn't you realize he was always feeding you 'material'? Doing shtick. He wanted you to write a great best-seller about him and his frivolous friends. About his fabulous, outrageous life. He had it all planned, right down to what he would wear for his talk show appearances.

"Don't you understand, James? We were all crashees. You and I and Bunny and Louie and all of the kids. Transients. Looking for a spiritual spa run by a good mother."

Jean never looked sad then, not in those early summer days when the loft was filled with people and the music was playing and the windows were open and Dutch was calling for rehearsals. "I had given up men. Sex. Who had the time? Occasionally one of the boys would start something, but I never let it get very far. I had always preferred adults."

"Exactly your problem, Jean Rice Halladay," Dutch would say to her. "When you realize it doesn't matter what you're fucking as long as you dig it, then you'll be cured."

"Of what?"

"Lifelong melancholia."

Everyone would show up for the rehearsals: the crashees, the kids, Bunny, Victoria and Morgan DeVine, fashion, "homosexualia" (Dutch's term), his entire world. There was always a party.

"We barely slept," Jean remembers. "Dutch didn't believe in sleep in the same way he didn't believe in time. We'd be dancing at 54 until five, six in the morning, come home, have coffee, collapse into our respective beds, and talk to each other from either end of the loft while Louie snored."

She'd get up at eleven to let the sewing girls in. They were attempting to finish the clothes for the show (his orders from the stores were being backlogged), but as often as not, as soon as a dress had its final seam sewn, Dutch was attacking it, ripping it apart again. "Darling, what can I tell you? It's not poifect."

She'd make breakfast for whoever happened to be there, the crashees occasionally sneaking back. "The crashees, dolls, do not get food in this house. When they are very lucky, they get a bed; no food." She'd feed them anyway.

Bunny was usually among them, and she'd make sure that he got to his job in the Pan-Sexual Boutique on Twenty-third Street by noon, though she would urge him to do something with his piano playing. "Darling, none of them low trash jobs for me. I have graduated out of the whorehouse. I am a shop girl now." After Bunny, she'd organize Louie so that he would get to his afternoon job at the meat-packing house on Fourteenth Street.

After Louie, she would take Dutch away from the telephone and the latest addition to his kids' collection and sit him down with the sewing girls (Lola, Carla, and Sylvia Einhorn) and force him to work.

Around five, she'd order lunch from The Deli Down the Street ("Everything in this town has to have a cute name," Dutch complained), and then she and Dutch would retire to the living section, where they would share a joint, salami sandwiches, and Doctor Brown's Cel-Ray tonic as they sketched dresses.

"You have genuine flair, dolls," he told her.

"No, I don't. I have fake flair. Picked it up from Lorraine and Lita and various boyfriends."

"Don't underestimate yourself, Miss Jean. You were a good, pedestrian decorator. But you got what it takes to be a great designer. Somewhere in that *goyishe* head of yours, you've learned to filter out all the worst that was Hollywood and keep all the best. And what business do you think we're in? Making what Hollywood decrees palatable to Mrs. Shopper. Just look at that little halter dress. Jane Russell and Audrey Hepburn and Farrah Fawcett-Majors could all wear it without a qualm. You understand construction, dolls. And that's ninety percent of the battle. Now if you'll just let me pin this adorable little top around—you have the most exquisite tits—because I think with a dart here and a nip there it can really be sexsational. There!"

She was his assistant, his model, his housekeeper, his favorite child. He loved her more than he loved anyone because she came closest to fulfilling his fantasy. "Did you ever see anyone, darling, who looked like that *off* the silver screen?"

I was spending a great deal of time at the loft, the Meade dining room now closed to me, the food at my various clubs not being what it could be, and the company of my uptown friends tending to the oversolicitous ("poor Grant") or the tongue-in-cheek ("Grant, you sly dog").

The circus atmosphere in Dutch's loft, especially during those two weeks leading up to the show, seemed designed to distract me from making decisions: what to do about the summer, about a car I owned and didn't use, about BaBa.

Designs were changing hourly; the sewing girls quit singly and en masse at least once a day; the models, chosen by Dutch from the ranks of the kids, didn't show up or showed up at the wrong time or called from phone booths around the city and the country, leaving cryptic messages.

"How do you stand it?" I asked Jean. We found ourselves sitting next to each other on the pink sofa, drinking coffee, after a particularly strenuous evening rehearsal.

"Stand it?" she asked, for a moment not knowing what I meant. "I thrive on it," she said, smiling.

"You do look wonderful," I told her. "I've never seen you so relaxed." And I hadn't. Her guard, usually in full play with me, had become increasingly less militant.

"Thanks, James," she said, putting her cup down next to the old radio that seemed to be one of the constants in Dutch's revolving furniture system. "You seem pretty relaxed yourself, lately." Then she was off, running across the loft to the work area, where Dutch was hard at work, ripping out a seam Sylvia had just hand sewn into a dress. Sylvia was screaming ("I quit") and getting into the jacket she wore whenever she had to go onto the streets of New York. Jean restrained her, steadied her, and eventually got her to take off the jacket.

Sitting Sylvia down at her sewing machine, patting that volatile woman on her shoulder, Jean happened to look up and across the loft at me. We both smiled, accomplices for the first time.

Three nights before the fashion show was to take place, while fifty people of various sexual persuasions were milling around the loft and the Bee Gees were singing their hearts out on yet another borrowed stereo, Isobel Barnard strolled in with several men, one of whom had been lunching with her at the Coz Club the day I blew up at poor Bernice.

Nothing fazes Isobel. "I heard you had been mixing it up with rather an outré crowd, James. Isn't this marvelous? Half of 54 is here. Do you know Tommy Ale?" she asked, introducing her former luncheon partner. "My God, there's my hairdresser. Ronnie!" she shouted, going off to talk to a short boy with a mop of unruly hair.

Tommy Ale, a balding man in his early fifties, unbuttoned his blazer, removed a salami hero and a beer from the table we had been standing in front of, and went and sat on one of the sofas. "Do sit down," he invited, and I did so.

"You have a place in Southampton, don't you?" he asked in mock transatlanticese. I allowed that that was true. "I used to see you on Job's Lane in a beat-up white Jeep. I thought you were sheer heaven."

I asked if he had a house in the Hamptons.

"All successful homosexuals my age have a house in the Hamptons. You might say it's the Number Two Station of the Gay Cross." He sipped at his beer and looked at me. I realized from the pinpoints of his beige pupils that he was high on something, probably speed. "When you're young and beautiful or young and anything, you go to Fire Island Pines and take enormous amounts of drugs and dance your ass off and go to fabulous parties dressed in fig leaves and fuck your way through your weekends, crazed and glazed with pleasure madness from late May until early September, when you start getting serious and look around for a winter love.

"When you get older, into your late thirties and early forties, say, depending on your looks and the salary the advertising agency you work for gives you, you renounce drugs (nothing ages a girl faster) except for a little speed every now and then. You've socked away a little money so you buy yourself a jazzy place in East or South Hampton (depending on the quality of your pretensions), a lot of smart, loose clothes, and a set of classic garden furniture. Then you procure yourself a lover who has a green thumb and a passion for Gilbert and Sullivan. You develop a taste for vodka and mildly deserted beaches where it doesn't matter what's become of your waistline. You spend Saturday nights having dinner and camping discreetly with friends in Sag Harbor, where they have a very lovely year-round gay community."

"What's next?" I asked, sipping my beer.

"Connecticut. And *that* is depressing. Connecticut is when you reach the age where it no longer matters at all. It doesn't matter what season it is, because you wouldn't be seen dead in a bathing suit, and the fur coat you bought on sale at Bonwit's makes you look like a femme dyke. Nor does it matter how your hair is cut, because you've had the last bit of surgery your face can stand and graying locks won't hide the tuck marks. So you give it all up and move to Connecticut. By now you have a lot of money, so you can afford a fairly grand place on a river in some dusty backwater where you find yourself making home cassettes from your old show albums and at last giving in and learning needlepoint. Your mother's spending more and more weekends with you and your lover only touches you when it's absolutely unavoidable (as when you fall down the stairs from mixing the vodka with the brandy).

"And suddenly you're back on drugs, but this time it's downs, because your heart isn't really much good and your main pleasure in life now is getting all dressed up and driving down into Manhattan, having a perfectly vomitous meal in the best gay restaurant (which is none too good), ogling the really low waiters, and getting so drunk you either have to stay at a hotel or bribe a friend to drive you and the Mercedes back to Connecticut.

"One night you decide to go to the baths because, after all, in the dark who knows or cares and there you have a heart attack in the steam room and half your estate goes to New York because you never made a will because you never thought you were going to die, leastways not in the baths."

"Has Tommy been talking your head off?" Isobel asked, coming back.

"I've been telling him the story of my life," Tommy said, sounding like Dutch, taking Isobel's white hand and kissing it.

"Go get your little friend, Tommy. I've promised Ronnie that we would drive him to 54 in the Rolls." Tommy shook my hand and went off. "She certainly is a knockout," Isobel said. "I just took a peek at her. No wonder Corea Medea is beside herself. Poor Christopher. Perhaps Peter and I should take a loft for a year and broaden our horizons.

"I understand," she said, as Tommy and his friend and Ronnie and a group of the kids came to claim her, "that BaBa's back in town. Your life's too complicated, James. Come and have dinner soon and tell us all about it."

She left, surrounded by Tommy and Ronnie and the kids, a slightly wicked suburban mother taking her decadent stepchildren for a ride.

The night before the show, Jean, looking translucent from lack of sleep, got everyone out of the loft except for essential personnel. At eleven, Dutch called and asked me to come up and do him a favor. He and Jean and Sylvia Einhorn were in the work area, all busy stitching away.

"Darling," Dutch said to me, "put on those little wrap trousers hanging on that screen—the yellow terry cloth —and that pale blue Eisenhower jacket. Louie, that despicable gigolo, hasn't turned up and I want to see how the trousers hang."

I started to protest but Jean, no longer relaxed or my accomplice, looked up from the sewing machines and said, "For Christ's sake, James, you've been hanging around here for weeks soaking up the atmosphere. He's only asking you to put on a pair of trousers, not to commit fellatio."

I went behind the screen. "Don't wear your undershorts, dolls," Dutch cautioned. "Those trousers were not meant for undershorts. Particularly the kind you wear."

I removed the offending undershorts and put on the yellow trousers and the blue jacket. "They look ridiculous with those clunky Church shoes," Jean said.

I started to protest, to tell her they were Peel's, not Church, when Dutch interrupted, asking, "Darling, put on these, would you?" "These" were a pair of straw shoes that looked like slippers mounted on three inches of wedged heel. "And take off that shirt. That little jacket was never meant to have a shirt under it. And try these."

He handed me a pair of mirrored sunglasses, the sort child rapists affect.

"Stunning. Isn't that stunning, Jean? James, you look twenty years younger. And sexy. Open that jacket. Where'd you get all those stomach muscles?"

"Pumping iron," I said.

"He runs around the track at the AC all day," Jean told him.

"How do you know?" Dutch asked, amused that Jean had such a piece of information about me and had withheld it.

"So does Buddy Ruben."

"I thought Jews weren't allowed into the AC," Dutch said, rearranging the way I was wearing the trousers. "Don't worry, darling, I'm not trying to cop a free feel. It's just that Louie wears his on the right and you wear yours on the left."

"They let a few in," Jean said, returning to the Buddy Ruben question, "just to show how liberal they are."

"Turn around, James. I want to see what that fabric does to your ass."

"Of course he still had a crush on you," Jean said recently. "He wouldn't give up after one tepid attempt. He used to talk about you all of the time. 'James J. Grant is the only straight man I have ever loved.' You think he kept you around for your witty patter? He wanted to get you into bed. Jesus, you are a naif. He and all the kids wanted you. They didn't know from six-foot-two Christian soldiers. You were Gulliver in Lilliput. They were all tiny and tight and skinny, New York gutter rats. You were the blond god from the playing fields of St. Paul's. What on earth did you think you had to offer?"

"The charm of the exotic."

" 'I'm going to have James,' Dutch would say. 'And I'm not going to rape him. He's going to come to me and beg me, darling, to get into his bed. I'm working on him all of the time. When he becomes a mensch, when he finally realizes that I'm the best thing that ever happened to him, that will be the day he'll come crawling. Naturally, I plan to be extremely, extremely magnanimous.'

"If it were possible," I say to Jean, "I would start crawling."

"I know you would, James."

CHAPTER 17

On Thursday, June the fifteenth, the white free-form telephone Cora had had installed at the side of my white free-form bed began to ring at six A.M. Aunt Alice's secretary, Judy Tuller, was on the line. She wanted to know if I would be able to attend Aunt Alice on her morning exercise and then join her in breakfast. If so, Thurmond would pick me up in a quarter hour's time. When it comes to time, Aunt Alice is like a great many very rich and very poor people, who tend to assume everyone runs according to their clocks.

I told Judy Tuller that Thurmond had better give me a half-hour. She said she didn't know if that would fit in with Aunt Alice's schedule and that she would have to make "inquiries." Rather than have her go through inquiries, I agreed to be ready in fifteen minutes.

I showered in Cora's plastic cube, assuming this early-morning meeting had been called to give me a lecture on my dissolute way of life. Thurmond was at the curb when I emerged some eighteen and a half minutes after hearing from Judy Tuller, looking guardedly at his watch. He drove up Park Avenue with a good deal more speed than his usual stately pace, exerting caution only when he wound his way over Grand Central Station. Even so, Aunt Alice was standing in front of the house on East Sixty-eighth Street literally tapping the toe of her stern white walking shoe.

"Good morning, James," she said, after Thurmond had helped her into the car. In addition to the white shoes, she wore a pale pink summer coat made of some light, fluffy material. Her hair, which is dyed a soft, natural red, looked as if it had been set with mortar. She wore little makeup and only one piece of visible jewelry, a gold bracelet pavéd with diamonds, a gift from Uncle Garfield.

"I'm surprised you're in New York at this time of year," I said.

"You're always surprised when I'm in New York, James. You act as if I made my permanent headquarters in Nepal. You find surprise convenient."

"For what?"

"For not spending time with me. Once you have gotten yourself to believe that I am never in residence in this city, then it's all too convenient for you to convince yourself that you never see me only because I am never here."

I looked out at early morning New York, which was deserted but still not innocent, and decided it was going to be a difficult day.

Thurmond turned into Central Park at Seventy-second Street and left us off at the southeastern end of the reservoir.

It was a cloudy, warm day, with the kind of sky that doesn't look like a sky at all but more like a ceiling in a municipal building. We climbed up onto the inner ring that circles the reservoir. It is a beautiful place to walk, the skylines of both sides of New York (East and West) seemingly equidistant, separated by the greenery of Central Park and the oval of water. Signs on the fence reminded us that that water was our principal beverage and that we should be careful not to throw foreign objects into it.

We shared the path with a great many joggers, who, in their satin shorts, ignored us much in the way aristocratic horsemen once ignored the pedestrian peasant. During a moment when we were almost trampled by a team of joggers, I suggested that we choose another walk. But Aunt Alice was adamant. "Your Uncle Garfield and I walked around the reservoir for thirty years and I have no intention of stopping now. If these people choose to run in this weather in those clothes, I certainly will make no objection."

Aunt Alice, who was born in 1900, believes in walking as my contemporaries believe in running. Her father was an admiral who became Secretary of the Navy during the First World War, and her mother was Old New York. (A woman I never knew, she was also my father's mother by an earlier marriage.)

During the twenties, during a long engagement to a man named Pierce, she managed to spend several years in Paris, where she met Gertrude Stein and Pablo Picasso and frolicked with the Murphys and the Fitzgeralds.

She is said to have been a beauty with an animated face, though there are only traces of the beauty and animation now. She returned to America reluctantly, married Pierce resignedly, and had two children by him unhappily.

Pierce expired in 1932, when Uncle Garfield's first

wife was divorcing him for real and imagined infidelities. He and Aunt Alice had known each other for most of their lives and, finding comfort in the familiar, promptly married each other aboard his yacht, the *Serendipity*.

The only burden in their marriage, Aunt Alice once confessed to my mother, was Garfield's money. After he died, the money became an even greater burden, taking on a life of its own, growing by leaps and bounds. Aunt Alice would be happiest, I think, in the nineteenth century, living in a castle on the verge of ruin in some Irish hamlet, gossiping, keeping her hands and mind occupied with busywork. "Don't you think that obese man in the persimmon shorts should be made to stop running?" she asked. "He's sweating fearfully and his face is dark red."

"I don't think he'd welcome interference."

"Perhaps he's right. Amelita Lizzardi tells me that all the doctors are making their patients run now, that age and weight are no barrier."

"Is Madam Lizzardi jogging?"

This query produced a giggle from Aunt Alice's thin, unpainted lips. "With those tiny feet and that torso? Dear me, that would be amusing. Though we mustn't laugh at poor Amelita. She has had her trials."

The latest of these occupied us while we completed the reservoir oval and climbed in Aunt Alice's waiting car. A school of joggers surrounded the car for a moment and then took to the trail, wingless butterflies determined to fly at any cost.

"Why are most of them so graceless?" Aunt Alice wanted to know, as Thurmond maneuvered the car up the drive and out of the park on Ninetieth Street.

Like Dutch, Aunt Alice is not shy about announcing

her rules. One of them—Nothing Serious Is to Be Discussed Prior to Breakfast—was in force that morning. She talked of her charities. Aunt Alice, meaning to do right by her husband's name, has given so much of herself to those organizations, to her special cases, that it seems she has little left for her family. Because my mother died when I was young, I have always felt as if I came under the heading of Special Cases. Like Amelita Lizzardi. Her own children, from both her marriages, are, for the most part, secure and happy individuals, regarding their mother with distant affection, keeping out of her path by living in remote places like Colorado and Michigan.

When we reached her house, an inherited member of her staff, a butler called Fredricks, opened the door and ushered us in. When Uncle Garfield was alive, all of the servants were required to wear uniforms. Immediately after he died, Aunt Alice banned them forever. "I've lived with uniforms most of my life. I never want to see another."

This decision led to an unfortunate incident, which occurred while I was still at Princeton. It was spring recess, and I had offered a ride to a freshman from Roslyn, Long Island, named Lenny Hertzberg. He had made arrangements with his father to pick him up in front of Aunt Alice's house. Lenny was very proud to be at Princeton and anxious to join a good eating club (he didn't). He thought that a ride to Manhattan with me was one way to get into one (it wasn't). He was a terrible snob (who went on to do well in the supermarket business), but I liked him nonetheless. Or perhaps because. We arrived at Aunt Alice's house, and, as there was no sign of his father, I invited him in. Fredricks, sans uniform, appeared at the door in mufti: a black suit, an even blacker tie, a white shirt.

Whereupon Lenny Hertzberg immediately extended his right hand and said, "Hi, I'm Leonard Hertzberg. I guess you're a relative of J.J.'s here. Let me tell you he's one heck of a guy."

Fredricks, always the perfect gent, extended his own pale hand and touched Leonard's. "I'm afraid not, sir. I am employed by Mr. Grant's aunt." He then touched my own hand as if it were the way things were done, mitigating the faux pas, as it were, and ushered us into one of the libraries, where a red-faced Leonard and I waited an interminable ten minutes for his father to turn up.

Since then, Fredricks has been the one member of the staff to be allowed to wear a uniform, which is, needless to say, an especially discreet one. He took Aunt Alice's coat, smiled his compassionate smile at me, and asked if breakfast were to be served immediately.

"Immediately, Fredricks," Aunt Alice said, touching the hard surface that was the back of her hair. "I'm famished."

"Would you care for tea?" she asked, once we were seated in the small breakfast room, which has an Oriental motif: pale gold wallpaper and dark, lacquered furniture. It is a serene, formal sort of room, and Aunt Alice is entirely appropriate in it.

Breakfast is a light repast, one that never varies: grapefruit juice, touted as fresh but tasting as if it comes from a can with Donald Duck's picture on it; thin slices of cinnamon toast, burnt to a crisp; and an endless supply of harsh orange tea. The last person who requested coffee received a tiny cup of weak instant Sanka.

After we crunched our way through the toast and I had admired a Chinese ancestral painting Aunt Alice had recently purchased at a private auction, she came to the point, abruptly.

"Why won't you see Barrett?"

"It's clear that *you* have."

"Don't take the Jesuitical line with me, James. There's no reason in the world why I shouldn't have seen her."

"I hope you gave her breakfast."

"She came for afternoon tea. But that's neither here nor there. She says she's done everything in this world to try and talk to you short of approaching you on the street, and you persist in avoiding her." She waited for me to say something, but I didn't. I drank the tea.

"Stop slurping, James, and listen to me."

"I haven't slurped tea since I was eight, Aunt Alice, and you sat me down and gave me extremely thorough tea-drinking lessons."

"You have a pattern, James, of avoiding anything unpleasant in your life. Of turning your back, of denying it even exists. Much like your mother, I am afraid. The least unpleasantness and you're closing your eyes, whipping out your checkbook. It's an unattractive trait, James —very angry-making. One longs for a good row with you, and you're out the door. James, I want to know why you won't see Barrett."

I looked up at her and finally told her. "I'm a coward. I can't face the pain. Do you have any idea of how hurting it was to wake up one day, after years of sleeping together, of trusting one another, to find that it was all a sham? I used to tell people, Aunt Alice, that I had married my best friend. I not only loved my wife. I liked her. But she wasn't only sleeping with her rock star. She was sleeping with her dentist and with her butcher. And then she'd come home to tell me we'd always be together, we would take care of each other in our old age, we would always love each other.

"I believed every goddamned word. When I found out, I felt as if I had fallen off the planet. All my supports had been kicked out from under me. I couldn't believe that someone I had known and loved for most of my life wasn't that someone at all. At first I wanted to kill myself. Of all the disappointments in my life, BaBa was the one that nearly did me in. Because she had made the other disappointments bearable.

"Afterward, I decided I didn't want to kill myself. I wanted to kill her. I'm still in the I-want-to-kill-her stage, Aunt Alice. I still hurt like hell." I turned away from those relentlessly inquiring eyes.

"I think," she said, after a while, "that when you can see Barrett, you'll realize that a lot of what she did came out of her own pain. Not that you have to forgive her. But you do have to see her, James."

"I don't want to, Aunt Alice."

"Dear Lord," she said, looking up at the Chinese ancestors studying their folded hands. "All of your life you've only done what you've wanted. And don't bring up that famous unpublished, unwritten novel. Your father didn't lop off your hands and burn the only existent typewriter. If you had wanted to write, you would have written. You've used your father as an excuse for much too long a time."

I looked at her again and realized that we were both growing older and softer.

"Do you think I would say any of this to you if I didn't love you, James?" Aunt Alice said, after a while. There were tears in her eyes, and I suppose there were tears in mine. The only person I could ever recall saying she loved me was BaBa, and she was too free with her avowals of affection. Certainly Aunt Alice had never said those words before. Not to me. Not to her own children, who claim she has willed her emotions to the American Cancer Society.

"I love you, too, Aunt Alice," I said, shocking myself. At that, we both rose, as if on cue, crossed the room, and embraced. It was a sublimely ridiculous moment, two grown-up Protestant sticks, clinging to each other, tears on our cheeks. Yet it is a moment I find myself treasuring.

As embarrassed and red in the face as Leonard Hertzberg, as the fat jogger in the persimmon shorts, we went back to our corners and put on our everyday masks again.

"You will come to dinner on Monday night, James, and see her? It's important to me that you do."

"Then I will."

We kissed good-bye in the usual lip-glancing way, and I went to my office while Aunt Alice had Thurmond drive her to a committee meeting.

I felt both rueful and peculiarly buoyant. "Up for anything, dolls," as Dutch might have said.

CHAPTER 18

It was raining on the day of the fashion show. I had lunched with a woman from Chicago, a lady novelist of uncertain years and a strict, disciplined talent, at the Italian Pavilion. Cora was there and stopped at the table to be introduced, to say "We must have lunch very soon, James." I remained noncommittal.

I escorted my companion to the St. Regis, where she was staying, and then walked back up Fifth Avenue, fighting the weather. It was that special New York June weather, featuring wind and rain and sudden gusts of unpleasant air. Umbrellas were being inverted by the wind, and frail lady shoppers were holding on to the posts in the vortex created by the Plaza and the General Motors Building.

I made my way west on Fifty-eighth Street toward Sixth Avenue and the Barbizon Plaza Hotel. The Barbizon has a small stage and auditorium, the kind of place where the University of Pennsylvania puts on its Mask and Wig Show for metropolitan alumni (e.g., Bernice's husband) fond of that sort of thing.

The fashion show had been slated to begin at two P.M.,

and it was close to three when I arrived. Dutch had assured me that the two other designers would present their lines first, and they would, according to the nature of the beast, be anywhere from a half-hour to an hour behind schedule. "Fashion shows, dolls, are notorious time wasters."

I don't know what I expected. I had accompanied BaBa to one or two during the early years, in Europe, and I suppose I thought I would see lots of paparazzi and women in sunglasses and silk dresses.

The auditorium was three-quarters full. Young men and women, ignoring the undrawn curtain on the stage, were talking and laughing and passing joints about. They seemed restive but alert, most of them dressed in an amalgam of loose-fitting brightly colored clothing, white scarves wrapped suicidally tight around their young and thin necks. Music, coming from two speakers placed on either side of the stage, was what Dutch classified as "elevator rock."

Two members of the Fashion Institute, elderly toothsome ladies wearing black dresses and false pearls, approached, identified themselves, and wanted to know if they could be of any help. They obviously approved of my suit, my briefcase, my air of professional well-being, which was in such contrast to the wild-eyed visages of the other members of the audience. Basking in their goodwill, I was about to ask a mild social question ("When do the proceedings begin?") when we heard a hissing sound from behind a curtained door. Bunny stuck his head through the curtains. His hair was braided in the most elaborate coif yet, a series of tightly woven strands that made the top of his head seem a perfect oval. He beckoned to me while I excused myself from the ladies, who no longer seemed so secure in regard to my respectability. I went through the curtains and found myself in a long corridor that led to the back of the stage. The smell of whiskey and musk was especially strong. "Do you have an idea where Miss Dutch is?"

"Not a clue," I said.

"*Vay iz meer.*" In the dim light I could see that Bunny was sincerely worried. However, not feeling particularly comfortable in that corridor with Bunny muttering Yiddish imprecations, I edged my way back toward the curtained door, saying something about finding a phone and calling the loft.

Bunny grabbed my arm and said, "Get your lily-white ass behind that stage, James Grant. We've been calling Dutch for hours. Right now we need help back there. Listen, *yankel*," he said in a more confidential, less angry tone, as I allowed him to escort me up the corridor, "only half of the clothes have arrived."

Pandemonium Reigned Supreme, as BaBa's mother used to say. Each of the three designers' entourages had been assigned to a separate area. Dutch's group was squeezed into a claustrophobic dressing room up a flight of narrow, steep stairs. A dozen people stood in the middle of it in varying degrees of nudity.

Jean was standing at the door, wearing a bathrobe, wanting to know "where the fuck" Dutch was. Louie was standing on a platform while Lola sewed up the seam in the back of the white Eisenhower jacket he was wearing. He was not, however, wearing trousers or undershorts. He stood perfectly still, looking bewildered, chewing gum. The sculptress, Tallulah, stuck a piece of gum in her mouth and cupped her hand around Louie's equipment. He pushed it away unconcernedly.

"You men," Tallulah said. "With your limp dicks."

The smell of marijuana pervaded the atmosphere. A tiny square of a window at the top of the room was open, but there were too many aromas—grass and tobacco, sweat and cologne, Juicy Fruit and hair spray—to allow any stale New York air in.

"Have you called him?" I asked Jean.

"Constantly."

"Where do you suppose he is?"

"On a slow boat to China. If he isn't, I'm going to kill him. He has half the clothes."

I left her leaning against the doorjamb looking like a young Blanche DuBois and made my way down the stairs. Dutch, with Sylvia Einhorn behind him, was just coming through the stage door, their arms filled with clothes.

"Could I help it, dolls," Dutch was saying to Bunny, "if I had a last-minute business conference? And what are you so crazy about? Those two *schlemiels* haven't even gone on yet? Hello, darling," he said to me, kissing me on each cheek. "How was your morning?"

"There's no time for that, Dutchette," Bunny said, moving him up the stairs and into the dressing room. I escaped into the auditorium, where I found a seat in the last row.

It was only later that I found out, from Sylvia Einhorn, that the business conference had been with Eddie Rabinado. "I don't know what they were saying," Sylvia told me, "but Dutch got all white in the face under his makeup. By the time Rabinado left, Dutch looked like a piece of unhealthy gefilte fish."

"Darling," Dutch said, "don't be ridiculous. The man was checking up on his investment. Sylvia Einhorn's a romantic from the *On the Waterfront* school. She's dying for a little mayhem."

The first two presentations were uneventful. Professional models moved up and down the runway, which extended halfway into the theater. They wore predictably outré outfits described by a lackluster female announcer who stood to the right of the stage and held onto the microphone as if it were a lifeline. More polite disco music backed her up. At the end of each presentation, the audience applauded, but no one was shouting "encore."

There was a ten-minute delay after the curtain went down for a second time. A group sitting several rows in front of me sent one of their number—a thin girl with tiny circles of rouge on her cheeks—to see if it was still raining. She reported that it was. They decided to leave anyway, when the disco music was abruptly replaced by the voice of Jean's mother singing "Mean to Me" in a jazzy, upbeat fox-trot tempo.

The lights dimmed as Lorraine sang *"each night when you say you'll phone . . ."* and a spotlight picked out a circle on the curtain. The curtain parted slightly, and Louie stepped through. He was shirtless under the Eisenhower jacket, though he wore a white collar and a dark red formal bow tie. His trousers were also dark red, terry cloth and formal with a blue stripe down their sides. He held his arm out and the spotlight followed it to the end of his hand. The curtains moved again, and Jean stepped out onto the stage wearing a silver dress that revealed most of her shoulders, back, and breasts. Lorraine sang as Louie twirled Jean into his arms and they danced out onto the runway. The only sound in the auditorium was

Jean's mother's whiskey voice, complaining of mistreatment in that perfect, masochistic song. Louie, with his sleek blackness, was the epitome of the man of the hour: slick, street-tough, and brilliantined. Jean, with that silver blondness heightened by the dress and the spotlight, looked as if she had just stepped out of a movie poster. They were very right together.

They danced back up the runway and off stage left to the kind of hysterical applause people reserve for rock concerts. Simultaneously, the music changed to Carmen Miranda as Victoria DeVine, Bunny, and Tallulah congalined onstage from the right. They wore matching Cariocan shirts, tight flowered shorts, bandannas around their heads, and six-inch high-heeled shoes. Afterward two lovely girls in pastel tea gowns danced a beautiful waltz together, followed by two boys with Rudolph Valentino hairdos wearing double-breasted terry cloth lounge suits who also danced a beautiful waltz together.

Somehow they—Dutch and Jean and the kids—had transformed the unspectacular stage into a genuine playhouse. The performance—because it certainly was that —had transcended the limits of a fashion show and created genuine entertainment. Everyone in the audience was moved, transported.

For the finale, all the participants came out on stage, dancing to "It Had to Be You." The audience stood up and applauded as Dutch came on, in a white silk shirt and turquoise terry cloth trousers, eyeshadow to match.

The music, tapes of thirties and forties songs, continued as the audience climbed up onto the stage and danced, sharing joints with the models. I went up to congratulate Dutch, who was dancing with Jean.

"Dolls," he said, embracing me. "Dolls!"

I tried to pull away after a moment. "Darling, where are you going?"

"Back to the office."

"And miss the party of the century? *Women's Wear* is going to be there. James, go right down to the loft and take off that ridiculous costume—really, a suit like that to a fashion show like this—and then run upstairs and help set up the bar. A few of the kids are probably already there. Don't let any of them near the scotch."

He turned to kiss an assistant buyer from Gimbels East and I found myself stage center, facing Jean. "Dance?" I asked.

It was a reprise of the first night we had met, at the Eye Ball. For a moment I thought she was going to refuse, and then she was in my arms. Her body, through the thin silver dress, felt vulnerable, too thin. But the all-night sewing sessions, the drugs, the terrible food, the dancing, didn't show in her face. She still looked incredibly young, innocent. I held her close for a moment and felt her respond. For a split second I was back in dancing school, eight years old, white gloved and blue suited, falling in love with a girl named Susan Anthony White. Then the tape ended, and Dutch pulled her over to talk to the Gimbels East buyer, and I was making my way across the stage to the exit.

"Listen, James," Jean says when I ask her why she didn't let up a little in the cold war she waged against me from the moment we met, "I had had men. Uptown men. 'Nice' men who fucked over me and under me and through me. The black limousine had evaporated along with Bert and Catherine and Buddy. I was free for the first time in my life. I didn't need anyone. I didn't want anyone. Let up? Man, I was increasing my guard."

Carmen Miranda was on the tape again. One of the boys who had modeled in the show asked me if I knew how to samba. I said that I did but that I would have to take a rain check. I had to go set up for the party.

CHAPTER 19

The only possession Jean had managed to rescue from her ravaged apartment was the photograph. "At least he left me that," she says, miming a gesture her mother was famous for: one hand on her hip, the other patting the back of her hair.

"Intentionally, do you think?"

"Meaning the photographs were left unharmed as some kind of punishment?"

"Sort of."

"He didn't have that kind of subtlety. He missed them. They were hidden under the sink behind the Ajax."

She keeps them in a large, fitted wooden box, one that was designed for her father by Abercrombie and Fitch. Lewis Halladay had been a fisherman. "He used to keep his worms in it," Jean claims.

The glossies of Lita and Lorraine are in the uppermost tray. The middle compartment contains the studio stills, photographs of actors and actresses who worked with Lita and Lorraine, people who knew Jean, who came to the Bel-Air house before her father was killed.

Below these, on the bottom level of the box, are the

snapshots. Pictures of Jean when she was young, taken by Lita, the governess, friends of the family.

The kids used to love to go through the glossies. They'd play a game, seeing how many of the stars they could identify. Brian Aherne. Broderick Crawford. Ann Miller. Herberts Marshall and Lom. Ronald Colman. Pat O'Brien. Marie Wilson. Eddie Albert. Lana and Ava and Marilyn were, of course, easy. They'd ask Jean questions. "When your mother did *Emerald*, was she sleeping with Bogart?"

Jean presented Dutch with the glossy he admired most. It is a photograph of Lita and Lorraine coming out of Chasen's, taken in 1954. Lita, with thin, penciled eyebrows and a good-humored, insolent smile, looks half her age. In a dark Dior dress, she comes off tough, but not unkind.

Lorraine, in black fox, is sullen and easy and fast, too young and too hip to be a mother. Baby Jean stands between them, holding on to each of their gloved hands, as if she's afraid to let go.

In the background, Clark Gable is talking earnestly to Lewis Halladay, who looks as if the answer to every question he was ever asked was no. He's the only person in the photograph who could conceivably be cast as a parent, and then it would be in the role of grandfather.

"The L.A. *Times*," Jean says about the photograph, "was trying to promote a family image for Hollywood. The caption said something about two generations of stars and a third coming up. The studio loved it so much they bought it and sent it out as a publicity still."

Dutch had it blown up to poster size and mounted. He hung it on the wall above Louie's piano. Later, Jean tried to clean the blood from it with a damp cloth, but the paper the blow-up had been printed on came apart in her hands.

When I arrived at the loft that afternoon after the fashion show, after I had changed from my suit into more casual clothes, I found two of the kids smoking joints, studying the poster as if it were an icon.

"Dynamite, isn't it?"

There were half a dozen kids in the living area, smoking marijuana, dancing to the Bee Gees tape that was constantly playing that summer, drinking punch from a large, formal crystal bowl that stood on a newly acquired, somewhat damaged circular Empire table.

I didn't recognize any one of them, but most of the kids look alike to me at the best of times. I had been prepared to help set up, as Dutch had instructed, but the setting up appeared to have been accomplished. The audience from the fashion show began to drift in. The rain was hitting against the windows with a constant beat, as if it were keeping time to the music. The garages and loft buildings were effectively blotted out by the fog. "Real mood weather," someone said, offering me a paper cup filled with punch.

I drank it without thinking, and filled my cup again, wondering when Dutch and Jean would appear, saying polite things to the guests who came up to the punch bowl. The punch tasted good and cheap, the kind I remember being served when Bernice and I were children. A woman who used to work for us during those Southampton summers, Evangeline, eschewed the fresh fruit drink mother ordered and would make a beverage from a

195

packet of powder and tap water. To fool mother, she would sprinkle lemon seeds on the top. Bernice swore, in her confidential voice, that the seeds were bugs. She called it bug juice and predicted imminent blindness as I rebelliously downed glass after glass.

I drank another cup of the punch, thinking of the bug juice, wondering if Jean's habit of taking out her past and scratching it until it erupted weren't catching.

For no special reason, I suddenly felt absurdly happy. I took my cup and sat down in one of the seating areas with four women in their early twenties who were discussing, intently, the merits of Peter Frampton. I went back to the punch bowl and brought everyone cups of the juice.

"Don't call it bug juice, man," one of the kids with a bad complexion, Sal, said. "That's so fuckin' unappetizing." A fat blond girl came up to where we were sitting and propped herself on the arm of the sofa facing me. She was crying, fat tears running down her cheeks.

"What're you crying about?" Sal wanted to know and the girl drifted away.

Some time later, Dutch, Louie, Bunny, Jean, and the models came in. I remember seeing Victoria DeVine's face and thinking it looked like the one in the "Portrait of Madame X" in the Metropolitan Museum, all powdered and pointy. Then I saw Dutch's face swimming across the loft toward me, disembodied, a Cheshire cat balloon.

"Dolls," he said, kissing me. "The most fabulous, fabulous success. If the orders that were placed are any indication, terry is next season's big resort fabric. Darling, it was worth every disgusting minute of preparation. And to put the icing on the cake, do you remember the tea gowns from the waltz? Jean designed them and Bloomie's wants them. I've launched a new star in my old age."

I looked up at him. I meant to express surprise that Jean had been designing, that his show had been a success. But nothing came out of my mouth. My tongue felt thick and salty. I was having difficulty breathing.

"James, you have the silliest expression on your face."

My eyesight seemed to be going. I wondered, idly, without alarm, if I hadn't been poisoned, if Bernice's thirty-year-old prediction had not come true. Dutch became a yellow, pink, and orange rainbow.

"Sal," Dutch said, and his voice seemed faraway and delightfully mellow, "have you been pouring your acid punch into James?"

Dutch turned purple and violet and blue then, finally, black, and I was out for fifteen hours, victim of the shortest acid trip Dutch claimed ever to have heard of.

"Nobody," he said later, "passes out on acid. People kill people on acid and people commit suicide on acid and people write operas on acid but nobody passes out. Darling," he said, as if I were arguing, "acid is full of speed!"

While I was out, my body responding to the LSD by sweating continually and copiously, ruining Dutch's favorite sheets (he and Bunny had gotten me to his bed), everyone present had a glass or two of acid punch, a hit or two on the grass laced with angel dust, a snort or ten of the cocaine that was making the rounds of the room. "That coke was lovely stuff," Dutch said, remembering it as if it were a rare old wine, laid down in 1920 by his godfather. "It was cut with really fine European borax. I'd swear it had only been stepped on two, at the most three times."

"Like me."

"We must have gone through two thousand dollars' worth of drugs."

"It's a wonder you're not addicted to one of them."

"Darling, they were all soft drugs, and I want you to know I never trust anyone who's not sensual about dope. It's like not really caring about food. Next time you do acid, James, try and get into it. Let it take over your body. Try and be sensual with it."

Louie, that evening, was merely feeling sensual about sex. I never supposed his sex life with Dutch was as satisfying to Louie as it might have been. It always appeared to me that Louie was more hetero than homo, that Dutch fulfilled more of his emotional needs than his physical ones. Jean, though she resists, agrees. "Louie was a kind of willing accomplice." He claimed that he was entirely passive, Dutch entirely oral. Dutch hotly denied this. "That Louie loves to throw his legs in the air the minute the lights go out."

Louie had a history of making off, every once in a while, with the girls who hung around with the kids. On several occasions, he was the cause of one or two being barred from the loft. "Drugs," he said, "make me horny, man."

He found Jean in her "bedroom," reclining on her bed, fanning herself, tripping, as she put it, lightly, fantasizing about becoming the next Chanel, wondering if she could legitimately omit the Hollywood section of her biography when she was being interviewed by *Women's Wear* and *Vogue.*

Louie, tuning into his own fantasy, took off his Eisenhower jacket and his terry dress trousers and zipped Jean out of her silver dress.

"Intellectually," Jean says, "I was perfectly willing to do it with Louie. He was a beautiful animal with a big cock. All rules and standards of behavior had been suspended by the drugs and the acid. I hadn't had sex in a long time. I told myself that I had to be horny. And then, you mustn't forget we had danced together on the stage. It's a Hollywood tradition that you fuck your leading man.

"But I couldn't do it. I experienced the female equivalent of impotency, of not being able to get it up. For the first time in my life I found myself not only not responding, I was beyond responding. I was incapable. 'I can't do it,' I told him as he was trying to force my legs open, as Dutch came barreling around the screen."

He didn't say anything. He stood staring down at Louie, who stood up and put on his trousers like a bad boy caught masturbating.

"What're you, man, some kind of superspy?" Louie asked, as he tried to zip himself into the trousers. "I'm fuckin' tired of you watching every time I take a crap. Slobbering over me like I was a piece of steak and you was the butcher. I'm going out to promote me some genuine live pussy. You got any objections, lay 'em on your mother here."

Louie stalked across the loft, making a path through the fifty or sixty people assembled there, wearing the Eisenhower jacket and the trousers Dutch had made for him. Dutch went after him, shouting at Louie as he ran down the stairs, "If you leave, you loathsome Puerto Rican whore, you never come back. You go back to the streets, to the hooker bar where I found you. Remember that."

"*You* remember, you cocksucking faggot scumbag,"

Louie said, continuing to run down the stairs. None of this fazed the kids, who continued to dance and dope and eat the Chinese food Dutch had had sent in.

"I couldn't move," Jean says. "I felt like a paralyzed Madame Recamier (Lita played her in one of the last silent films). I lay there nude, on that bed, with a black feather fan in my hand, ridiculously happy with myself. For the first time I could remember, I hadn't responded to a man who wanted me. It was a wonderful, incredible feeling and it had nothing to do with the acid punch. I lay there digging it and after a while Dutch came back around the screen, puffing on one of his cigar-sized joints, and sat down next to me. I managed to say I was sorry. He kissed me and held my hand."

"He'll be back," she assured him. "Louie loves you, Mister Dutch. We all do."

"I wish people would stop loving me so much," Dutch said, "and start wanting me a little."

CHAPTER 20

"Had I taken two minutes out to think about it," Jean says, indulging in a little hindsight guilt, "I would have known something was terribly wrong. Jesus, he had just come from the most successful event in his life and he couldn't be up about it. Yes, there was the Louie scene, but that wasn't unusual or unexpected. And yes, there was Eddie Rabinado in the background, but Dutch was determined not to let him worry him.

"It was something deeper. The cracks in his happiness facade were beginning to show. Only I wouldn't see them. I had a vested interest in keeping my image of Dutch—Mister Happy, Mister Perfect—intact. I was so fucking involved with myself, James."

"I didn't see the cracks then, either, if that's any consolation."

"It's not."

She spent the early part of the evening coasting on the LSD while the kids downed blues and reds and purple hearts, smoked grass, and snorted. I wondered why they didn't all die from overdosing, when a couple of glasses of Sal's punch put me out for hours.

"Your system's not used to high living, dolls," Dutch explained.

Someone's tape deck was playing at full volume when Lorraine's version of "Body and Soul" came on, sung in her offhand, lowdown voice.

"Are you crying for Louie?" Jean asked him.

"Darling, vampires never cry. But if I did, I'd be crying for what I wish Louie had been."

"Dutchy," Jean often says, "was as much a victim of Hollywood as Lorraine—or even I—was. He never saw Louie except in the glow of a cameraman's cheesecloth. Louie wasn't a sensitive young poet of the street. He was a big, dumb, sweet boy. He wasn't going to be the love of anyone's life, let alone Dutchy's. Not at their respective ages. None of Dutch's lovers or loves were what they were supposed to be. They were John Travolta or the Midnight Cowboy . . . he wished."

The cutting table collapsed when two couples joined them, and then it was decided that everyone go to Studio 54. Dutch called the limousine hire service he occasionally subscribed to (seventy-five dollars per hour, two-hour minimum), arranged for a car, and he and Jean got dressed while the kids went on ahead.

The crowd outside Studio 54 was larger than usual for a Thursday night. When Jean and Dutch alighted from the limousine, they saw that most of the kids had already arrived and were standing on the sidelines, behind the police barriers, unable to get in.

For a moment, Jean thought she and Dutch were going to be rejected, the bouncer being a man she didn't know. But he waved them in as he held back a group of people behind them.

"Something was definitely and obviously off," Jean

says. "To start with, the lights were up and the music was being played several decibels lower than usual. For another, there was a definite dearth of local color. The boy waiters in their underwear were on duty, but the jockstrapped men who usually stood around the bar weren't, and the kids—they always let a few kids in, that was the point—weren't there. Most of the men were in black tie and the women in designer dresses. We were on the dance floor, neon lit, before we realized there was a private party going on."

"54 is going down the tubes," Dutch said, looking around him. "Where it came from."

It took one of the boy waiters, a friend of Dutch's, to tell them that the party was for an octogenarian movie star who had just had his thirtieth film released and that everyone in the room had been to a thousand-dollar-a-seat benefit showing of the film.

"54 looked and smelled, suddenly, like Hollywood. I began to pick out faces," Jean says. "Producers and directors and front-office johns and the stars who managed to survive. The guest of honor's career only began in earnest when he turned seventy. Hollywood rewards its survivors. I looked at them looking at me. It was as if the photograph collection had come alive and were sitting in judgment."

She told Dutch that she wanted to leave, and he realized she meant it. They were making their way out of the main room when a group of the kids surged in, Bunny in the lead. He grabbed Dutch, pulling him toward the dance floor. "Darling," Dutch said to her, "I can't *fargin* Bunny a dance."

Jean went to the bar and ordered a gin and bitters à la her grandmother. "I thought it was you," a huge, red-haired man, a producer who had given Lorraine a break in the fifties, said. "Sorry to hear about your ma. One of the great greats."

Jean laughed. "It was almost reassuring, hearing the Hollywood bullshit again."

"I have this crazy idea," Irv said.

"Save it."

"Make a test for me. I'm going to do Lorraine Rice's life. I've wanted to do it for years. You'd be sensational."

"I won't sign a release, Irv. Neither will Rank."

"I swear I'll play it straight. No ballyhoo. We'll put it all up there, just as it was. I could put a package together tonight with that story and you."

"And the release and the night and the music."

"Jean, fly out to the Coast with me tomorrow. On me. Strictly first-class. We'll go see Howard . . ."

Jean set the drink on the bar and walked away from Irv. The Hollywood bullshit was beginning to sound less reassuring. She was headed for the ladies' room, going to see if she could find one of the girls, to borrow taxi money. Kirk Douglas and his son were standing just inside the entrance, talking to one of the more famous Hollywood alcoholics.

"Don't tell me it's Jean Rice," Kirk Douglas said, anxious to get away from the drunk, taking Jean by her shoulders, leading her back into the room.

"He looked as if he were wearing a Kirk Douglas mask," Jean said, disengaging herself, answering questions. "He wasn't meaning to be unkind. But I was paralyzed. A Vincent Price nightmare movie, one of those neo-Poe jobs he specializes in, was being produced around me. The atmosphere was full of that same shtick, zombies rising out of their coffins, acting as if it were all part of a day's work. People I had thought dead, killed in airplane accidents and felicitous falls from hotel-room windows, were drinking martinis at the bar. It came to me that I was hallucinating, that the LSD was having a delayed effect. It sometimes does, you know. I thought if I could just get out of 54 and onto the street, they would all go away. I wanted to push past Kirk and Irv and Dotty and Arlene and all of those walking, talking ghosts and get out. Somehow I couldn't. A woman who had played the wife in an Orson Welles film joined us and talked about Sybil and Rank, about real estate, about Film.

"She seemed to go on for hours. I closed my eyes, and when I opened them, I saw Bert coming for me, a New York Galahad. Now I realize that the big Manhattan parties had just broken and the guests who could make it were coming on to 54. But then, at that moment I imagined that everything that had gone before me in my life was overtaking me, in chronological order.

"I can't exactly verbalize what the feeling was. Claustrophobic, as in a dream. I suppose I was feeling the kind of horror one of the Price/Poe heroines is supposed to be experiencing when she opens the moldy old casket and discovers her own face on the decayed body lying inside.

"Bert put his arm around me and I could see Catherine behind him, sitting down at a table with Marian Javits and a man whose face was familiar from newspaper photographs.

"Bert was being marvelous. He introduced himself to Kirk and the Orson Welles wife, said a few words about 54, and then asked if he couldn't 'steal Jean away for a few minutes.' With his arm still around my shoulder, he piloted me out of the room and up to a private office which was paneled in what seemed to be black velvet.

The only light came from a small, deadly-looking coil of chrome.

"Baby looked as if she were having trouble," Bert said, holding her. He kissed her while she rested her head on his shoulder, enjoying that familiar aroma of club talcum. While she rested, her eyes closed, he fumbled with his trousers.

He pushed her down on her knees, clasping his hand around her neck. "He was forcing me to go down on him. Just as he did the day I first met him in the mayor's bedroom in Gracie Mansion. But then the sight of his cock excited me. In that office on the second floor of 54, it made me ill. I tried to push him away when someone with a key opened the door and came in, switching on the overhead light."

It was Buddy Ruben. The two men looked at each other. After a moment, Bert took his hand away from her neck, put himself away, and buttoned the fly of his exquisitely tailored dinner trousers. He left, Jean still on her knees, Buddy Ruben, pale and serious, standing next to the door. "She's all yours, Fauntleroy," Bert said. "You've waited long enough."

Buddy helped her up and led her down a set of private stairs and out to the alley behind 54. A long black familiar limousine was already there, waiting. Buddy stepped in first and she followed, allowing her head to rest against the soft plush.

"He took my hand as the Caddy drove across town. He had a nice, square hand. It was reassuring to be riding in the back of that car, all quiet and black and noiseless, with Buddy sitting beside me, holding my hand."

They went to his apartment, the top two floors of a converted town house in the East Sixties. "I don't think

Lilli had anything to do with the decoration. It was all Spartan luxury as opposed to Lilli's sybaritic restraint. The bedroom had gray walls, a serious platform bed, industrial carpeting. No paintings or wall hangings. No art of any kind. And no sofas or chairs. I remember wondering how he put his socks on in the morning. When he lit the candles, I thought: This is it; this is romance; this is love.

"I know it's insane, but I still believed, in the back of my mind, that Buddy Ruben was the man I was going to marry. I had been waiting for him to break away from Bert, to come into his own. Just like Dutch and Lorraine, I had been seduced again by Hollywood, by Gary Cooper, Jimmy Stewart, Hank Fonda: the soft-talking man is the good man.

"Buddy Ruben beat the shit out of me. That was Buddy's fantasy. That's what he had been saving me for."

We were standing in the rain that had been soaking New York for several days, not relieving the humidity. Walking was like swimming upstream in a polluted river.

Jean was still wearing the silver dress. It was torn and there was blood on the hem, which, like all of Dutch's hems, eventually came down. I was in a business suit, suffering an LSD hangover, asking myself if my mental faculties had been permanently damaged, headed uptown for an early breakfast with a neurotic author at the Plaza.

I fidgeted with my briefcase, wondering how she could still be so good to look at when, at the same time, she looked as if she had been raped by the Russian army.

"Your eye," I said, uncomfortable.

"It was Buddy who did the number on my apartment. Not Bert. I should have known. Bert wouldn't jeopardize his chances like that. It was always Buddy. He followed me in the limo and he rang my bell in the middle of the night and he called me at three, four, and five in the morning.

" 'You're not fit,' he told me, 'to lick the shoes of a man like Bert Brown.' "

"You really should do something about that eye," I said, and tried to touch her, to somehow comfort her.

She pushed my hand away and went on. "He put a dog collar around my neck. He made me crawl around on my hands and knees. He used a horse whip. You should see my back, James. You should see my—"

"Jean, let me—"

"Every time I begged him to stop, he used more force. Do you want to know something? He didn't believe me. He thought I was digging it. 'Here, bitch, chew on this.' He dragged me into his bathroom, dropped his trousers, and pissed all over me. Then he threw me out into the hall along with my dress and my shoes."

"Jean, you've got to—"

She pushed my hand aside again. "Poor Buddy Ruben. He had Bert go to all that trouble, taking me up to the upstairs room at 54, setting up Buddy as a hero. 'I wash Bert's back,' Buddy told me. And he was so proud. 'Bert washes mine.'

"The really terrible thing, James, is that he couldn't get a hard-on. Buddy Ruben couldn't fuck me."

She stopped talking and started to cry. "Darling," Dutch said, getting out of a taxi. "Darling!" He put his arms around her, and she buried her face in his neck. He held her for a moment, and then he took her inside the building, up to the loft.

I stood around on the street, my briefcase in one hand,

my other (useless) hand in my pocket. After a while, I went upstairs. The door was open. Dutch had cleaned her up and forced her to lie down on the white wicker bed, a camisole comforter over her. She looked sixteen, virginal and helpless.

"I want to die, Dutch," she said, not seeing me.

Dutch shook his head, motioning for me to leave. They didn't need me then. Jean didn't. I went on up to the Plaza and placated the author, who was on his fourth cup of black coffee.

Dutch sat with Jean, holding her perfectly shaped hand, until the sewing machine girls arrived.

CHAPTER 21

"We're recuperating, dolls," Dutch said several times during the following weeks. "Attending to business."

The dark circles under his eyes and the cough accompanying his French cigarettes made him seem like some bizarre consumptive, ailing rather than recovering. Jean was remote and pale, especially in contrast to the rest of New York, sporting their weekend tans.

I offered to take them to Chinatown, Dutch's favorite neighborhood outside his own, but he declined. "Do you know how many back orders we have?"

Dutch Unlimited's business problems seemed to have been worked out with the fashion show. One afternoon, having given up on my office, I was in the loft, watching Dutch and Jean and Sylvia and the girls working away in the un–air-conditioned heat. The phone rang. "Darling, could you make yourself useful and get that?" Dutch called.

"Is Mister Cohen there?" a cold, male voice asked.

"Whom may I say is calling?"

"Mister Rabinado. If he's busy, don't bother. It's no big thing. Just tell him I called, huh? Tell him I'm going to get back to him." For all of its careful, polite tone, there was something especially chilling about that conversation.

"Darling, he's a paper tiger," Dutch said, dismissing Eddie Rabinado. "Idle threats."

I didn't pursue it. Material was being ordered. Girls were being hired to work the sewing machines. The loft had been spruced up for the blitzkrieg visits the out-of-town buyers were beginning to pay. "Business," Dutch announced, "is thriving."

As far as I could tell, Dutch and Jean were spending solitary evenings together, having food sent in or going round to Max's, smoking joints, taking taxis to midnight movies on Forty-second Street.

"Darling," Dutch said, "that's the only time to go to the movies."

I asked after Louie and was told that "that *chazer* moved himself out a week ago." I offered sympathy, but Dutch wasn't having any. "I needed that *schlemiel* like I need a hole in my head. Darling, I want a real lover, someone with a brain in his head and a touch of the poet in his makeup. I want someone, dolls, who can respond to genuine love, generous affection. I do not want someone, James, who allows me to blow him on odd Thursdays."

Jean was standing at the reassembled cutting table during this conversation, putting together a pattern, her silver eyes concentrating on the flimsy piece of paper she held in her hand.

I left them, for the most part, alone. I was spending the weekends with friends in Montauk, pleasantly drunk from Friday night to Monday morning, avoiding the Southampton set, allowing myself to be taken to faintly literary parties where attractive women with unattractive haircuts made themselves agreeable. Of course, I was having problems.

Aunt Alice had called the Monday morning of the Monday night dinner party where I was to "confront" BaBa to say that it was being called off.

"Any particular reason?"

"BaBa thinks you're not ready to meet her."

"She couldn't be more right."

"Apparently she knows about that Halladay person."

"I wish I did."

Aunt Alice had me promise that I would see BaBa when "I was ready" and then announced she was off to Hawaii for the remainder of the summer.

"Is this the season for Hawaii?"

"I'm not sure Hawaii has a season. I've never been interested in 'seasons', James."

This was not strictly true, but I didn't want to argue and instead asked her where she planned to stay.

"I do not understand," Aunt Alice said in her aggrieved, querulous voice, "why I cannot go somewhere without all of my acquaintances having to know how I plan to travel, where I plan to go, and with whom I plan to stay."

"I'm not exactly what one would call an acquaintance, Auntie."

That kept her quiet for a moment, and then she confessed she was going to stay on the King Ranch, which takes up all of one of the lesser islands. I knew Adolph King slightly, a man in his late sixties who took his handball seriously and was almost as rich as Aunt Alice. His wife, a gracious and vital woman, had died the year before, and Aunt Alice had seen a bit of him in Palm Beach during the winter. Invitations to his Hawaiian ranch were as difficult to come by as they were desired. I forebore from putting two and two together.

"Your silence needn't take on that sort of tone with me, James. I am not considering marrying Adolph King."

We talked about other matters (Madam Lizzardi was in Switzerland, where it was definitely *not* the season), and when they were exhausted, I wished Aunt Alice godspeed and rang off.

I also wished her, mentally, good luck. Whether the trip was a trial get-together or merely the visit she insisted it was, I never found out. Aunt Alice still considers Adolph King a dear friend. He is always invited to her winter fête in Palm Beach. But whenever she speaks of him, her voice takes on a peculiar mournful tone, and he is not asked to sit at her table at the Eye Ball. I think Aunt Alice is disappointed. Or perhaps Adolph King is.

All summer, BaBa stepped up her typically convoluted campaign. My agreeing to attend a dinner party at which she would be present was clearly not enough. At first, when the party was called off, I thought she had given up, that she had found another fish to fry. Not so. She was attempting to get me to come to her.

I was being fed enough information about her comings and goings to make me realize she was still in the game. I knew she was living in a sublet on Fifth Avenue in the seventies because one of the younger agents in the office, a socially acceptable type, had been invited for cocktails and let me know it. "Had drinks with your wife Thursday afternoon, James. Extraordinary woman."

I knew BaBa was using the Southampton house, because the bills were rolling in and one of Lilli Ruben's lesser lights called to ask if I minded whether BaBa had the south dining room repainted a "pale, pale sea-blue, to reflect the colors of the ocean."

I had firsthand information that she was looking for a job, preferably "editorial," because the editor-in-chief of a publishing house I habitually lunched with mentioned the fact. "Damned attractive gal," said the editor-in-chief.

I knew she looked "divine" and "fit as a fiddle" because Madam Lizzardi, back from Switzerland, called to ask for Aunt Alice's address (I did not give it to her) and mentioned that she saw "dear Barrett at the Maidstone Club in East Hampton, breakfasting with that terrifically handsome Dicky Duane."

By July, when BaBa had given up looking for a job, editorial or otherwise, when she had left the Fifth Avenue sublet and moved out to Southampton with everyone else she knew, when I had still not called, or evinced any interest in her movements, she evidently realized—correctly—that I never would.

Thus, I was not unprepared for Bernice's dinner invitation. "Just a few pals, stuck in New York during the week," Bernice said. "I have to come down to the dentist, anyway, J.J."

I decided to get it over with.

Bernice has what BaBa once accurately described as the largest and least amusing apartment in Manhattan. It is on the top floor of River House, and the view from its windows, if one can get past the tiers of draperies Bernice is addicted to, is almost worth the price of admission. On a clear day, which happily seems to be becoming less of a rarity in New York, one can see Staten

Island and the Verrazano Bridge. The East River runs along Manhattan Island like one in a fairy-tale illustration. One expects a friendly dragon to come sailing along, accompanied by the red and blue boats and barges that inhabit the river.

I was inspecting this charming and unexpected view when the silence in the sixty-foot room behind me announced that BaBa had finally appeared, some forty minutes late. In a dress that was too simple not to have cost several hundred and perhaps even a thousand dollars, she looked as upper-class as ever. An aristocratic Barbie Doll. Her green eyes were as open as they could be. "No bullshit here," they said. "Just plain American privileged class straight-from-the-shoulder talk." Her blonde hair, lighter than it had been when we kept house, fell straight down her back, reaching her waist. It wasn't fashionable or even all that attractive, but it was appropriate.

"I hear you're running with a racy crowd, James," she said, giving me what appeared to be an obligatory kiss, setting the hard-hitting, frank tone for the evening.

"Any objections?" I asked, immediately on the defensive.

"The best thing that could happen to you, James," she said, laughing in a way that I had once enjoyed. She left me to greet the guests Bernice had managed to assemble during a difficult social week, the one leading up to July Fourth weekend. They included: three stockbrokers whose wives were on Nantucket; a lawyer and his pregnant wife, afraid to leave the proximity of her Manhattan doctor ("We invited him for the weekend but it was no go"); and a couple from France whose Newport rental did not begin until July the seventh. The latter bemoaned their late rental in that annoyingly cranky way Parisians have.

It wasn't until after the overdone lamb, the over-cooked and not entirely defrosted asparagus, and the heavy and sodden vanilla mousse that BaBa asked me to step into the library. "For a little chat, James."

Once inside the library—a room in which, as far as I know, a book has never been cracked—I poured myself a brandy and sat in a green leather chair that had belonged to my father. BaBa lit a cigarette and propped herself up against a bookcase. "If you wanted to see me, BaBa," I said, "why didn't you simply call? Putting us through all that"—I gestured in the general direction of Bernice's dining room—"wasn't necessary or even kind."

We looked at each other. I don't suppose either of us was pleased with what we saw. "You haven't changed," I said.

"You have."

She seemed content to let that statement lie there between us, so I asked in what way.

"You seem somehow less respectable. A touch less sure of yourself. You look more casual, younger, and a little belligerent. I'm not sure I like what I see." She put her cigarette out in a glass bowl not made for that purpose (BaBa loathes decorative bowls) and said, "I'm willing to try again, James."

"Why?" I found myself not really caring, staring at the rows of red leatherbound volumes with their gold tooling, wondering which of BaBa's neuroses was forcing her to go through this and why her psychiatrist hadn't cleared it up.

"We still have a lot going for us, James." This was said bravely, her voice breaking only slightly, and then on the

217

last two words. I was much too well acquainted with BaBa's theatrics to take any of this seriously. For reasons of her own, she had decided to cast herself, again, in the role of spurned wife.

"What about Randy?"

"That wasn't important, James. It was *why* I went off with Randy that was important. *Why* is the real issue, James."

After a few silent moments I said, "All right. *Why* did you run off with Randy?"

"It's obvious, isn't it?"

"Not to me."

"I was being made a fool of all over town. I now understand that your little relationship, if that's what you want to call it, was going on way before I caught onto it. Remember the day we had lunch together at La Petite Ferme and she was sitting a couple of tables away, pretending she had no idea who we were. You must have had fun with that one. And turning up with Buddy Ruben and Bert Brown at the Eye Ball, having one little dance with you. Oh, I fell for it. I fell for all of it. And at the same time, you were screwing Corea Medea.

"A woman's confidence begins to ebb, you know. The only reason I responded to Randy was because you were making me feel so damned unwanted."

"You don't seriously believe all or any of this? Do you, BaBa?"

"Of course I do, James." She stood up, her defense established, ready to get on with the prosecution. "As I've indicated, I'm willing to try again. With the proviso that you give up that woman and that you see Marcie Hitchcock."

MIDNIGHT MOVIES

"Who the hell is Marcie Hitchcock?"

"A marvelous person, a psychiatrist who saved my life. I met her in the Scilly Isles when Randy was giving me a terrible time."

I stood up. I'd had enough. I felt as if I had been watching a film based on my life: just recognizable. "I'm bored, BaBa"—I said. She looked disappointed. I think she thought I was going to kiss her—"with your continuing parade of self-serving deceptions. But the nice thing is I don't hate you anymore. For a long time I did. I felt you had betrayed me. Now I realize you never knew who I was. So there was no betrayal. Only a lot of incredible insensitivity." She started to say something, but I wouldn't let her. "For the last seven, eight months, I've been with people who, God knows, have problems. But underneath all the shit, they have the ability to care about other people, about me. You know, BaBa, I never really thought anyone could care about me. Certainly you couldn't. I don't think you can now."

"And that movie star's daughter can? James, I always suspected you confused screwing with loving. . . ."

"No, BaBa. You do."

I looked at her and saw the weakness that led to such strength. She was frightened and alone and I felt sorry for her, but I didn't want to be with her. I walked out of the library.

"Where are you going?" she asked, as I stepped around Bernice's guests, neatly placed in the sitting room. "What am I supposed to do?" she shouted. I still couldn't decide if her hysteria was real or calculated, one more move in her need to establish herself as my victim.

Poor Bernice. People always seem to be letting loose

in her Puritan presence. "You can go fuck yourself, James," BaBa shouted after me. I took irrational pleasure in hearing one of Bernice's coffee cups fall to the parqueted floor as the nonplussed servant shut the door after me.

CHAPTER 22

Whenever Dutch talked about his mother, he spoke in a fan's voice, adoring and childlike. One came away from the anecdotes, from the stories of her fabulous Reno lovers, with a vision of a glamorous, tough woman, a cross between Barbara Stanwyck and Joan Crawford.

Jean's version differs. "She was short and dumpy. Her lipstick went up but her lips went down. She looked as if she spent her life complaining."

I saw her but once. She was being whisked in and out of a rented black car, her face buried in her hands.

"The lover wore a gold-plated watch chain and featured manicured fingernails, highly polished. He worked a toothpick around his teeth for a half-hour after dinner, carefully inspecting each scrap of food he found on its tip. He was as unlovely a piece of work as I've ever seen. They seemed perfectly matched.

"And all the time Dutch was trying to impress them. 'I sold a dress to Ohrbach's this week, Ma.' "

" 'I wouldn't go near Ohrbach's if they were giving away those *schmatas*, free. *Dreck!* That's all they sell in that goddamned shithouse, *dreck.*'

"This, while she was slamming plates on the table, shoveling knives and forks and spoons around like a demented waitress. It was wildly unpleasant."

I was having my little chat with BaBa in Bernice's library about the same time Dutch and Jean were entering the beige-and-white living room of the small apartment his mother, Faye, and her lover, Marty, called home. It fronted Thirty-fourth Street and was between Second and Third Avenues.

"I always have dinner with Faye when I break up with a lover, darling," Dutch had informed Jean when he invited her to accompany him. "It's a family ritual. And you can use the diversion."

Faye opened the door for them, wearing a yellow-and-white caftan that bore an olive-colored stain where a button should have been. "My son, the successful woman's clothing designer. To think I should have lived to enjoy such rewards. You're looking more like your father every day."

"She was mean to him," Jean reports. "Absolutely cruel. It was so desperately unfair. There was Dutchy, a veritable balloon of humanity and kindness. And there was his mother, who clearly hadn't a scrap of decency. She was really, as Dutch used to say, the pits. And he couldn't or wouldn't see it. He could not stop trying to prove himself. He needed so badly some tiny piece of approbation, some drop of affection from her.

"But she wasn't a woman capable of giving it. She couldn't see anything but her own little miserable world. To her, Dutchy was just one more plague visited upon her by a hostile God. And the terrible thing was, he wanted so little from her. He wasn't begging for hugs and kisses—just a little pat on the back.

"Faye served the dinner in the apartment's dining alcove on white dishes with a blue border. It was Ronzoni spaghetti topped with sauce from a jar.

" 'It's delicious, Faye, ' Dutch told her.

" 'Bullshit. But what do you want when I work eight hours a day and have to keep house in the bargain and that bastard next to you won't even do me the courtesy of marrying me?'

"She knocked over the bottle of Lafite Rothschild Dutch had brought, spilling the wine over her cotton caftan, onto the floor. When Dutch offered to run downstairs and get another bottle, she told him to 'forget it. Who do you think we are that we have to have wine? Water's good enough.'

"It was obvious—or at least *I* thought it was—that she was going out of her way to be offensive because I was there. For some reason, I made her angry. She never said a word to me beyond hello.

"And Dutch would not let go. He could not stop playing up to her.

" 'Oh, Faye,' he said, after the wine was sopped up. 'Jean and I are thinking of running over to Bermuda for a week in September, just to give ourselves a little break. You were there, weren't you?'

" 'Yes,' she said. 'There's no dessert. You want coffee?'

"Marty hadn't said much. Throughout the ordeal he sat at the table, staring at my blouse, studying my breasts, his fingers working the toothpick. 'I heard a joke from Murray Meisselman today,' he said, when Faye accused him of never saying a word.

" 'Don't tell it here,' she said, pouring sugar into her coffee. 'I know Murray and his filthy jokes.'

" 'One faggot's talking to another and he says, "Why

223

don't you think they call it a cunt?" The other faggot, the smarter one, says, "Listen, Bruce, you ever see one?" '

" 'Jesus, Marty.'

" 'One more. What do they call a cunt with a zipper?'

" 'I give up.'

" 'A zunt.' He laughed so hard he had to put his tooth-pick down. 'That Murray Meisselman. He's got a million cunt jokes. Though I don't suppose you'd appreciate them,' he said to Dutch."

"They were having an off-night," Dutch had claimed, as they rode to the gold-flecked lobby in the gold-flecked elevator. "They're usually much, much better."

Jean put her arms around him and kissed him.

"You have to catch Faye on a good night," he said, as if she did a nightclub act. "When she's feeling up and she has her makeup on and that pasqualnick isn't doing his number. She's a totally different person, believe me."

He hailed a cab at Park Avenue South and put Jean in it. "Where you going?" she asked him. "I thought we were going to work on the spring line tonight."

"Darling, you work on the spring line. I'm going to get laid."

He went to the baths. "The serious baths, dolls."

The serious baths are located on the top three stories of a yellow-brick office building in the East Forties off Third Avenue. They are, according to Dutch's eyewit-ness account, a grim and desolate place. Ill-lit corridors crisscross each other, ending in square "rest" areas with blacked-out windows and cracked leatherette chairs. The corridors are lined with cubicles furnished with iron cots and paper-thin mattresses.

"It's like a set from a grade-Z girls-in-prison movie.

But it's the smell, dolls, that is so disgusting, in a kind of sexy, stomach-turning way: grass, poppers, sweat, come, cologne, and Top Job or whatever they use to disinfect those holes.

"And then there are the noises coming from behind the closed doors. The sounds of men getting fucked. Fifty-year-old fatties stand in front of the closed doors, getting off on the sounds."

The sprinkler system, installed when another baths burned down with half a dozen clients in it, makes the place resemble the gas chambers at Auschwitz. "The whole business reeks of death."

The patrons make their rounds in towels wrapped around their waists. When not walking along the corridors, they lie on their cots in seductive poses. "Them that wants to get fucked traditionally lie on their stomachs and show a bit of ass. Them that wants to be butch sit on the edge of their cot, their elbows on their knees, pretending they're not interested, that they happend to have wandered in by some devious mistake." The walkers move from cubicle to cubicle, shopping, waiting to be invited in. What little light there is comes from painted bulbs hanging in the corridors.

"Your average night in hell, dolls. Everyone is desperate, seething at the mouth. Nothing uglier than naked neurosis. Some nights, of course, are better than others. That night the joint was filled with a bunch of aging body builders and teen-aged mimps."

After showering in the communal shower and draping his towel around his waist, after walking up and down the corridors for over an hour, he found what looked like a young, tough boy sitting on the edge of a cot in one of the cubicles, smoking a cigarette. "At least he looked young. Who could tell in the light of a fifteen-watt bug bulb?" The boy was staring at the floor. Dutch coughed. "Want a little company?" he asked.

The boy looked up, stared at Dutch, and said, "Move it, honey. We're not into fat and ugly this season."

Dutch turned and went to his own cubicle ("And I had a little trouble finding it, yet"), dressed, and checked out of the serious baths as quickly as possible. The attendant, a fellow with rampant acne and a T-shirt that read "Christian" over the heart, said, "Come back and see us again, big boy."

"I wasn't finished. I wasn't going to let some bitchy queen deflate me. I was determined to get laid. And I was determined not to pay for it. You know me, James, when I'm determined."

He took a taxi down to the Christopher Street docks, where danger-seeking homosexuals cruise between the trucks parked there. But it had been raining fairly heavily that evening, as it had been most of that summer. There was no one standing behind the trucks except for a pair of bored cops, who ignored him.

He walked up Christopher Street and went into a bar called The Toilet. In the front room, young men in their early twenties stood around a circular bar, drinking beer, talking with their friends, "doing a little cruising on the side. The dreariest bunch of middle-class fags you ever saw in your life. And when I say dreariest, dolls, I mean dreariest. Little pleated chino trousers and Chemise Lacoste shirts. Every single one of them had a Coppertone tan and an Ipana smile."

In the dark back room, under a pressed-tin ceiling, men with their trousers down around their ankles were having sex with one another.

"Of course it's dangerous, darling. That's all part of it. Who knows what exotic disease you're liable to pick up in that back room? Who knows what kind of cuckoo bird you're going to meet there? They're very into fist fucking. And Bunny swears on a stack of Bibles that a dear friend of his got castrated there one night. It's a San Francisco trip."

The men in the back room of The Toilet made it clear that they, too, weren't interested in "doing it" with Dutch. "Every single one of them a size queen. So what was I supposed to do, James? I'm fifteen pounds overweight. I don't look like Warren Beatty. And I don't have a ten-inch cock. *What* was I supposed to do?"

He wasn't expecting an answer, but I gave him one. "You could have come home and masturbated. You could have looked for someone your own age with your own interests, someone you could develop a genuine relationship with. You've introduced me to dozens of gay men who don't demean themselves at the baths or the docks or The Toilet, who have good, solid relationships going for them. Why don't you try working at one of those?"

"Darling! Do you think my being gay has anything to do with it? That's just one more wrinkle in the onion. If I were straight I'd be going to massage parlors and picking up *curvas* on the corner of Forty-second Street and Eighth Avenue."

"If you know that, why don't you see a psychiatrist? Why don't you find out why you always have to go after people who don't want you?"

"The answer to that one is spelled F-A-Y-E and maybe someday I will go to a shrinker, but it will be to find out why, if I know the answer, do I still go out and do it. Besides, can you imagine me, preshrunk and pre-faded, sharing a house in Fire Island with someone my own age, getting into heavy cooking and macramé, both of us wearing little outfits that came off the same rack? Darling!"

He went to Le Dirt, where he picked up an angry black hustler who took him outside and around the corner into the filthy alley that separates Le Dirt from The Oklahoma City Chicken Corp. "All I could smell was that rancid fat they murder those chickens in." The hustler pushed Dutch up against the brick wall and put a knife against his Adam's apple.

"He didn't even have the courtesy to let me blow him."

"I'd as soon stick you as look at you, man. Just give me your wallet and the watch."

Dutch handed over the wallet. He didn't own a watch, which for some reason evoked the hustler's sympathy. "You got to be careful who you pick up in that shit hole, man."

"I know, darling."

"You crying, man?"

Dutch didn't answer.

"Jesus, he is crying. Jesus Christ." He knocked Dutch down and ran out of the alley, up Sixth Avenue.

"No, I did not call the cops, James."

We were sitting in my loft on one of Cora's backless, sideless, colorless units. He was smoking a joint, thanking God the hustler didn't take any of his rings.

"He probably thought they were worthless," I said, taking a sip of the brandy I was drinking and wasn't sure I wanted.

"That dummy."

It was four o'clock in the morning. We had both finished telling each other the stories of our evenings. I hadn't minded Dutch ringing my doorbell. I had been tired but unable to sleep, the image of BaBa being "reasonable" haunting me.

"Those are very cute pajama bottoms," Dutch said. "I love white pajamas with blue piping."

"Aunt Alice bought them for me at Abercrombie's before they went bust."

"How is she?"

"Disappointed in love."

"James," he said, not looking at me. "Let me sleep with you." The mascara or whatever he used around his eyes had gotten smudged, making him look like a bandit in a cartoon.

"I can't, Dutch."

"No sex. We don't have to have sex. We'll just get into bed together and see what develops. Please, James."

"I can't, Dutchy. I wish to God I could. I just can't."

"Well, then," he said, sighing, getting up, putting the joint out and carefully storing it in his pocket, "I think I had better call it a night, Mister James."

I walked him to the door and watched him as he went up the stairs to his loft. "No hard feelings?" I called after him.

"No hard feelings, darling."

CHAPTER 23

"Louie called," she shouted when she heard him come in.

"What'd that cocksucker want?" He went directly to the cabinet where he kept his scotch and poured himself a tumblerful.

Jean put on a negligee they had bought together in the basement of Alexander's, a pink nylon one with red feather trim, and went out into the living area. She, too, hadn't been able to sleep. She kept thinking of that terrible meal at his mother's, of how desperate he had seemed when he put her in the taxi.

"He wanted to know how you were doing," she said, going up to him. "Louie wants to be friends."

"Next time he calls, tell him all my friends have to have IQs over eighty-six."

He turned and she saw his face, mascara smeared, infinitely sad.

"I'd never seen him look like that before. You know how we all saw him—Mister Dutch, the Big Smile. It was only beginning to dawn on me that he was even unhappier than I and a lot more desperate. I wasn't at all sure I liked that. I was the child of Hollywood, doomed to, at the least, suicide. Kids from Brooklyn aren't doomed. They're funny and freaky and crazy and lovable. But they're not supposed to be doomed."

There was a cut on his cheek where the hustler had hit him. "You'd better clean your face, Dutch," she told him.

"Darling, I don't have the energy."

"I'll do it for you."

She made him lie down on the white wicker bed and put a pillow under his head. Then she swabbed his face with a cotton ball soaked in Clinique Clarifying Lotion 2 while he told her about the baths and the docks and the bar and the hustler-thief. She cleaned the cut with hydrogen peroxide and then patted his skin with Clinique Dramatically Different Moisturizing Lotion, 100% Fragrance Free.

"Now you're going to take a warm bath."

"Jean, it's five o'clock in the morning. I've taken half a dozen showers today, including two at the tubs. I never needed a bath less."

"Sure you do. Auntie Mae Bonita used to say it was the only way to cure the Hollywood blues."

"So that's what I have. And here I thought I was only horny."

"She used to dunk Lorraine in one regularly, every time she came to do our hair."

"It didn't seem to cure Lorraine."

"She was a special case."

Somehow she got him into the ancient footed bathtub he had painted with blood-red enamel and filled it with lukewarm water and two caps of Sardo.

"There I was having a perfectly divine tragic evening and she's turning it into a game of wash-the-baby. May I have that glass of scotch, dolls?"

"Just relax, Dutchy," she told him as she sponged his back with a scratchy Swedish sponge. "Do you know that in the twenties they used to ship stars with nervous breakdowns to a place called Les Bains down in Baja to dry out? Grandmother Lita used to fake hysterics so they'd send her. Every time Mother had to check into Silver Hill, they used to make her spend two or three hours a day in a Jacuzzi. Her doctor once explained it: we were born surrounded by liquid; getting into a bath is a kind of rebirth, washing the spiritual as well as the physical dirt from one's person."

"Thank you Aimee Semple McPherson. Is that why all those Indians jump into that filthy river every year?"

"I would think so."

"Well, darling, I am ready to be reborn. Rebirth me."

She helped him out and dried him with a huge red-and-blue beach towel which featured an illustration of Spider Man over the legend I've Got You in My Web.

"I asked James to sleep with me tonight," he told her.

"He wouldn't."

"He couldn't."

"Well, you're going to sleep with me tonight, Mister Dutch," she said, bundling him up in a terry cloth robe, taking him behind the screen, and putting him in the white wicker bed.

"I felt so tender toward him," Jean says. "I was bursting with tenderness. I wanted to hold him and kiss him and hug him as if he were my brother or my child. I couldn't stop touching him. He was so adorable without that shield he habitually wore. He was so vulnerable. Our roles were reversed. For the first time in my life, I wanted to protect someone else besides myself.

" 'No funny stuff,' he said when I got into the bed and

put my arms around him. It was his first time with a woman. I didn't set out to seduce him. It wasn't a mercy fuck. And I wasn't playing *Tea and Sympathy*. I had no illusions about his going straight. But somehow seeing him so down and sad and lonely made me realize how much I cared for him, in a way I had never cared for anyone else.

"And he had given me so much, always there for me from the moment I had met him, sitting up with me, holding my hand during my various self-induced traumas, teaching me his craft, teaching me how to live a little, how to enjoy—as he would say—the trip. 'Darling,' he once said to me during one of the rented limo evenings, 'getting there is always more fun than being there.'

"I put my arms around him and he put his arms around me and I began to move a little and he began to move a little and both our bodies began to respond. I did, not to put it too nicely, all the work. I got up on top of him. I made love to Dutch.

"If it was the first time he was ever in bed with a woman, it was the first time I ever made love to a man in the sense that I didn't just lay there being pummeled, accepting whatever was being handed out. I was the active one, the initiator, the aggressor.

"It wasn't exactly a trip to the moon on gossamer wings. But in its unthrilling way, it was a totally satisfying experience. What they call in the ladies' magazines 'fulfilling.' That sexual episode with Dutch, only one of thousands in my life, was a revolution for me."

For Dutch it was, like most of his sexual episodes, a solitary event, a never-to-be-tried-again experiment. "A real, genuine experience, dolls." He slept afterward, still in her arms. She lay awake, watching the sun come up through the windows that surrounded her, feeling, for no reason she could put her finger on, good about herself.

Characteristically, she examined the feeling. "There I was, living in a loft on Twentieth Street furnished with the leftovers of other peoples' lives. I hadn't a penny to my name. I smoked dope and chatted up gum-cracking buyers from second-rate department stores and fought with sewing machine girls from hunger. For the first time in my adult life, I was not trying to pretend I was in love with some bastard who hated me. The only sex I'd had in the past month was with a sadist who worked me over and a sad, fat, gay dress designer whom I had to seduce.

"This was not what I was led to believe would bring me happiness and contentment by my grandmother and my mother and the films they made. This was not Glamour or Romance or even Life with a capital L. I wasn't living in a penthouse with someone else's husband, drinking gin and going to hell with myself in a roadster. Nor was I wearing dark glasses to avoid my fans or singing the blues in a spotlight at the Coconut Grove. I was being, if not ordinary, at least not sensational. And I was feeling divinely, exquisitely happy. And I wasn't afraid to admit it. Either something was very, very wrong or very, very right."

She dozed off after the sun was up, and by the time she was awake again, Dutch was already in the living area, dressed in his terry cloth trousers and a green satin smoking jacket, serving coffee to two buyers from Bamberger's, Newark, showing them the current line.

"It was as if," Jean says, "nothing had ever happened. He had on his full daytime makeup and his delightful, charming smile. He was selling. And he loved to sell. He loved to charm the buyers, to have them try on the dresses, to give them advice on nail polish and cheek blushers. 'Darling,' he would say, 'you could be ravishing, and I mean ravishing, if you just had the slightest suggestion of a curl to your hair. And I know exactly the right hairbender who can give it to you.' "

Later, when they were alone for the first time that day, he became formal and serious. "I want to thank you very much, darling. It was a wonderful experience and it could have only happened because of the love we feel for each other. But it's only fair to tell you that I've made a decision: from now on, I'm swearing off sex of any kind. Boys and girls. Sex has never brought me anything but misery and I think I'll have a better time without it."

"Just how do you plan to cut it out of your life?"

"No surgery, dolls. Merely an effort of will. I'll make it a mind exercise. I'll concentrate my energies on our career."

She was hurt. "I hadn't thought it out but it seemed to me we could have had something. We cared about each other so much. And there he was denying me. I should have gotten angry. I should have told him he was afraid, a coward, that he was aborting what could have been the making of both our lives. I didn't. I allowed him to run away."

That week, two more designs—one by Jean—were picked up by Neiman Marcus's central office and later by Altman's. *Women's Wear* called to arrange an interview and *W* mentioned Dutch's name in an article on up-and-coming designers. The article also said, ". . . and working with him is Jean Rice Halladay, the daughter of the notoriously fabulous Lorraine Rice."

"You could be the next Gloria Vanderbilt," Bunny told her, waving the issue around in the air. "To think I have such famous friends."

They were working twelve-hour days and enjoying them. I was spending more time upstairs (by then BaBa was calling daily), playing gin rummy with Dutch while Jean sketched. The kids had disappeared for the summer, taking jobs on Fire Island and in Provincetown.

"Quite the extended family," Dutch said, as he called the Chinese restaurant and asked them to deliver egg rolls, lobster Cantonese, spare ribs, and fried rice. "Just the three of us and that no-good *schvartza*, Bunny."

"You talking about me, Miss Scarlett?" Bunny asked.

By the first of August, New York was depopulated, its native citizenry taking to the mountains and the beaches and the charter trips to Paris, France. I myself had never spent a summer in New York and—despite the heavy, filthy air and the demoralizing humidity—found it a pleasurable experience. The city was filled with foreigners from Europe and aliens from the Midwest. The latter were in shirt-sleeves on Fifth Avenue, their women in ill-advised shorts. Their cameras clanked against the gold medallions they wore around their necks as they trudged dutifully around Rockefeller Center, up and down the steps of Saint Patrick's Cathedral. None of my family or friends were anywhere within a hundred mile radius. I felt as if I, too, were on vacation, as if I had traveled to another city.

At the end of the first week in August, on an excruciatingly hot night, Dutch received a phone call from Bunny. "She's having her much-publicized nervous breakdown," he explained, putting on his green shorts. "At last. I suppose I have to run up to that hideola apartment and hold her hand." He borrowed money from Jean and left, saying, "See you later, kids."

It was the first time we were alone together in a long time. I asked her if she wanted to go uptown to have dinner.

"I have nothing to wear to Lutèce."

"Why is it that whenever you and I are alone, you turn into a first-class box?"

She looked so young and fragile in the light from the bulb hanging over the sewing machine. There were two straight pins in her mouth and she was concentrating on some problem in the construction of a new design Dutch had failed to work out. I got up from the pink sofa and headed for the door.

"I'm not first class, James," she said. "I'm strictly second-class in the box department."

I went up to the University Club, which looked as if it were the victim of a poison gas attack, and had a perfectly awful meal.

CHAPTER 24

As August wore on, as the air became thicker and
moister and more unbreathable, as New York became
less habitable, Dutch took to spending more nights away
from Jean and the loft. He was, as he put it, "carousing"
with Bunny.

The thermometer had been hovering around the hundred mark for several days when I stopped up at Dutch's.
The pale blot that was the sun that afternoon could be
seen through the windows, playing hide-and-seek with
the grimy clouds. The windows were open, but no air
was passing through. The sewing machine girls, their
clothes dark with sweat, were working away at their
machines. Jean stood at her usual place at the far end of
the cutting table, a babushka around her hair, a pair of
cutting shears in her hands.

"Now I understand what they mean by a sweatshop," I
told her.

She put the shears down and looked up at me with
those incredible, celluloid-silver eyes. "It is awful, isn't
it?" she asked with good humor.

"I don't know how you all stand it."

"Dutchy inspires devotion. He would have made a marvelous general."

"For the Rockettes," Sylvia Einhorn said, snipping a thread in two with her two front teeth.

"Give yourself a break, Jean, and come downstairs for dinner tonight. Air conditioning is a marvelous invention, and Peters is back from holiday. He'll do us up a steak in the Radar Range." She hesitated. "Bring Mister Dutch as duenna."

"Mister Dutch isn't likely to be around."

"Don't tell me he's breaking his vows of chastity, so recently taken?"

"He's trying."

"Very trying," Sylvia Einhorn said. As head sewing machine girl, she viewed Dutch's absences as a personal rejection.

"Will you come?" I asked Jean.

"Yes, James. But I probably won't be able to get away from here until late."

She wasn't, she says, really hurt by Dutch's defection. "I was pissed, but I wasn't taking it personally like Sylvia Einhorn. Yes, we had a zillion back orders and I *was* working my ass off every day with the girls, trying to fill orders while Dutch was off with Bunny every night, doing heavy drugs, strolling in at eleven or twelve in the morning, heading straight for his bed. If Sylvia felt like Dutch's cast-off mother, I felt like his discarded wife.

"But that was Dutch. One couldn't expect him to design a successful line and then follow through on it. He never wanted his fantasies to come true. Look at Louie, the divine and perfect boy he had been after all his life. He kicked him out, refused to have anything to do with him after what was only a mini-battle in Dutch's book of warfare.

"And look at me. He used to tell me how he jerked off over Monroe, of how he always wanted a female lover. 'One with tits, dolls.' The morning after we went to bed, he's explaining that he's finished with sex. He couldn't handle success on any level, any more than my mother or my grandmother could. They all had built-in self-destruct mechanisms."

"And yours?"

"It got defused."

She didn't really want Dutch to come back to the business. She was having too good a time with it. "I loved it. I loved the work and the girls and the buyers and the tumult. I loved the pressure. I loved putting a line out knowing I did it from scratch, from the design to the last final stitch in the hem. It was boring and aggravating and it made me crazy but I loved it. I still do."

That night, when Peters cooked us his special, thoroughly gray Radar Range steak, she seemed tired but not unhappy. "I suppose Dutch is having his little vacation. He's had a difficult summer," she said, drinking white wine from a glass with an almost invisible stem, sitting back, reveling in the air conditioning. She was wearing white pajamas she and Dutch had concocted, based on the set Aunt Alice had given me. I was always amazed at the mundane objects that served as their inspiration. Their version of the pajamas was made up in white satin. They were loose and elegant and the kind of outfit Jean could wear without looking costumed. She put her head back and sighed. She is the only person I've ever known who can contrive to look comfortable in the furniture with which Cora filled my loft.

I was drinking my wine, thinking of how incredibly attractive she was and other thoughts, when she said, letting the bombshell drop gently, "Your wife came to visit late this afternoon, right after you left." She popped one of the heavier-than-lead tiny cakes Peters's wife had made for the occasion.

"Full of her usual charm?"

"It reminded me of a film Mother made with Margaret Sullavan that Father liked to show in the screening room after midnight because it contained the word *adultery*. I used to sneak up into the booth and watch it with the Mex house boys. It was called *Reflected Glory* and was banned in half a dozen states before it was taken out of release. There was Mother, in a black satin slip, sultry hair, and that look of sheer decadence only she knew how to manage, standing in the doorway. The husband, Robert Montgomery I think, was behind her, lying on the bed wearing trousers and an undershirt. La Sullavan, who was a touch too old for the part, was wearing a little Adrian suit and had just been shown in by the irate Irish landlady. It was all terribly steamy. Maggie Sullavan said a few well-chosen words to Bob Montgomery ('The children, my dear, want to know when you can be expected home') and Mother slammed the door in her face. The audience rooted for Lorraine. The bad and the beautiful was more sympathetic than the good and the refined. I think the film was even on the Index for a time."

"Do you want to tell me what happened between you and BaBa or do I have to wait for it to be shown on television?"

"It wasn't unlike the film. She was Maggie Sullavan and I had Mother's part, the scheming husband stealer. She said things like, 'How much would you take to leave

James alone?' I burst out laughing and Sylvia Einhorn was red in the face from the exertion of trying to over-hear us. I would've been furious if Sylvia had a stroke because of BaBa.

"After a while I took your wife into the living area where I patiently explained that you and I were not an item and had never been an item and that I had a shipment to get out.

" 'Don't hand me that,' your wife said. 'He ditched Cora Meade for you. Everyone knows that. And you gave Bert Brown the heave-ho.' "

"She never said that."

"The substance is all there. I think it was then I laughed again. I shouldn't have, but I was so fucking busy and I promised that the delivery would be ready by five, and there was your wife in a Kenzo, playing a scene in a film my mother had made twenty-five years ago. 'I thought I could talk to you as one woman to another.' I could have sworn old Barney Meyer had written the dialogue. She finally left when I told her I was too busy to play but if she wanted to, I would meet her in the Palm Court after the summer and we could do it up right."

"Poor BaBa."

Jean put the wine glass on the plastic table and lit one of her occasional cigarettes. Her hands seemed steady enough. She has a theory that European cigarettes aren't cured with sugar and thus won't give her cancer. "Why on earth do so many people think that you and I are having it off?"

"Because we live at the same address. Because they cannot conceive of either you or me living a celibate life. Because, in a great many ways, we're a very natural couple."

She took a final sip of wine and stood up. "A year or so ago, definitely. Maybe six months ago. But not now, James. I don't want it."

"I do," I said, not getting up, not looking at her. "I think I want it more than I've ever wanted anything else."

"I refuse, James. I won't fuck up my life again." She went to the door. "I absolutely refuse." I heard the door shut after her.

Later, she told me that had I stood up, had I made a move toward her, she would've crumbled like a stale fortune cookie. "I was so vulnerable at that moment, more hurt by Dutch's apparent defection than I was prepared to admit, feeling the weight of the business. I wouldn't have minded some of the old comfort. And there you were, big and blond and beautiful. All you had to do was reach out and touch me, James."

Dutch didn't return from his evening with Bunny until late the following afternoon. "Several hours after the shit hit the fan," Jean says prettily.

"Hi, kids," he said, and immediately took off his Cornel Wilde shirt. Sylvia cornered him in the bathroom as he removed his eye makeup, asking him an irrelevant question about a pattern for a wrap skirt. Jean, she implied, had not answered it in sufficient detail. Sylvia was proving that she knew who the boss was and where her loyalty lay. This exercise took a good half-hour. During it, Jean stood against the cutting table, her arms folded, patiently waiting her turn.

Finished with Sylvia and the makeup removal, he went into the living area, heading for the telephone. Jean beat him to it, putting her hand on the receiver. "Hard day's night?" she asked.

"I'm *plotzing*, darling." He sat on the pink sofa, removing, with difficulty, his Moroccan high-heeled dancing boots. "Bunny and I carried on till dawn. Have you ever had ether?"

"No."

"The most divine trip. And you'll be happy to know Bunny's greatly recovered from her latest bout of delirium tremors. She dragged me to the cutest new dance club on Fourteenth Street where we danced with the funniest, smartest bunch of *schvartzas* you ever met in your life. They all wore little gold earrings and had brilliantined hair and the sweetest, whitest smiles. No one wanted to go home, so we all went on to the seediest—and I mean the seediest—after-hours club in the West Fifties, where a bunch of West Side queens in drag were having a birthday party. The place reeked of poppers. I stayed two minutes and left by myself—Bunny, that *chazer*, wanted to wait for the birthday cake to be cut. I ended up at the Bagel Chateau for a little bite to eat, and who do you think I ran into but those two adorable Puerto Rican kids Charlie and Kelly brought over last week. They literally insisted I schlepp up to One Hundred and Fifty-fifth Street to see their apartment, which is, even I have to admit, spectacular. Absolutely spectacular. A doll's apartment with at least ten of the tiniest rooms you'll ever see in your life. Each with its own nostalgic theme. The Bobby Darin Room. The Sandra Dee Room. The Twiggy Room. The Christine Jorgensen Room. All Puerto Rican pink and blue with lavish—and I mean lavish—amounts of style, not to mention the most meticulous attention to detail. They forced me to have breakfast with them. Chicken and ham and black beans and fried bananas and the most delicious bread I've ever tasted appeared out of nowhere. And all the time they were chattering away with the cutest, idlest, funniest gossip and patter, half in New Yorican, half in Yiddish. We laughed for hours. By the time I knew it, it was noon. I had to borrow seven bucks from them to get home. Remind me to send them a check, darling." He was massaging his feet, taking the armory of gold chains from his neck, counting them before storing them in his carved, wooden jewelry box. "I must get their address from Bunny if that *mishuganah* ever turns up again."

She had waited for him to stop, and eventually, finally, he did.

"Dutch, what's a factor?"

"Darling, you know very well what a factor is. Everybody knows what a factor is."

"I'm not certain I do, Dutch. Enlighten me."

"Darling! A factor is a man who lends money to a manufacturer so that that manufacturer can buy goods to get his line out. The factor makes a little gamble that the new line will be popular and that the manufacturer will be able to pay him back. Naturally all factors charge ball-breaking interest rates."

"Could Mister Edward Rabinado be classified as a factor?"

"That's what he calls himself. Personally, I call him a loan shark."

"Whatever he is, Dutch, Eddie Rabinado and three thugs appeared here at nine this morning. They took every ounce of material we had on hand away with them. I threatened to call the police. Rabinado laughed and showed me a contract he had signed and so had you. Before I called the police, I thought I had better wait to find out from you whether or not he was within his rights."

"He was definitely within his rights, dolls."

"The girls are sitting there sewing belts from scrap material for dresses we can't turn out, for orders we promised we'd fill. We won't. Not unless we get that material back."

"I had a little inkling, darling, that something like this was in the cards."

Dutch Cohen, Unlimited, owed Eddie Rabinado ten thousand dollars.

"Where did you think we were getting the money to buy material, darling? From the tooth fairy?"

"Your father's estate . . ."

"And what did you think we were living on? A thousand dollars a month in drugs begins to make a dent after a while, darling."

"What're we going to do, Dutch?"

"We'll just have to miss the September shipments." He yawned. "And hope with all our heart and soul that Bloomie's sells enough of the little wrap dress to give us capital to start again in October."

"Are you out of your mind?" The yawn had gotten to her. "Do you think any buyer in the world would place another order with us after we reneged on these shipments?"

"Darling, in this business they forget in a minute. By the time October comes around, we'll be the hot new house again."

"You fucker," she said, standing up, following him to his bed, which he proceeded to make. "You goddamned destructive bastard. My first designs aren't going to get manufactured because you took what you thought was the easy way out and went to some loan shark instead of going to a bank."

"Darling, who could be bothered to *potchka* with banks? And what bank would lend *me* money? Be serious."

"You asshole! What bank wouldn't lend you money with all those orders in your pocket?"

"Darling, calm down. Have a joint. I have this regusting drug hangover—not to mention the scotch I drank—and you're shouting in my ear. Besides, I went to Eddie Rabinado long before all those orders came in."

"Dutch, is there anything we can do? Anything? Isn't there someplace we can go for material?"

"Short of paying Eddie Rabinado back his gelt, nada." He got into the bed and looked up at her. "Jean, don't look that way. It's not the worst thing in the world that could've happened. We'll cool it for a couple of months and start over." He closed his eyes.

"What're you doing?"

"I told you, dolls: I'm *plotzing*. I have to get my beauty rest."

"Go fuck yourself, you fat, lazy, dumb cocksucker. I'm getting out of here. What am I doing, wasting my time with a nowhere queen like you? You want to know something, Dutch? You're a person with a lot of past, very little present, and no future."

He opened his eyes and sat up, leaning on one elbow. "You mean you only just found that out, darling?"

He watched her pack a wicker suitcase with some clothes, her designs, and the photograph collection. "Good-bye, Dutchie," she said, not able not to cry. "If success were all you couldn't handle, I might be able to deal with that. But you're just like Lorraine—you've never learned to handle love."

"*Vaya con dios,* darling."

"Tell me not to leave, Dutchy. Somehow we can find a way to get the orders out."

"Darling, I can hardly keep my eyes open. I would never fargin you a parting scene but don't make it the last act of *Aïda.* I think you should leave. I'm always gong to disappoint you in the end. I don't want what you want. When you get settled, give me a ring. We'll have dinner and yenta a little."

She stopped at the door and looked back. He was either already asleep or pretending. One of his thick legs was hanging out of the bed and in his arms he had a pillow. She slammed the door as hard as she could on her way out.

CHAPTER 25

"There are no children in New York or Hollywood," Jean said, sitting herself down in the mock-Gothic visitor's chair facing my desk, suspiciously watching Miss Lustig leave the office, as if she were the reason there were no children in New York or Hollywood.

"It seems to me," she went on, the pupils in her silver eyes dilating, "that there was a time when there were kids everywhere. Before Father was shot, I used to go to two birthday parties a week. Once, when I came to New York with him, when Lorraine was off in Tahoe with Jeff Chandler's stunt man, we were invited out every night to dinner by the New York honchos and there were always other kids at the table. What have they done to the kids, I'd like to know? And don't tell me about Cora's kids, prep school monsters competing for grades in kindergarten. They're not children. They're tiny automatons with frozen personalities."

She stopped talking and looked at me for the first time since she entered the room rather than at the grandfather clock ticking its heart out in the corner. "Does that thing ever stop ticking?"

"Not that I know of."

"James, do you think I might have a glass of water? I'm dying of thirst. Parched." I recognized a southern-belle voice her mother had used fairly effectively in a series of steamy plantation films made when I was in college. I rang and Miss Lustig brought in a glass of water. "Why, thank you so much, darlin'," Jean said. Miss Lustig is difficult to startle, but I think Jean got to her.

"What's the matter with you?" I asked.

"Speed," she said in her ordinary voice. "I'll be all right if you can get me a cup of black coffee."

"You're sure you wouldn't like something else? Food?"

"No, James. Black coffee. Better make it two cups."

Miss Lustig brought in the two cups of black coffee, and for the first time in our long association, I saw her poise slip as she stared at Jean knocking down the two cups and blotting her lips with the accompanying paper napkin.

"Anybody ever tell you, Miss Lustig," Jean said, "that you have two of the biggest, brownest, bedroomiest eyes in the whole wide world?"

Miss Lustig left as quickly as she could.

"Would you like to lie down? There's a sofa in my uncle's office."

"James, I ate three reds on the plane. I won't be sleeping until a week from next Thursday." Her hand shook as she picked up one of the Stryrofoam cups and drained the last drop into her mouth.

The interoffice telephone rang. Miss Lustig wanted to know if I wanted her to announce a spurious visitor, to get rid of Jean. I said that wouldn't be necessary and that I wouldn't be taking any calls until further notice.

"What were you doing on a plane this morning?"

"Flying." She laughed too loud and too long.

"What role of your mother's are you playing now?"

"I suppose, as Mother said in at least six of her films, I had better tell you everything." She sat up, crossed her legs, and made a visible attempt to sober up.

She got as far as the moment when she left Dutch's loft with all her belongings before she asked to use the bathroom. She didn't have time to close the door. I heard her throwing up. When she came back into the office she looked paler but healthier, her pupils more normal, that manic look beginning to fade.

"Feel better?"

"I feel like Sophie Tucker after her last stroke. Do you think I could have something to eat? Little white-meat chicken sandwiches with the crusts cut off, brushed with mayo? If you could send dear little Miss Lustig over to the Dorset dining room, they do them fabulously well there."

I sent dear little Miss Lustig down to the coffee shop on Fifty-fifth Street. "They'll only have chicken loaf," Jean predicted.

It turned out to be chicken salad, but she was beyond protesting. After she wolfed down the sandwich, she went on with the story. From Dutch's, she went to the De-Vines, where she left her belongings with Piers after discovering Victoria and her husband were sailing around Maine for the month of August. "Victoria would've given me the money in a second." From the DeVines, she went to the Women's Bank on Fifty-seventh Street and Park. A kind woman executive named Joan Carlson told her how much she loved her mother ("I've seen every one of her films on Channel Eleven") and that Jean didn't have a chance of getting a loan on a business she didn't own. Her own personal credit was not what it could have been, for that matter. She went to Chase Manhattan just to make sure.

She unearthed an old pal of her father's in the telephone book, Mookie Schneeweiss, a man who once dictated long-distance studio policy. She found him in his Central Park West apartment, chewing on a stogie and making life miserable for his companion. "Make out a check for five hundred bucks, Dolores. This isn't a loan, darling," he told Jean. "This is a gift. For old times' sake. That father of yours was a pisser. I never saw a guy with a straighter face. I tell you, I was all broken up when he bought it."

She forced herself to go to Lilli Ruben, who couldn't have been more welcoming, more noblesse oblige. "My dear girl," Lilli said, after the preliminaries, "I would sooner put ten thousand dollars on a horse." She walked Jean to the elevator, an action she took only with Princess Elizabeth of Yugoslavia. It was then she offered Jean her old job. "At a cost-of-living increase, of course, my dear."

At that moment the elevator, full of decorators and their clients, opened, and Buddy Ruben stepped out. Jean got into the elevator, faced front, and put her finger on the open button before the door could close. "You can take that increase, Lilli, and use it to ask a shrinker why your retarded son's a golden shower freak."

"It was a very silent ride down to the first floor of the D and D Building," Jean admits. "All the occupants seemed to be engaged in a breath-holding contest. They could hardly wait to discuss what I heard one little decorator, unable to keep quiet a second longer, describe as 'Lilli Ruben getting hers.'"

She took a taxi to Kennedy and called the DeVines to see if they had checked in with their answering service, which they hadn't. "So I got on the first plane to L.A. What else could I do?

"It wasn't so terrible. I saw *What's Up, Doc?* for the third time, I had a couple of glasses of domestic champagne, I shot the shit with Rita Moreno. Soon as we landed, I put myself into another one of those Hertz Fords and drove straight out to Malibu. I knew Rank would be there. I even felt, as I knocked hell out of that white meatball I was driving, suddenly up, euphoric. I would get the money. I would return to New York. I would save Dutch Unlimited. I would get my picture on the front page of *Ms.* I was no longer in one of Lorraine's films. Now I was in one of Lita's.

"And L.A. looked so good. It was cooler and drier than New York. The palm trees and the pink stucco houses and the navy blue Mercedes were all clean and bright and new, as if they had been recently issued by the prop room. It was early evening, the smog was invisible and the red glow that covered the horizon was from the sun going down, not from a brush fire. For a moment I wondered why I had ever left. Only for a moment.

"Sybil's getting used to my bursting in. She looks like she's had a nip and a tuck recently. Her skin has that face-lift texture. But her eyes seemed terribly old. She didn't make a fuss. All she did was introduce me to the new butler. 'Randolph, this is Jean Halladay, Mr. Rank's stepdaughter. Jean, this is Randolph, who's working for us now.'"

Rank was in his bed, a long, low, flat affair. It lay under a retractable smoked-glass ceiling through which he could see the stars. "I think I am really dying this time, Jean," he said, sending a man with pale hair and a blue nurse's uniform out of the room.

"It was too much like a set for me to feel real sympathy. But he looked terribly thin and frail. I told him I had seen Mookie Schneeweiss in New York and he brightened visibly, wanting to know how that 'old bastard' was doing. We were feeling very companionable. There was the kind of comfort that comes from being with old enemies."

"I need fifteen thousand dollars, Rank," she told him. "Not a gift. A loan. Strictly legit and on the up-and-up. Whatever the going percentage is. It's not for me, Rank, it's for—"

"For Christ's sake," he said, turning mean, "I'm dying, Jean!"

"I'll pay it back to your estate."

He started to laugh until he started to cough. "The spit and image of Lorraine," he said, recovering. "The spit and image."

"I'm nothing in the world like her."

By the time she got back on a plane, she had lost her L.A. buoyancy. First class was filled with members of an acid rock band making their last tour. The lead electric guitarist passed her the reds. She took a taxi from Kennedy to my office.

"I didn't want to have to come to you," she said.

"Why not? Too easy?"

"Much too easy. For you, James. You've spent your life dismissing people with checks. I won't be one of them."

I opened the desk drawer and pulled out my personal checkbook. "Is it ten or fifteen Dutch owes Rabinado?"

"Ten. I wanted the extra five from Rank to give us what Dutch calls a little maneuverability."

"Whom should I make it out to?"

"Put it away, James. I don't need your money. I got it from Rank. A gift. He said he owed it to my mother."

"Have you been to Rabinado?" I asked, feeling foolish, the thin checkbook in my hands.

"No," she said, looking away.

"What're you waiting for?"

"He scares the shit out of me, James. He has the same exact look Bert has. I knew the second I saw him what he digs."

"What does he dig?"

She didn't answer. "I'm afraid of him. And I'm afraid of me. Part of me wants Eddie Rabinado to fuck me. He could tell. He read the vibes. As his thugs were taking the bolts of fabric out of the loft, he stood watching me. At one moment, just before he left, he put his hand on his crotch. He had a hard on. I almost followed him out into the corridor."

The telephone rang. Miss Lustig told me it was Richard Gordon at the Palm, wanting to know where the hell I was. I told her to tell him something had come up, an emergency, that I would speak to him the next day. I took Jean down to my bank where we sat in Charley Grayfield's office while he did whatever he had to do to certify the check, and then we took a cab down to Thirty-seventh and Seventh where Eddie Rabinado made his headquarters.

The building was yellow brick, built in the late fifties and filled with tenants in businesses related to the garment industry. I left Jean standing in front of the paper stand and went up to the fortieth floor where the last bleached blonde in the world asked me to have a seat in the waiting room, which boasted a Danish modern sofa and a coffee table on which sat a plastic plant in a plastic cachepot.

The waiting room was cool and damp, as air-conditioned, windowless places are apt to be in August in New York. The blonde occupied her time by chewing at the nail polish on her thin, long fingers. I watched her, enjoying the period of inaction, refusing to allow my mind to wander along the long list of reasons entitled *Why I Should Not Be Getting Involved in All This*.

Eddie Rabinado, in a tan silk suit, looked like an exotic reptile, one that had been preserved but was nonetheless dangerous. I handed him the check. He asked me if I spoke Sicilian for no reason I have ever been able to come up with. I said I spoke some Italian. He asked me, in English, to sign a paper, politely inquiring if I had power of attorney. I said I did—which, of course, I didn't—wondering how many years of lawyers and courts that lie would entangle me in. But the paper we both signed and which the blonde notarized was as legal as a four-dollar bill, which was reassuring. I asked him when we could expect delivery of the confiscated material. He answered by pushing a button on the phone and saying into a speaker, "Get that shit over to that blond broad on Twentieth Street right away."

I said if we didn't receive it by six, we would stop payment on the check.

"You will receive it, good buddy. Nice doing business with you people. You ever need another loan, you come to Eddie Rabinado. I'm here to serve you. You remember that."

I told Jean what had transpired, in the taxi on the way to the loft. Sylvia Einhorn was the only one there, sitting in the work area, a paperback entitled *Jade* ("a gripping tale of love and treachery—and of a beautiful young bride abandoned on her wedding night") propped up on her sewing machine.

"Where's Dutchy?" Jean asked.

"He left here a couple of hours ago. Told me he was going to paint the town red. Now what I want you to tell me, your highness, is what I should do with all those belts we've been making for the past two days. If the answer is nasty, remember, I can always get a job in a union shop." She folded her fat arms and smiled her fat smile.

Jean told her to go home, to call the other girls, to make sure they would all be in first thing in the morning. "I've got the material back."

"I'll see it when I believe it," Sylvia said, putting her book in her Estée Lauder carryall, exiting as if she were leaving a house of mourning.

Jean tried to locate Dutch by calling several likely places but couldn't. Bunny's phone, the operator reported, was off the hook. She wouldn't sit down, and I couldn't stop looking at the Baby Ben traveling alarm clock Sylvia had brought in to keep near her machine, to tell her when it was time to go to lunch and when it was time to return to Queens.

At a quarter of six I asked Jean if she could possibly stop pacing. "The reds are still working," she explained.

At ten of six I asked her if it were possible Rabinado might not deliver, and if so I would have to call the bank manager at his home in Riverdale and stop the check.

"Anything is possible."

At five after six, three young men who looked as if they had just that moment jumped parole began carrying bolts of material into the loft, dumping them just inside the door. "Do you think you could put them in the work area?" Jean asked. They didn't answer. They continued to drop bolt after bolt just inside the door.

"Put them in the work area," I said, after a while.

They still didn't answer.

"Put them in the work area," I said, walking over to the leader, a thin young man with greasy shoulder-length hair.

"If you say that once more, man," he said, "I'm going to stick a knife in your ear."

"If you don't put those bolts in the work area, I'm going to stop payment on the check I gave your boss. He won't be happy." We stood there for a couple of dangerous seconds, looking thoughtfully at one another. Finally, he turned away and said to his two compatriots, "Put them in the work area, guys. Put them in the fuckin' work area."

When they left, I asked Jean if she wanted to have dinner. "I'm too jumpy," she said. "What I'm going to do is go up to the DeVines' and have a sauna and a bath and get a good night's air-conditioned sleep. There's no one there but Piers and Eve and they'll pamper me like crazy. That's just what I feel I need. I have a lot of hard work tomorrow. As it is, we're going to be late with our deliveries."

I went with her downstairs. She kissed me on the lips before she got into the taxi. "Thank you, James," she said.

I watched the taxi go east on Twentieth Street,

wondering why I was letting her go off like that, wondering why *I* wasn't pampering her like crazy.

I went back up to Dutch's loft and waited around for him. By eight, I decided he wouldn't show and went down to my loft, where Peters informed me Aunt Alice had called. Twice. I called her house, and for the first time I could ever remember, she answered the phone herself.

"Could you come up and see me, James?" she asked, in a voice that sounded weary. "I'm just back from Hawaii and I need some company."

Aunt Alice never made requests like that one. I told her I'd get into a taxi. She said she'd send the car.

CHAPTER 26

So Jean had a bubble bath in the DeVines' ten-foot bathtub and a roast beef sandwich and a scotch at their twelve-foot dining table, and Piers and Eve tucked her into the canopied bed in the air-conditioned room with the new French windows and the old terrace, and she fell asleep immediately.

And I had cold chicken in Aunt Alice's paneled dining room, and afterward we sat in the library on the tufted leather sofa and watched an old Bette Davis weeper on the television and halfway through I found Aunt Alice's hand had crept into mine and there were tears running down her patrician cheeks.

"I'm a very lonely woman, James." I put my arm around her stiff shoulders and she allowed me. "And a foolish one." There didn't seem to be anything to say, because of course she wasn't going to give out with the details of why she had come to those conclusions (though it had something to do with King and his ranch and what had taken place in Hawaii; that much was obvious) so I held her for what seemed like a very long time while she cried.

Finally, she stood up, borrowed my handkerchief, dried her eyes, and said, "James, do you think you could sleep here tonight? Just tonight?" At that moment she didn't look like one of the five richest women in the world. She only looked like a woman who had just stepped over the border into acknowledged old age, resentfully, unhappily, but finally.

So I ended up in my old room with a glass of iced tea by my bed and a copy of *Moby Dick* in my hands, dressed in a pair of Uncle Garfield's purple silk pajamas, which smelled slightly of mothballs and bay rum. Long after I lost interest in *Moby Dick*, I was still awake, the vision of two women dancing around the empty ballroom in my head: one had artfully dyed red hair and more money then she could count and had decided, or so it seemed to me, to give up; the other was a platinum blonde and had decided, or so it seemed to me, to keep trying. I loved them both in very different ways.

And while Jean was sleeping in her luxurious bed in the Dakota and I was attempting to sleep in my rather more stoic one in the town house on Sixty-fourth Street, Dutch Cohen—my best friend—was setting about the task of destroying himself.

As Bunny was later to say at the funeral, ashes to ashes, Le Dirt to Le Dirt.

The following is what I believe happened to Dutch during that day and that night. It is a narrative pieced together from Bunny, the police, Jean, the trial transcripts, my own surmise.

When Dutch left his loft on the afternoon of August

the twentieth, he believed his business bankrupt and Jean
permanently out of his life. He stopped down at my loft,
where Peters informed him I was still at my office. He
arrived at what Bunny calls his apartmentette looking
"as if Judy had died all over again. I asked him if his
world had fallen apart or if he had the crabs and he
asked me if I had any dust. Asking me if I have any dust
is like asking Tinkerbelle if she has any wings."

They spent the afternoon smoking marijuana laced
with angel dust, watching Mary Tyler Moore reruns on
Channel Four, schmoozing. "I kept getting more ripped,"
Bunny says, "and he kept getting more straight."

Later, they went to a gay restaurant on Bleecker Street
in the Village, where Dutch had three double scotches
and Bunny had a five-course meal. "I was feeling,"
Bunny says, "no pain. Dutchette was hardly saying a
word. I figured he was in the same state of grace I was."

They went to visit a gay couple Bunny knew who lived
in a studio apartment above the Orange Julius on Eighth
Street. They smoked hash in a corncob pipe, and one of
the boys, a hairdresser, gave Dutch a haircut. By the time
they left it was eleven o'clock. They ran into one of the
kids on Sixth Avenue, who said he had been fired from
his waiter job at Fire Island Pines and wanted to know if
he could crash at Dutch's loft.

"I don't think so, darling," Dutch said. "The Dutch
Cohen Hotel for Kids is closed for repairs until further
notice." The kid moved on, and Bunny announced he
was going to the baths. He and Bunny kissed on the lips,
good-bye.

Dutch went to Le Dirt.

A hustler in his early twenties was leaning up against
the side of the building in a way that was supposed to

make it unclear whether he was interested in Le Dirt or in The Oklahoma City Chicken Corp. His name is Anthony (Tony) Galvez. I saw him once. He has broad shoulders, thin lips, a headful of black curly hair, an incipient mustache, an absolutely blank twenty-year-old face. Anything could be written on it.

When I saw him he was wearing a heavy, dark blue suit, a white shirt, a black tie, black lace-up shoes. But it was a hot August night when Dutch alighted from his taxi, and then Tony Galvez was wearing painter's overalls, sandals, no shirt. For some reason the fact came out at the trial that he works out in a gym five times a week, lifting weights. His muscles must have shown brightly in the neon light given off by Le Dirt's discreet sign.

Reportedly, they came right to the point. Tony Galvez said he would give Dutch "a good time" for twenty dollars, a suspiciously low starting-out price. Dutch wanted him to be more specific about what constituted a good time, but Tony wasn't that verbal. "I never said I was going to have sex with the guy," he has sworn, as if that statement exonerated him from everything else. "I never promised him anything. Just a good time."

Dutch offered to take him to the Monte Excelsior, that hotel on Lexington Avenue, but Tony said no, he was with a friend and the friend didn't like those kind of shithouse hotels. Dutch asked where the friend was, and Tony pointed, with his thumb, at Le Dirt's door. "He's not going to do anything, man. He'll keep himself busy while we're otherwise occupied."

As wrecked as he was, Dutch apparently didn't like the setup and started to walk away. But Tony took Dutch's hand and placed it on his bulging crotch. "Come on, man, I could really use a good time."

Dutch said they could go to the roof of a loft building he knew, and Tony pushed Dutch's hand away and said, "Okay, man, let's forget it, huh?" He turned and walked away from Dutch into Le Dirt. Dutch, hooked, followed. He got himself a much-watered scotch and stood at the end of the bar watching Tony Galvez talk to his buddy, a thirty-two-year-old man named Thomas Massoth. He has been described in the *Daily News* as a drifter and in court as a vagrant. At the time of his most recent arrest, he was wanted for pistol whipping a boy in Detroit. I have never seen Thomas Massoth, but I understand that he is short and muscular and mean. He is said to pride himself on his masculinity, to be a macho man. Dutch must have hated him.

Still, after fifteen minutes or so of Dutch staring and Tony ignoring, Dutch walked up to the two of them and said okay, they could all go to his place.

He must have known then. Even with all the drugs, the dust, and the hash, he must have realized he was breaking his Number One Rule with a terrible vengeance.

It was well after midnight when they arrived at the loft. "The place was a dump," Tony has testified. "It looked like a circus." Dutch turned on one of the lamps, a ceramic swan, in the living area, and the three of them smoked two of the doctored joints Dutch was carrying in his cigarette case. After they finished the joints, which were smoked in silence, Dutch asked Tony to come with him into the sleeping area. Tony began to get himself out of the pink sofa, but Thomas Massoth pushed him back and stood up. "I'm first, faggot," he said. Dutch refused, and Thomas Massoth punched him in the mouth.

Bleeding, Dutch got down on his hands and knees as Thomas Massoth undid his trousers. Dutch began, tentatively, to blow him. Thomas Massoth pushed himself completely into Dutch's mouth and forced Dutch's protesting head up against his body while Tony tied Dutch's hands behind his back with one of the worthless belts the girls had been working on while waiting for the confiscated material.

Dutch started to retch, but Massoth pushed himself in and out of Dutch's mouth, forcing him to finish. Afterwards, he gagged him with a piece of scrap material and used the belts to tie Dutch's ankles to his wrists and his wrists and ankles to his neck. Dutch was in the position known as the Cradle. If he tried to move, he would strangle himself. "Man," Tony Galvez, forgetting himself, said in court, "that fucker was as still as a dead turtle. Only his eyes were moving around in his head. It was creepy, I'll tell you."

The two men smoked the last of the doctored joints as they went through the loft, opening drawers, boxes, pulling down bolts of the fabric Jean had rescued, causing random damage, becoming angry and frustrated because there was so little of visible value to steal.

While Dutch lay in the corner, next to the pink sofa, forcing himself not to move.

When they finished rummaging through the loft, when they had drunk from the bottle of scotch they had unearthed, Tony Galvez turned on the radio (which they had already decided was too old and too large to take) and turned up the volume. It was WPIX, an Oldies But Goodies station, one specializing in instant nostalgia, 1950s and -60s music. A Creedence Clearwater Revival song was being played—"Bad Moon Risin'."

Thomas Massoth stood over Dutch, looking down at him thoughtfully. He told Tony to turn the volume up and Tony said the volume was nearly as high as it could go and Thomas Massoth shouted at Tony to turn it all the way up. "Don't you hear the man, Galvez? There's a bad moon out tonight." He took out his knife. It was a long-handled knife with a short, sharp blade. "We got to have us a ritual for that bad moon, Galvez."

Tony Galvez has said, has testified, that he was under the influence of unfamiliar drugs, that he didn't know what Thomas was going to do.

He, Tony, just did what he was told.

Massoth undid the belts but left the gag in Dutch's mouth. The two of them laid Dutch out on the floor. Tony sat on Dutch's legs, holding him down, while Thomas sat on Dutch's chest, pinning his arms to his side. He undid Dutch's terry cloth trousers. Tony pulled them down to Dutch's ankles and over his shoes, balling up the trousers, tossing them under the Empire table (where they were found, several days later, by Sylvia Einhorn, who then had to be given a tranquilizer and sent home).

Thomas Massoth and Tony Galvez faced each other over Dutch's exposed, pathetic genitalia.

After Thomas Massoth finished hacking them off with his short-bladed knife, they both had to stand up and get out of the way of the blood. "It was like a fuckin' geyser," Tony says.

Dutch reached up, pulled the gag out of his mouth, and began to scream. Startled, their responses slowed by the angel dust, the two men stood back as Dutch somehow got to his feet and ran out the stairwell door, holding onto the wound between his legs.

There was, according to Tony Galvez, a lot of blood. It was all over the living area of the loft, covering the blown-up photograph of Jean and Lita and Lorraine, the pink sofa, the mock Empire table. For weeks after, little spots of it would show up in unlikely places, as if the loft had its own stigmata.

They followed him up the iron steps, onto the roof, edging him into a corner. "He was like an animal. Screeching his fuckin' head off," Tony Galvez testified in court.

Thomas Massoth closed in on him and punched Dutch again in the mouth. Dutch fell back against the crenu-lated parapet wall, still holding on to his wound. "What we going to do with this faggot?" Thomas Massoth, ac-cording to Tony Galvez, asked.

It was a rhetorical question. Thomas got hold of Dutch's ankles, Tony told hold of his wrists, and they stood on the parapet surrounding the roof, swinging Dutch out and back like kids playing at the edge of a pond.

"*Uno,*" Tony shouted, and he could hear his echo coming back to him from the alley, six stories below.

"*Dos.*"

"*Tres.*"

"Man, he was still screeching his fuckin' head off when we dropped him."

CHAPTER 27

She woke at midnight, refreshed, surprised to find herself in the DeVines' canopied guest bed on the second floor of their Dakota duplex. She was thinking about what she had come to call The Back Orders. "Actually, I wasn't thinking, I was obsessing." If Sylvia Einhorn had contacted all the girls and they were all going to appear at eight thirty in the morning at the loft—if they were, indeed, going to fill and make ready for delivery all of the back orders—she would have a great deal of preliminary work to do.

She threw back the satin sheets, thinking not for the first time that Victoria DeVine would have made a great set designer. Eve had unpacked her suitcase, pressed her dresses, and hung them in the closet during the day. "I had this sudden rush—I had to get back to the loft. I had a million things to do. Long lists kept compiling themselves in my mind. And there were a zillion decisions to make. Like who was to get what and when? Like which girls were to work on which orders? Like which buyers would I have to call and stall?" She chose the first dress that came to hand. It was the famous backless, frontless silver one she had worn in the fashion show, the one Dutch had designed for her.

"Of course it was inappropriate. Who cared about appropriate at that moment. I had this compulsion to get back to the loft, to start sorting orders and fabrics. I didn't care what I was wearing. I would've gone dressed in Victoria's *peau de soie* bathrobe if I thought a cab driver would've picked me up if I were wearing Victoria's *peau de soie* bathrobe." She stopped and looked away. "Anyway, that dress turned out to be appropriate, after all."

Piers and Eve, bored without the DeVines' all-night demands to keep them on their toes, were eating melted cheese sandwiches in the kitchen, drinking beer. Jean told them she would send round for her things the following day, that she had to get back to Twentieth Street, would Piers find her a cab?

Piers, who is short and stout and beautiful like a Russian icon, insisted he be allowed to get the car out, to deliver Jean home. He drove quickly and with expertise.

"All the time I was sitting on the edge of the backseat, as anxious as a thirty-year-old virgin. I kept telling myself it was the back orders, but you know as well as I do that it wasn't. Dutchy was calling me and I was hearing him. Don't give me that pitying look, James, I beg you. You want to dispute it, open up your mouth and say something. Spare me your knowing looks. Oh, I know it smacks of my grandmother and her midnight séances. I don't care. I have no explanation. I simply know that Dutch was calling me."

Piers pulled up in front of the building on Twentieth Street and rushed around to open the door for her, but she was already out, looking up at the sixth floor which was dark except for the dim light coming from the swan lamp. The radio was still at top volume, Dion singing "Runaround Sue."

Over the radio sound they could hear Tony Galvez counting out in Spanish (*"uno . . . dos . . . tres"*), and over that they could hear Dutch Cohen screaming, falling, screaming. The radio went blessedly silent (it shorted itself) as they stood there, the singsong counting stopped and so did the screams. In that one moment, all she could hear were two sounds. The first was Dutch's body hitting the canopy Tallulah had rigged up on the fire escape of her second floor loft. The second one was his body slamming against the pavement of the alley between the loft building and the garage next door.

Piers went back into the car for a flashlight, but Jean didn't wait. The bad moon was still shining brightly. She found him at the foot of the fire escape, in the middle of the garbage that had been so casually dumped there. She knelt down in her silver dress and took him in her arms. For some reason she expected him to be cold. "But he was hot. His body was sweating, as if he had OD-ed on heavy acid. He was still alive."

She shouted at Piers to go up to my loft, to wake me, to get an ambulance, a doctor.

"Too late, dolls," Dutch said.

"Bullshit."

"I broke my own Number One Rule, darling." He closed his eyes.

"Don't you die on me, you fat bastard. Don't you dare die on me."

He smiled. "You know something, Jean? It didn't matter."

"What didn't matter?"

"That you weren't a movie star," he whispered.

"No shit," she said, holding him closer, realizing that what she had thought was sweat was blood, hot and sticky.

"It didn't even matter that you weren't a boy." He stopped, and his body made a convulsive movement. She couldn't feel him breathing. She thought he was dead. She bent her head down to kiss him. It was then he whispered, "I loved you anyway, Jean."

EPILOGUE

Jean refused, point blank, to attend any of the trials. "They'll hold you in contempt," I warned her. "You're a witness." She wouldn't look up from the pattern she was working on. "Don't you want justice?"

"Justice was done. Dutch killed himself. Now be quiet. I have orders to get out." She looked up and waited for me to argue, and Sylvia Einhorn and the girls looked up and waited for me to argue, but they're all too tough and too right.

"Those beasts," Jean went on, pushing fabric around the cutting table, "may be guilty of a lot of crimes, but Dutch's murder wasn't one of them. I've told you a million times, James—that fucker killed himself." She pulled a cigarette from the Newport pack Sylvia left on the table and lit it, hands trembling, but less then they had been.

Uncle Elwyn helped to pull the right strings—Bert Brown was at the end of one of them, but Jean isn't to know that—and she was never subpoenaed, never forced to sit in a chair in front of a judge and a jury and repeat what she had found that night.

Nothing could stop the newspapers. August was a quiet month, and New York's three survivors aren't still around because of their soft hearts. The *News* and the *Post* featured Jean's photograph on their front pages. "Movie Star's Daughter's Lover Castrated," read one of the subcaptions. The *Times* printed photos not only of Jean, but of Lorraine and Lita as well. A story accompanying the photos detailed Jean's history and rehashed the mystery of her father's death.

"He killed himself," Jean says now, about her father. "Lorraine should have told them from the beginning, but at first she saw possibilities in the role and then, when she was scared and did say it, no one believed her. He walked into the library, shot the lover, and then put the gun to his head. Lorraine thought it might give her career a little boost to be thought of as a murderess. She loved to misrepresent herself. They all did."

The night after Dutch died, after she had been up a solid thirty-six hours, when she couldn't possibly light her own cigarettes, I got her to leave Dutch's loft and come down to mine. She ate half a corned beef sandwich and drank a little tea, Peters hovering in the background with the mustard and the sugar and other unwanted attentions. I finally sent him home.

"You'd better get some sleep," I told her. Her skin was almost transparent. One of Cora's free-floating chairs turned into a bed; Peters had made it up.

"Where the hell were you?" she asked, trading a cigarette for a joint. "Where the hell were you, James?"

I told her.

She stabbed the joint out, went to the bathroom, came

out wearing the brown-and-red satin robe Dutch had given her, and went to the narrow bed. I went to mine and touched the switch that dimmed the lights.

Two hours later she came to me without the robe, and we gave each other what comfort we could.

By the following January, things had begun to even out, to quiet down. Dutch Unlimited had become more then merely solvent. Jean's designs were on every fashion page in and out of the business, and sometimes they even forgot to mention who her mother was. A show at the Waldorf featuring half a dozen Kennedys, Lena Horne, Lilli Ruben, and Diana Vreeland in the front row helped. A Coty Award (for "up and coming," even though it was clear she had already arrived) made her feel, she said, "like Kate Hepburn in one of those career women movies."

She had an interior stairway built between the fifth and sixth floors so she could "pop down and watch."

"You're not supposed to watch a writer write," I told her. "It's distracting."

"We all need a little distraction every now and then," she said, kissing me.

"I've never been kissed so much in my life."

"You don't like it?"

"I love it, Jean. I love it."

Early on, I bought her a satin teddy bear to replace the one Buddy had destroyed. She was furious. "Man, you're my teddy bear now," she said, handing the thing to Bunny.

We talk baby talk. We make love—the passionate kind both she and Dutch accused me of never being able to feel—a lot. We hold on to each other every night as if we were afraid that one of us might slip away.

"Why do you think we're such children with each other?" I once asked her.

"Because we had such lost, fucked up childhoods. We're making up for them now."

It was that January when BaBa announced she had achieved a quiet Mexican divorce and remarriage (not to her rock star) in the same weekend. Jean and I and Aunt Alice went out to the Southampton house, ostensibly so that I could finish the last draft of the book. Jean and Aunt Alice get on. In fact, they are alarmingly friendly. They thoroughly approve of each other.

Peters and his wife had been sent out to Southampton the moment we heard from Baba, to turn up the heat, to push furniture around, to stock the various larders.

We were married in front of the huge marble fireplace in what is known as the grand salon by a local judge, Bill Mercer, on a bleak Sunday morning. Through the French windows that surround that room, we had a perfect view of the deserted winter beach and the green-black waters of the Atlantic.

Aunt Alice gave the bride away ("It's a feminist age," she informed Judge Mercer) while Peters and his wife acted as witnesses.

After champagne and an inedible cake concocted by Peters's wife, we drove Aunt Alice to the East Hampton airport, where a much-bundled Madam Lizzardi had been waiting, we were told, some forty minutes. *"Cara,"* she said to Aunt Alice, holding a handkerchief to her nose. They were being flown to Palm Beach in David Littlefield's Lear jet.

MIDNIGHT MOVIES

That night, upstairs in the ducal bed my great-grandfather had carted home from Italy in a whimsical moment in the nineteenth century, Jean said, "This house reminds me of Bel-Air. Only it's the real McCoy, isn't it?"

"Well, there aren't any screening rooms."

We hugged and kissed and drank more champagne. The light from the fireplace made us feel conspiratorial and safe. "This is the way Lorraine's—as well as grandmother's—movies always ended," Jean said. "For the other woman. Marriage and a mansion and a gorgeous, rich, adoring husband. Lita and Lorraine always had to slink off through the back door at midnight. That or commit suicide."

She stopped talking and turned away from me.

"I've been thinking about him all day, too," I admitted, taking her hand so she couldn't reach for a cigarette.

"He was exactly like them," she said, getting one with her free hand, lighting it with the gold table lighter. "Always into a role. Never accepting help. Never even letting on he needed help. Who knew how desperate he was? Why couldn't he have opened that yenta mouth? Why couldn't he have told me?"

"Maybe he didn't know."

"He knew all right."

"You're still angry with him?"

"I was never angry, James." She put the cigarette down and turned back toward me. Tears were in her silver eyes, but she ignored them. She moved closer to me, if possible. "He left me a terrific legacy, but he left me. Dutch Cohen. He was sad and fat and he had that terrible, all-consuming need to have his heart stepped on a few thousand times. No one was going to stop him from having it kicked in."

I pulled her head close to mine. I could taste her tears. She said something I didn't hear. I had to ask her to repeat it. "I loved him anyway," she whispered.